I0561921

Snowbound

A HOLIDAY MYSTERY

AGNES TAYLOR MYSTERY
BOOK THREE

EVA BERNHARD

Books by Eva Bernhard

Agnes Taylor Mystery Series

Absent Beauty - Short Read Prequel

Silent Sands – Book 1

Writer's Death – Book 2

Snowbound – A Holiday Mystery – Book 3

Stormy Night – Book 4

Louise Penfold Mystery Series

Death at Rosewood Manor – Book 1

Death at Eagle Roost – Book 2

Copyright © 2024 & 2025 by Eva Bernhard

All rights reserved.

No part of this book may be reproduced in any form or by any electronic or mechanical means, including translations, information storage, retrieval systems, and AI training, without written permission from the author, except for the use of brief quotations in a book review.

ISBN 978-1-997787-11-2 (Standard Font Hardcover)

ISBN 978-1-0690966-0-9 (Standard Font Paperback)

ISBN 978-1-0688740-9-3 (eBook)

ISBN 978-1-0688740-8-6 (Large Print Hardcover)

ISBN 978-1-0688740-7-9 (Large Print Paperback)

Editorial Services by Pam Clinton at pccProofreading

Cover design by EB Press with an AI generated cover image used under license from Pixabay. Back matter image used under license from Unsplash.

This is a work of fiction. All the names, characters, businesses, institutions, places, events and incidents in this book are either the product of the author's imagination or used in a fictitious manner. Any resemblance to actual persons, living or dead, or actual events is purely coincidental and unintended.

 Formatted with Vellum

For my son, my best friend and ski buddy. Let's hit the slopes again...and again...

'Twas The Day After Christmas...

Of things to come...

Prologue — Of Things to Come...

A clearing blanketed in fresh powder snow opened as Gabriel emerged from the shelter of the pine forest. Out here, the snow came down thickly in tiny flakes. Forty yards ahead, the cabin sat in silence—deserted. No smoke curled from its chimney. No sound broke the stillness.

Gabriel slapped his fleece-lined work gloves together to boost his circulation after dawdling in the freezing cold on his walk over from the main lodge. Not using the skidoo gave him extra time by himself. He loved being out after a heavy snowfall, making fresh tracks. The mandatory steel-toe work boots, part of the resort staff's outfit, weren't meant for hiking. Bound to cause blisters again.

Reluctant to disturb the virgin white vista, Gabe allowed another minute to laze by.

Better get on with the snowplowing job the boss's son Phil had assigned him to. As he headed across the clearing toward the old wood-shed next to the weathered log cabin, his glance idled on the piled-up snowbank where he knew the path to be. He'd have to shave off some of it. With the huge amount of new snow to clear, there was no more room on this side of the path, and the adjacent forest crowded in right behind it.

Would be easiest to dump it into the open space toward the center. Not a viable option, as Phil hated to spoil the view from the cabin, though he rarely stayed there himself. Lately, he mostly lent it to friends. No good arguing with the boss's son. All the lodge resort employees agreed. Both father and son had a short fuse these days.

Gabe kicked fluffy snow out of the way to wrestle open the creaky shed door. A dancing shower of flakes rose to meet their more stately falling cousins. The sight threw him right back in time to racing out into the backyard as a kid in Montreal's west end. Freak October snowfalls were not unusual in Quebec. First snowfalls of the year sent him into early morning ecstasy. Left to himself, kicking the white stuff like mad in his tiny boots was pure bliss.

He'd always been a loner. A trait which served him well now as a graduate student and aspiring writer. This stint as groundskeeper over Christmas ended his parents' dispute about whom he should join for the holidays. Since their divorce during his late teens, they'd put him on an annual guilt trip. The lodge's vast forest stretching into Mont Tremblant's National Park buried all worries under a thick layer of snow and allowed his mind to roam creatively.

The dreamy smile faded when Gabe dragged the aged snowblower outside, hoping the blasted thing wouldn't let him down today. He unscrewed the fuel cap. Still half-full. Time enough to refuel later. With a last yearning look at the undisturbed white-scape, he brushed off the snow that settled again on his sleeves and shoulders. Focused on the blower, his eyes fastened on the resort's sticker Phil had stuck to the battered chassis as if the red devil in the logo could ward off mechanical failure. He held his breath and yanked the starter grip.

The engine roared into life and shattered the afternoon silence of the woods.

His left hand reached for the heavy-duty earmuffs dangling from his neck and wedged them over his hat. The roar died to a dull droning. It gave Gabe a strange sense of disconnect with the world.

The self-propelled blower ate its way into the path, spewing white spray onto the bank. It carved a neat furrow into the untrammeled canvas. The machine throbbed under his gloved fingers.

Later, he could not have said how long he'd been pushing along, self-absorbed, lost to the world. He'd just tackled the snowbank about twenty yards from the cabin's front stoop when the blower's rumble gave way to a high-pitched whining that penetrated his ear protectors. The blade caught at something. Maybe a thick branch.

In practiced reflex, Gabe hit the off switch. The engine died. Hands tingling from long exposure to vibration, he pushed the earmuffs down his neck. Relief at the sudden stillness flooded his nervous system. Before he stepped around to dislodge whatever choked the blades, he glanced up at the darkening sky. Another storm was moving in. Better get on with the job. Gotta get back to the lodge, he thought. Robert, the boss, was sure to grumble—

Gabe froze. His throat constricted. Acid rose from his gut. He staggered back against the snowblower. Saliva pooling in his mouth, he wrenched his eyes away from what lay before him. Blindly, he stumbled a few yards along the track he'd just plowed.

His own moaning brought him to his senses. Go back and check. Make sure before raising the alarm. It took all his strength to pull himself together to face it. The few steps felt like miles.

Not looking at the mangled mess in the snow, he bent down and used his gloved hands to free more of what lay buried in the snowbank. A shoulder emerged beyond what must have been a left arm before the blade caught. Then a neck and the back of a head, short hair frozen in streaks.

Teeth chattering now, he removed his right glove and inserted his fingers under the neck. Useless, but had to be done. No pulse. Just icy skin. Still, he had to suppress the impulse to take off his coat and cover the naked shoulder.

Like an old man, he scrambled to his feet and stumbled away into the clearing. His stomach heaved and disgorged all it held. Weakened, he sank to his knees.

*Twas Three Days
Before Christmas...*

CHAPTER 1

Late afternoon of December 22

AGNES

"Spy on them? How can you spring this on me last minute, Jac? With one foot on your plane to Paris, and me—" Dr. Agnes Taylor sputtered to a halt, too angry to continue.

She swung around to face her friend and academic colleague, Jacqueline Xavier, in the driver's seat. The tiny Yaris wasn't designed for grand gestures of outrage, especially when one wears a bulky winter jacket, Agnes found as she dropped her hands onto her jeans-clad thighs with a slap.

As if in protection from the onslaught of Agnes's wrath, Jac's petite figure huddled deeper into the stylish black wool coat when she replied, "Please, Agnes. Hear me out. I'm not asking you to spy on my family. It's just..." Jac's voice trembled, and Agnes noticed how the small hands clad in elegant leather gloves tightened their grip on the steering wheel.

Don't freak the driver, Agnes told herself. In a tiny car, boxed in by humongous, slush-spitting semi-trailers on the icy six-lane Highway 401 to Toronto, their safety depended on Jac. Though Agnes was no longer sure she wanted to catch her flight to Quebec, ending up in hospital or the morgue didn't appeal. To quarrel on the eve of Jac's departure for a year in France would be terrible. Plus, Jac had gifted her the week's accommodation at the Xavier Lodge near Mont Tremblant, Quebec's premier ski resort.

She sucked in a steadying breath and said, "Okay, let's start all over. I just wish we'd discussed it days ago instead of you waiting 'til we're heading for the airport."

"I didn't know until today," said Jac, a notch less anxious. "When I Skyped with Dad, he sounded so worried and looked stressed out."

"Stands to reason when his daughter takes off for swinging Paris, doesn't it?"

"Don't be silly, Agnes. I'm 34 and not some irresponsible teen. Dad's proud of me getting the visiting professorship at the Sorbonne. No, he was angry at my brother Philippe for pushing to sell the lodge. Dad loves the old place." A momentary smile softened Jac's profile as she added, "*Maman* used to say he's married to the lodge." Her eyes swiveled to Agnes. "You know Phil. He's very strong-willed. So is Dad."

"Yeah, well," Agnes mumbled and shifted uncomfortably. Her only recollection of the man was from Jac's Bachelor of Arts convocation ten years ago, where a beaming and booming Robert Xavier had invited her along for a celebratory dinner in a Toronto restaurant. Sadly, Jac's mom had passed while Jac was on a student exchange year in France as an undergrad.

Over the years, Agnes had encountered Jac's brother, Phil, several times. Four years Jac's senior, he'd struck Agnes as self-absorbed on his last flying visit to his sister, same as back when he was in his twenties. Quite accidentally, she'd overheard him asking Jac for a loan. Didn't sound like the first time, either. Not a good sign for someone in his late thirties.

Agnes stifled a heartfelt sigh. Here, she'd been determined to enjoy Jac's gift, a special Christmas treat, despite the dreaded cold. Her mother, Sera, seemed touched by Agnes wanting to spend Xmas together at the Xavier lodge and loved the prospect of a ski trip. Mont Tremblant was her mom's favorite ski resort. Though Agnes was less than fond of careening down slippery slopes, a peaceful time with her mom somewhere quiet sounded nice. Now, it came with tough strings attached.

Still aiming to evade involvement in family affairs, she suggested, "If your dad doesn't want to sell, why not simply say no thanks? End of story."

As though Agnes hadn't spoken, Jac said, "I wish my mother had never willed her share in the lodge to Phil and me. Things would be so much easier if Dad would own it outright since *Maman* passed away."

"Oh? In all these years, I'd no idea you were a lodge owner, Dr. Xavier. Fancy," said Agnes, aiming to lighten the somber mood. In the dozen years she'd known Jac, she'd always assumed the place belonged to the dad. She imagined it being some outdoorsy lodge. They'd never gone to her friend's francophone home province together. A lifelong urbanite by conviction, Agnes always found excuses to block Jac's suggestions they might visit the Xavier's home base. If Quebec, she'd rather stay in Montreal or enjoy the European flair of Quebec City. The lodge didn't even have a functioning website. Just a header image of an old cabin in the snow.

"Ownership only on paper," Jac said after another mammoth truck had swung by, making the Yaris shake on its pint-size wheels. "It paid for my education. Now, Dad reinvests all profits because it's costly to run the place against growing competition. The Mont Tremblant area attracts developers and investors in the hospitality industry like a giant sales magnet. Our lodge is dated and needs modernization. Phil and I own 25 percent each and Dad the other 50."

"Umm, a rather uncomfortable impasse if you and your brother want to sell. Unless, of course, your dad buys you out." The malfunctioning heater of the subcompact came to life and hit Agnes with a blast of hot air.

"I've never thought about selling and paid no attention to the legal intricacies. This came out of nowhere. All I know is the three of us must agree for the property to be sold. Besides, Dad doesn't have the funds to pay us off. It would break his heart if I were to side with Phil against him."

"Then the answer is simple: just don't," said Agnes. "From what you say, your brother can't put the lodge on the market against your dad's and your will."

"It's far more complex, Agnes. I'm seriously worried about my dad and Phil fighting. Once Dad gets riled—He grew next to incoherent when I asked for details."

"Do they live together up there?" Agnes saw herself thrown to the family wolves wrangling over the lodge bones with herself playing monkey in the middle. The mental image made her wince. A whiff of resentment at Jac for landing her in a family mess mingled in.

Nose close to the windshield, Jac spoke while fiddling with the wipers that fought to combat the slush spurted by a passing SUV. "No, Phil's there for the holidays. He lives in Montreal and goes to help Dad off and on for a few days."

Agnes stared out into the snowy twilight gloom of HWY 401. They still had an hour and a half to go, even without getting stuck in the usual gridlock once they hit the Greater Toronto Area. Pearson International Airport, situated north of the city, connected to the major arteries fatally clogged with vehicles of all types. Traffic in the GTA environs was always at its most treacherous in drifting snow.

She wriggled her back against the passenger door, uncomfortably aware of the cold radiating from the side window. Her eyes resting on Jac's profile, she said, "I'm sorry, but I still don't get what you want me to do. If the place is not on the market, and your brother can't list it for sale without you and your dad agreeing, why don't you just tell Phil it's no-go? I mean, there's nothing I could do."

Jac tugged at the fringe of her blue-toned silk scarf, destroying its artful arrangement that offset the black of the coat. "My father sometimes gets fixed ideas and misinterprets things. I'd have preferred if you went there with a completely open mind."

"Ha-ha, open mind? Me?" said Agnes.

Jac shot her a lopsided smile and continued, "This is what I piece together from Dad's, I guess you'd call it, rant. The party interested in buying our property is staying at the lodge over the holidays. And an agent is pestering Dad."

"What do you mean? Whose agent? I'm confused."

"So am I, Agnes. That's why I need you on the spot. Dad didn't say who the agent works for or who's interested in the lodge. He fumed about Phil. Said my brother invited buyers and gave the agent the run of staff-only areas without telling Dad."

"Not much to go by," remarked Agnes when Jac hesitated.

"I realize that. This sounds weird, but Dad also hinted someone's leaking confidential info about the business."

"Yikes."

"Yes, rather. I told Dad you'd show him how to fingerprint protect his new laptop. He's a little computer-challenged."

"Sure, that's no problem. I'm no tech wizard but can manage." Pretty bad if Jac's father didn't trust his own son with a simple thing like security settings. The info leak might be close to home, Agnes figured.

Next to her, Jac spoke again but kept focused on the road. "I texted Phil to ask why he didn't mention the dispute about selling when we spoke to say goodbye yesterday, but he merely said not to worry. My brother always waits for a *fait accompli* and then expects me to side with him against Dad. Oh, he said he looks forward to seeing you."

Can't say the feeling is mutual, commented Agnes silently. Sometimes, she suspected Jac of playing matchmaker.

Aloud, she said, "So, what are you asking me to do? Pour oil on the raging waters? Play arbiter? No thanks, Jac."

"All I'm asking is for you to give me an unbiased view of who those prospective buyers are and if anyone is bullying my father. Who knows, you might find who has info they've no business to have."

"Hey, you're punning."

Jac shot her a tiny grin. "Dad wants to have you and Sera over for coffee. And your friend Polly, of course. Have a casual chat and tell me."

"Be realistic, Jac. Your father is not going to share his worries with me, a total stranger. You'd be better off Skyping with him."

Wrong thing to say, Agnes realized, as Jac's face swung around in renewed agitation. "People always confide in you. You don't get it. My dad won't tell me what's going on. He and Phil treat me like a little girl, no matter how many degrees I've got. It's so frustrating!"

"Watch the road, Jac," warned Agnes as the little car went into a slight skid on the sludgy surface. "If we end up with a fender bender, we'll both miss our flights."

While Jac concentrated on maneuvering the Yaris in the worsening weather, Agnes mused her friend stood a better chance of catching the plane scheduled to leave for Paris two hours after her own departure for Quebec. Her mom, Sera, had texted earlier to say she and Polly checked in at the lodge and would pick up Agnes from Tremblant Airport.

At the thought of Polly Holt, whom she and Sera had met during a fateful week of their past summer vacation in Germany, Agnes groaned. Unfinished business. More strings attached to the Christmas gift horse.

11

She smiled wryly but only at mixing cliché metaphors. Time to deal with Ms. Holt once she'd arrived safely in Quebec.

Right now, she needed to decide what to say to Jac's plea for help without being ungrateful. What was she letting herself in for? Exasperated, Agnes sighed. They were both still reeling from the effects of Jac's last request for Agnes's aid.

Just a month ago, Jac had urged Agnes to disprove a malicious rumor at Bowman College, where they both worked as professors. While Agnes only held a one-year contract teaching philosophy, Jac was a tenured professor and coordinator for the Humanities department's creative writing program. During the "investigation," as Jac insisted on calling her blundering efforts, Agnes thought ruefully, she'd come close to losing everything—including her life.

Never again. Agnes shivered in memory rather than from the chill of the Yaris's temperamental heating.

Outside, she could see the hazy lights of the western outskirts of the GTA. The traffic volume increased bumper to bumper for some stretches. Agnes glanced at her friend. For a moment, the glaring lights of an interchange with another major highway threw Jac's profile into relief. The winter-pale skin, taut over the edgy cheekbones and pointed chin, was framed by icy blond hair recently styled into a layered bob. It gave Jac an ethereal vibe, Agnes thought, as she looped strands of her own heavy dark tresses behind her ears. Or maybe it was just the light coming in.

The closer they got to Toronto's major airport, the slower their progress. Organized as usual, Jac had insisted on leaving early from their shared place in a small town a few hours west of the megacity, as Torontonians were fond of calling the conglomerate of multiple cities joined into one gridlock mess.

The silence contracted the atmosphere in the little vehicle, cramped full of Jac's luggage for her one-year sojourn. There'd been barely room to squeeze in Agnes's suitcase, bloated with winter wear. She didn't own skis and boots. Sera would know where to rent them, she figured. Unlike her exercise-challenged daughter, Sera was an avid skier even in her seventies.

Oh, God, thought Agnes, I don't even like skiing. She cleared her throat without an idea of what she was about to say.

It prompted Jacqueline to throw her such a pitifully pleading glance, Agnes's heart melted.

"Okay, Jac. But I make no promises. And I won't get involved in family affairs. I just casually chat up whoever I'll come across."

Jacqueline's hand reached over to squeeze hers. "Thanks, Agnes. You are truly my best friend. We'll talk via FaceTime once I get settled in Paris."

"You bet," agreed Agnes.

Why then did she get this feeling her best friend was hiding something from her? Was there more involved than Jac let on?

As if in afterthought, Jac now said, "Of course, don't mention to anyone what I'm asking you to do or what I've told you. Promise?"

"What do you take me for? A bleeding amateur?"

CHAPTER 2

Evening of December 22

AGNES

A few hours later, Agnes stood agape at the top of the mobile boarding stairs that led right onto the wet tarmac of Tremblant's La Macaza airport. What she saw was a show-stopper Christmas fairytale.

Instead of a utilitarian airport building, there stood a brightly lit, massive gingerbread house powdered with fresh-fallen snow. Mellow round logs in natural cedar tone joined horizontally by cream-colored mortar might evoke pioneer days of yore if it weren't for the state-of-the-art high-pitched metal roof set in geometric sections.

Behind her, a steward of the Air Canada Express urged her to disembark.

"Do you need help with your bag, ma'am?" asked a stewardess in a sweet Quebecois accent on Agnes's other side.

"No. No thanks," stammered Agnes, still dazed. It's just such a culture shock after boarding at Toronto's Pearson, she wanted to say but thought it might be taken amiss. She shouldered her backpack and cautiously descended the steep metal grid stairs to follow the passenger herd meandering into what must be the terminal. A ground crew unloaded luggage onto carts to be reunited with their owners.

Once inside the building, Agnes felt transported into some rustic hotel foyer. Roughhewn trees served as posts and beams supporting a soaring pine ceiling. A fieldstone fireplace, logs ablaze, and cushiony sofas invited weary travelers to rest. The lofty gallery above must give a panoramic view of this unique arrival hall.

Then Agnes saw them straight ahead. Her mom, Sera, slim and tall next to Polly Holt, waved and smiled. As Agnes moved forward to hug her mother, Polly hung back. The imp, as Agnes had dubbed the enigmatic Polly, seemed tinier than in memory. Not that there was anything demonic about Ms. Holt or whatever her real name might be. But Polly's mischievous grin used to bring a smile to Agnes's face. Well, Polly wasn't beyond an impish trick or two.

Swaddled in a thick, charcoal jacket, skinny legs stuck in tan UGGS, Polly didn't grin now. Matchstick-short wispy hair, no longer ash-blond but green, stuck out in all directions. Polly stood twisting a red Pom-Pom hat between her child-size fingers. Down to the green leggings, the androgynous little person reminded Agnes more than ever of Santa's elves.

They stood awkwardly. Didn't hug. Just said, 'Hi, how're you doing?'—like casual acquaintances.

The unique airport should serve as a welcomed icebreaker, Agnes hoped. An instant conversation piece to lessen the tension.

"Can you believe this place? Just out of this world," she said.

"Quebec style," said Sera. "Wait until you see our place at the resort."

"Yeah, it's awesome. Thanks so much for inviting me," said Polly almost shyly as they walked out to the parking lot. Not at all the vivacious person Agnes remembered from their time on Bosum half a year earlier.

Don't think of that now, Agnes urged herself, when the thought of the North Sea Island inevitably summoned the gruesome image of a body half-buried in sand. Playing Watson to Polly's Holmes was a thing of the past. Well, in the end, the imp had walked out of her life without a backward glance. Left them in the lurch Agnes felt back then and never expected to see secretive Polly again.

But Sera and had kept contact with their summer acquaintance. Agnes found out when calling her mother about Jac's gift. Ski holidays were her mom's passion. Her own holiday spirit evaporated when Sera asked with atypical diffidence, "Would you mind if we'd squeeze in one more, dear? Polly is visiting over Christmas." No way to be churlish and refuse. So, Polly had come to stay.

Jingle Bells on the airport's sound system brought Agnes back to the present. Oh, what fun it is to ride headlong into Jac's family affairs with the imp in tow, she thought as the cold hit her outside.

In the slushy parking lot, Sera unlocked a large SUV from afar, its lights blinking a greeting. While Polly hopped into the back, Sera pulled Agnes into another brief hug, murmuring how good it was to see her.

Then, with a sideways nod to the rear of the SUV, Sera said softly, "It's time to forgive and forget. Isn't that the real meaning of Christmas?"

"Mom, you're not going religious on me?" Agnes joked, not committing herself. "Hey, I'd no idea you went in for off-road luxury motors."

In the weak light, Agnes saw her mother's sculpted face crinkle into a smile. Well-cut short hair, the original black still showing among the gray, her mom remained an attractive woman.

A silvery tinkle swung in Sera's laughter as she replied, "Adorned with borrowed plumes, my dear. I still drive a little hatchback in Nova Scotia. A friend lent me the Explorer for the trip up here to have room for skis and Polly's snowboard. I picked her up at the airport in Montreal last night, and we stayed over at Gwen's place."

"How nice," said Agnes as she settled into the passenger seat.

Once installed comfortably in the roomy vehicle, her mother drove out onto the lonely road before asking, "You remember my friend Gwen, don't you? She was the department chair when you came to the conference in Halifax a few years ago but now lives in Montreal."

The last thing Agnes wanted to remember was her first brush with murder on her brief visit to the Canadian Maritimes. Nor was she going to tell Sera about the death of a creative writing student just last month at Bowman College. A vision of being stalked by death sent a shiver along Agnes's spine. She hugged herself in reflex.

"Are you cold, dear?" asked Sera. "Is the heating set too low for you?"

"No, I'm okay," Agnes assured her and huddled deeper into her winter jacket. Just someone walking over my grave again, she wanted to joke but thought better of tempting fate.

As though checking her non-existent makeup, Agnes flapped down the visor and slid the cover to reveal the vanity mirror. In its light, she could glimpse Polly's profile. Hard to believe she's in her late twenties, Agnes thought, as she studied the younger woman's unlined features that probably had changed little since girlhood. Though Polly's antecedents were anyone's guess. Notoriously cagey about herself, Ms. Holt had no inhibitions about digging into the lives of others.

Stood to reason in a journalist, freelance or not. Just to say something, Agnes asked, "You okay back there?"

The mirror told her Polly still stared out at the snowbanks lining the Trans-Canada Highway they were now zooming along. "Yeah, sure. Just jet-lagged. Think I'll have a little snooze."

"Grab the cushion and fleece throw from behind you, Polly," Sera said, and with a glance at Agnes, "We had little sleep. Polly's flight came in late, and highway construction zones slowed us down. By the time we got back to Gwen's, it was well past one o'clock."

"Oh, Mom. I'm so sorry. You must be exhausted."

"Don't worry about me, dear. I napped when we arrived at the lodge this afternoon. Very comfortable beds." Her mom gave Agnes's arm a quick pat. "I'm so thrilled to spend the holidays here with you, dear. Our first Christmas together in ages. Ski trips were never your kind of thing. I truly appreciate this treat."

Agnes laughed uneasily. "Well, I'll stay on the bunny run, I guess, or on my bum. Haven't skied since you moved to Halifax twenty years ago."

"Oh, I see." The stiffened posture and flat tone told Agnes more than Sera's words.

A moment ticked away before her mom added more upbeat, "Well, it's never too late to relearn."

"We'll see," muttered Agnes, aware neither one of them wanted to pursue the thorny topic of Sera taking up a professorship in the Fine Arts Department at a Halifax university, leaving Agnes to live with friends in Toronto while finishing high school. At a not-very-sweet sixteen, Agnes had felt abandoned. Resentment at being left to her own devices when she needed her mom badly stewed for years and years after and bubbled up each time on their rare and perfunctory encounters.

Their summer holiday, the first in two decades, marked a decisive change. In the end, they'd bonded. Sort of. Yet, even during those final harmonious weeks in Berlin, Agnes hadn't felt ready to confide the serious trouble she'd been in back in her teens when Sera moved to Atlantic Canada.

Another memory to bury deeper, she thought and closed her eyes.

The vehicle's sudden slowing down jerked Agnes awake. She swiped at her eyes to clear her vision. In the silence of the Explorer, the ticking of the turn signal sounded unnaturally loud. Ahead, a red '*Arrêt*' octagon marked a T-junction. Straight across, their headlights illuminated a brown sign: *Parc national du Mont-Tremblant.* A wooden one with a mini-roof next to it hailed—*Bienvenue Welcome*—with an arrow to *Versant Nord 5 km.*

Still sleepy, Agnes had to clear her voice to ask, "Are we there?"

"Not quite," said Sera. "We turn right toward *Lac Supérieur* but head further up along the river."

The mention of Quebec's namesake of the Midwest great lake did not improve Agnes's sense of orientation. Nose to the side window, she glanced out. Not much to see. Except for a driveway off and on, the vista remained identical as far as she could tell. In a curve, the headlights reflected on what might be a stream. They passed too quickly to be sure.

A few kilometers later, Sera swung onto a one-lane road. A green street sign—*Chemin de l'Avalanche*—boded ill. Surely, there were no avalanches in Quebec, or were there?

The snowbank-lined forest encroached yet closer on the asphalt with not even a hint of a shoulder to pull over in case of a flat tire or something.

No one spoke as they continued at low speed to—literally—the road's end.

"Truly out in the boonies." Agnes hadn't meant to sound so negative, but disappointment welled up. "Jac said nothing about the lodge being in the middle of nowhere."

In the twilight, Sera glanced over before swinging into a private drive. "It's close to the slopes, Agnes, which is the main thing for skiing, isn't it? You'll love it," she said in her no-nonsense tone.

"Yeah, it's sweet," came a voice from the back. The dark interior of the car hid Polly's expression when Agnes swiveled and forced a smile. She felt outnumbered by the enthusiasts.

At the mouth of the drive, an advertisement board hailed visitors in yellow and flame-red on black. '*Va au Diable*'—a deep red devil with horns and club foot right next to it. Below in smaller lettering: '*Sur réservation seulement—Chalets, Cabines, Restaurant.*'

"Well, let's 'go to the devil,' then," said Sera.

"Reservation only—for your seat in hell," said the imp.

A sarcastic 'haha' stuck in Agnes's throat, drowned by the heavy vehicle's clatter when they crossed a bridge and came to a halt halfway across.

Her startled, "What's wrong?" raised a chuckle from the backseat.

"Not to worry, dear. It's just the *diable* in its full splendor," said Sera, lowering her window to let in the roaring from below. "After the flooding a few weeks ago and the recent mild spell, waters are running high."

Since her own breath fogged up the side window, Agnes opened it to peek out—and recoiled.

"Sera! Mom, please—can we go on?" Never one for heights—though the bridge likely rose merely twenty feet above the foaming torrents lined by ice and snow-crusted rocks—the sight of the racing cataracts worried her.

A small face squeezed in beside the front headrest. Close to Agnes's ear, Polly's excited voice rose over the din. "The river of Tartarus, eh, Aggie? Quite hellish, isn't it?"

Distracted, Agnes wondered if Tartarus, the lowest underworld of Greek mythology, involved torture by water among its horrors. In parallel thought, a memory flashed in of a major bridge collapsing during a flood —TV footage watched with horror.

To judge by the sound the bulky Explorer had made, this bridge was mere wood rather than concrete. How could it withstand a raging surge like this?

"What if it undermines the bridge? And SUVs weigh tons," said Agnes.

"Don't exaggerate, dear. The lodge, I'm sure, receives its supplies by the truckload. Snow ploughs cross here too. Earlier, when Polly and I arrived, we passed one close to here."

Sera put the car in gear, and they rolled on.

CHAPTER 3

Late Evening of December 22

POLLY

Count on Aggie for tummy first, Polly Holt quipped to herself as the three of them trudged along the footpath to grab a late-night supper at the *Va au Diable*, the resort's bistro. Nothing had changed from the summer in that respect, Polly thought wryly. A wee person like her could do without constant refueling. Not so for foodie Agnes. Soon as they'd arrived at their cottage chalet type of thing and Agnes got over all the oohing and aahing at how awesome it was, she'd craved food.

Funny how the friend, the proprietor's daughter to boot, had never told Agnes what a grand place the resort was. From what Polly had seen on her reconnoiter this afternoon, there must be close to twenty buildings of varying sizes, tastefully set among conifer trees and some decorative split-rail fencing.

Aggie's open-mouthed gape when they got out of the SUV was a perfect photo-op for a Google ad. Their glass-fronted chalet-style cottage looked darn pretty. All lit up, Christmas tree twinkling behind the sparkling floor to rafter windowpanes, it bowled you over.

The tree was in the communal space of the four-apartment cottage, flanked by a couple of sofas and armchairs. They got the larger of the two downstairs apartments, with another two upstairs. She'd already met the guys from upstairs this afternoon when the dudes had come back snow-covered from skiing. Man, Polly thought, can't wait to hit the slopes tomorrow. Not like the Alps for sure, but what she'd googled about Mont Tremblant had her excited, like a little kid waiting for Santa.

The image put a happy skip into Polly's booted step. With all the cottages along the resort's central lane shiny with fairy sparklers and string lights along the pathways, the place oozed Christmas magic. If only she could shed this awkwardness at meeting Agnes again after the radio silence since last summer, this could be a fun holiday.

A nice break before heading west to interview a group of gutsy teens who were suing the Canadian government for climate change inaction. Nothing high profile like the September climate protests spearheaded by Greta that she'd covered. But a good excuse to visit friends on Vancouver Island. Some fence-mending there, too...

Why must life—and people—always be so complicated? For the few days she'd known Aggie during the summer, their friendship seemed to grow by leaps and bounds. Made you think it could grow into something more.

Yah? Don't kid yourself, Poll, something in the back of her mind scoffed. You blew it the moment you ran from the place your ex-lover died. Agnes never got in touch, did she? Wasn't keen on ever meeting again, was she? If it hadn't been for—

Sera's voice saved her from sinking into hated introspection.

"There's the main lodge. From what we saw when Polly and I arrived this afternoon, it must have been the original lodge, with later additions to the back."

"Wow, this is quite impressive," Polly heard Agnes say from Sera's other side.

The main lodge threw its lights far out onto the snow, with a massive Christmas tree right out front. Same as the rest, the place was built from round logs. Stands to reason, Polly thought, the whole province is nothing but woods, or so it looks on Google satellite.

"Shall we venture inside?" Sera asked rhetorically.

Though she and Sera had seen the place when they picked up the key at reception, the foyer's mellow, glowing wood charmed Polly again. They sure liked soaring ceilings around here. On one side, a row of windows and glass doors let you look right into one of those white-linen dining rooms, now dimly lit after closing. The reception staff called a friendly *bonjour* as they followed the sign to the bistro in the back. Some people in ski jackets were just leaving and held the door open for them.

Polly dawdled, her eyes eagerly scanning the place. While what she glimpsed of the main restaurant seemed sort of fancy, the bistro was for causal meals and chatting over a glass of wine. Quite a few tables were taken. What else could you do out here away from the ski resort but sit in your own cottage or come to this bistro at night? Or the bar. A sign pointed to it at the end of the room.

"Hey, are you coming?" Agnes called her from a table at the window.

No white tablecloths here. Glossy from decades of use and polishing, the tabletops' naked wood shone. The upholstered seats of the chairs were quite cushy, Polly found as she sat down across from Sera instead of facing Agnes squarely.

While they'd ordered, Polly's eyes roamed in tandem with her thoughts. All the punters dressed casually in jeans and sweaters or in classier après-ski wear. Her glance strayed back to Agnes, who faced the window. Still parted her wavy hair in the middle, glossy and dark against her creamy skin. A Raphaelite madonna face so prone to make a person's heart ache. Polly suppressed a sigh.

Perhaps aware of her scrutiny, Agnes said, "You're mighty quiet tonight, Polly. So, tell me, did you fly in from Germany? Or what's your base now?"

Put on the spot, Polly mumbled, "Oh, been here and there. I don't do permanent base." Why does everyone ask personal questions? Always want to know who you are, what you do, where you live, and so on. Can't one just be without being slotted into someone's mental pigeonholes? Agnes hadn't asked about personal stuff back in the summer. Or did she?

"Makes sense for a freelance journalist, I guess," said Agnes, arching an eyebrow at her. "Did you come to Canada on another of your assignments? Plenty of environmental issues for you to investigate."

They'd found out about her being a hack from the article she'd pseudonymously published after she'd left them in the summer. Or so she'd understood from Sera. She'd meant to come clean. Eventually.

"Yeah, sort of," Polly prevaricated and dropped her voice to a comical whisper, zipping her lips with her fingers. "Prefer to fly under the radar. All hush-hush stuff, you know."

"Ah, I wondered," said Agnes.

But Sera intervened. "How's the teaching at Bowman College going? Did you enjoy the fall term there?"

Why Agnes blushed, rather engagingly, at the question beat Polly. Seemed innocuous enough. But Aggie downright waffled in answering.

"It's been...different. I mean, it's not like university teaching. But I guess you could say exciting." Agnes ended on an uncertain note.

Something's brewing, thought Polly. Wonder what scrape she's got into.

"*Excusez moi,*" a waitress leaned in to serve their orders. Food looked appetizing.

With a '*bon appétit,*' the server withdrew.

"I see our neighbors are also enjoying a late snack," said Sera. "The couple from downstairs, Maria and Gino. I met them this afternoon when you were unloading the SUV, Polly."

Swiveling to follow Sera's nodded greeting, Polly's gaze zoomed in on the girl. Her heart skipped a beat. There sat the prettiest porcelain doll-faced brunette. Early twenties, at a guess, and a wee slip of a babe. Of the guy, she only saw the back. Dark hair and probably medium height once he'd get up. Their table was at the far end, diagonally across.

When the girl looked up, and their eyes met, Polly felt herself beam like silly. The teeniest nod and the girl smiled like unsure they'd met before. Then, her dude distracted her again.

"Do you know who's in the upstairs apartments?" she heard Agnes ask.

"I've spoken briefly to one couple, Cheryl and Matt. Apparently, they and the two young men upstairs form part of an extended family who rent the largest chalet."

"Holy mackerel. Quite the holiday spirit," commented Polly, glad her staring went unnoticed. Or so she hoped. Honestly, she couldn't imagine belonging to a vast family. Never mind spending a vacation with a clan. "Speak of the devil," she added under her breath as the males in question sauntered in. They'd said hello to her when they came home snow-covered from the slopes late this afternoon.

The guys came up to their table now.

"No, no—don't get up," said the skinnier and shorter of the two as Polly rose. He stretched out his hand to greet Sera and Agnes. "Thought we'd say hi. I'm Josh. Meet my partner, Greg. We're the elephants above you."

Pleasantries exchanged, they made for the bar, giving the Gino person a high five in passing. The petite brunette—Maria—ignored them pointedly. Her man turned out a twin of Michelangelo's David as he rose.

"What time should we say for skiing tomorrow?" asked Sera. "Polly, you are an early bird, aren't you? We need to persuade Agnes to rise for a vigorous morning outing."

"Huh?" Polly said, still distracted. "Me? Any time is dandy."

"Argh, no sleeping in on the holidays?" Aggie groaned comically.

Sounds from the back of the room and Sera's serious expression diverted Polly's attention. The Gino person jumped up, hissing something at Maria, who snatched at the cuff of his sweater. The girl beseeched him, it seemed. He yanked free and strode toward the bar door.

With an agonized glance at his retreating back, tiny Maria grabbed a Hermes handbag and sprinted for the exit without even slipping into the jacket she clutched to her chest. As she passed them, Polly saw tears coursing down the girl's cheeks.

"Oh my," said Sera.

"Yikes," commented Agnes. "Not a good omen for their merry Christmas, is it?"

Polly would have given anything to rush after the damsel in distress. Awoke all your protective instincts, she thought.

Instead, they ordered a round of decaf coffee.

The waitress had barely served it when another guy came straight for their table. Must have missed him coming in. Tall, broad-shouldered like Greg, not much of a looker. Except for startlingly blue eyes, which now zeroed in first on Agnes, then politely on Sera.

"Good evening. I hope you found everything to your liking," the dude said in a sonorous voice. Which made Agnes almost jump. And blush.

"Hey, Phil. Was going to text you to say we got here alright. Nice to see you," said Agnes, but the smile looked kind of fake.

There's a history and not the most pleasant one, thought Polly when

Agnes introduced Sera and her. The guy declined the offer to join them but asked the usual things about the flight and drive. His eyes seemed to scrutinize Aggie's face more than politeness recommended.

"My dad," he said, "would like to have you over for coffee. Would tomorrow afternoon suit you? After the lifts close? I'll pick you up at your apartment. My dad's private place is a little difficult to find."

"How very kind of your father," Sera said.

"Yes, please thank him for us. We look forward to it," said Agnes.

Man, do they ever get formal around here. Hope it's not one of those stiff 'tuck in your pinkie' affairs, Polly mused. Well, it wasn't tea and scones the invite asked them to partake in.

The outer door opened with somewhat of a thud as the door handle banged the wall. For Pete's sake, how many broad-shouldered six-footers do we get tonight? Polly wondered as another man in a parka and one of those pilot hats with furry ear flaps strode in.

Phil excused himself and went to shoulder-slap the man in greeting.

As the guys passed, Phil said to Agnes, "I'll text you tomorrow. My sister gave us your number. I hope that is alright."

"Yes, Jac mentioned it. Well, see you tomorrow, and thanks again," Agnes said with another forced smile.

They all said goodnight, but the newcomer hardly glanced at them. His eyes were on the bar. Can't wait to get at the booze, Polly figured.

When the two males were safely into the bar, Agnes said softly, "I wonder who Phil's friend is."

"I can tell you his name," said Sera. Aggie ogled her mom in surprise. Sera's tinkling little laugh lightened the somewhat strained atmosphere this Phil had left behind. "That's Matt, who's staying upstairs with his wife. The one I mentioned earlier."

"Hmm." Agnes looked thoughtful. "So, Jac's brother is friends with the other guests in our place. Interesting."

Now, what was behind that remark? Polly wondered as they waited for the waitress to bring their bill. There's more to this trip than meets the eye.

Twas Two Days
Before Christmas...

CHAPTER 4

Afternoon of December 23

AGNES

The next afternoon, Agnes stood at the floor-to-ceiling window of the great room in their log house. Dressed in her winter jacket, wool hat in hand, she stared out. The snow swirled and blew in a thick curtain of tiny flakes, collecting on the grid of the panes. Picture perfect for the season's greetings. So much more picturesque from inside, next to the crackling fireplace, as far as she was concerned.

No desire to venture out. Much less to go to Robert Xavier's for afternoon coffee. Last night, Phil had sounded polite and formal. Past encounters when he visited his sister in Toronto were far from pleasant. Jac obviously loved her brother, but Agnes thought him moody and self-centered. Her impression hadn't improved over the years. A few times, he needed to borrow money from his younger, financially cautious sister. Not a sign of a responsible character. Jac adored clothes but spent strategically on quality rather than quantity.

Agnes sighed. This holiday wasn't shaping up well. The morning had been pretty awful. First, getting rental skis and boots, which took far too long with lineups. When they finally tackled a green run, Agnes's skiing ability had proved non-existent. Sera did her best to teach her again the basics, but the past 20 years of a sedate academic lifestyle had taken their toll. Meanwhile, snowboarding ace Polly hovered, clearly bored by their slow progress. At midday, Agnes told them she would practice on the bunny run and meet up when the others were ready to call it quits in the afternoon.

During one of her frequent breaks at the cafeteria of Tremblant's North face base lodge, she'd emailed Jac to tell her of the afternoon invitation for coffee. Whereupon Jac's instant reply reminded her to help Robert with the laptop fingerprint access and to get a sense of what was going on. The former was awkward while Phil was around, Agnes had said. But Jac simply responded, use your ingenuity, and don't make it obvious. Yeah, right.

Agnes shuddered at the prospect of plumbing the depth of Jac's family affairs. Her own experience with family was so limited. After all, Sera was her only blood relative. Can't even imagine where to start, she fretted.

A couple of skidoos pulled up noisily.

Shoot, she thought. Sera wanted to walk despite the weather. Snowmobiles held no attraction for Agnes, the urbanite. Give me a romantic sleigh ride, she thought and grinned in self-mockery. Or the Explorer, at least.

The droning of the engines ceased, and a moment later, the outer door opened to reveal two snow-covered, helmeted figures. They stopped on the rubber-backed welcome mat, shedding snow and droplets as they raised their visors. Both wore black parkas with the lodge's red devil logo above the heart.

Agnes went over to greet them. "Hi there." She smiled at the younger guy before addressing Jac's brother. "Nice to see you, Phil. How are you today?" Silently, she cursed her habit of babbling when uncomfortable. "I'm afraid my mom wants to walk." Figuring it sounded rude, she laughed as if indulging a parent's whim. Which she was.

"Hello, Agnes. Okay by me," he said. "Gabe and I don't mind. It's not far. He's ground staff and out in all weather."

"Hi, Gabe," Agnes spoke pointedly to the much younger man. "Kind of you to come along." The kid looked a little embarrassed, twisting his gauntlet gloves around in his large hands. He was just as tall as Phil's six foot, if not a little taller.

"Hi, Dr. Taylor," he said diffidently. "You won't remember me. I was in one of your philosophy classes at U of T. I'm Gabriel Gagnon."

"Wow, what a surprise running into you here. Yes, I recall. Must have been two years ago. A pleasure to see you again." With so many students, her recollection of them was rather dim, but of course, she remembered her one term teaching at the University of Toronto. "What brings you out here working at Tremblant?"

"I'm from Montreal. My father still lives there. Phil got me the vacation job at his dad's, I mean, at their resort." Gabe glanced sideways at his employer, who was growing impatient at their prolonged exchange.

"I'll get my mom and Polly, then. We'll be ready in a moment," she said.

It turned out to be less than a ten-minute walk, taking a shortcut through the woods next to their log house. The guys left the skidoos behind to be moved by Gabe later. Phil walked in front with Sera. Snatches of their conversation, mere conventional small talk, carried back with the icy headwind.

The drifting snow made talking a chore. Flanked by Gabe on one side and Polly on the other, she said, "Too bad you can't be with your family over the holidays."

The young man shrugged. "Makes things easier. My parents are divorced. If I'd spend it with Dad and his girlfriend, Mom would feel hurt. She's a cop and transferred to Toronto when I got accepted at U of T. Now I'm back in Montreal for my MA in creative writing, and she's stuck in Ontario."

As Agnes sensed Gabe's unease over his family issues, she switched topics. "How come you got the gig up here? Aren't there jobs in Montreal?"

"Sure. I work at a pub downtown. Phil's the manager. He knows I love being outdoors and hired me for the holidays at the lodge."

Hmm, interesting, thought Agnes. So, Phil worked in the hospitality industry. Yet, he didn't see his future in running the resort his dad felt married to, which would explain the rift between father and son. Worth checking into the son's ambitions for the future. It only struck her now how little Jac ever talked about the Xaviers.

A vicious gust of wind caught Agnes's hood and pushed it back to bare the wooly hat she wore below. Twilight descended rapidly. The dark clouds, blurred by blowing snow, were even less defined against the darkening sky.

From a few steps ahead, Phil's voice fought against snow and wind, calling, "Here we are."

They stood in front of a small Quebec-style cottage set in a clearing no larger than an urban backyard. The steeply sloping roof formed a canopy over the front porch, supported by wooden pillars. Two latticed sash windows shed mellow light to welcome the guests. They flanked a solid, red front door decorated with a wreath. A twinkling Christmas tree glimmered behind the snow-rimmed glass panes.

"C'mon in out of the cold," urged Phil.

When he opened the door to let them pass, loud, irate voices penetrated to the outside. Taken aback, they stopped dead on the porch.

Phil waved a hand at Gabe, who made to leave, with a murmured "Merry Christmas." Agnes wasn't sure if it was sarcastic or resulted from embarrassment. She called after him, "Thanks, Gabe. See you around."

Polly, who'd been silent on the way over, now said, "Nice kid," which sounded funny to Agnes. Gabe was probably a mere four or five years younger than Polly and towered over her by a foot and more.

As Phil ushered them through the entrance into the living room, the voices, ebbing and flowing in varying degrees of animosity, appeared to come from another room farther back.

"Oh, bother, not again," grunted Phil and kicked off his boots. "Ignore them. Let's get you into the warmth," he added with artificial cheer.

Subdued, they removed their footwear and stepped farther into a masculine living room. Furnished with northern pine antiques, rawhide leather armchairs, and a tartan sofa in forest green, blue, and beige, it spelled relaxation. The obligatory wood stove radiated welcoming heat. As Agnes stepped closer to warm her freezing fingers, the accusing eyes of a stuffed moose head stared right at her from above the rough-hewn mantel.

She turned her back on it and sauntered to the Christmas tree by the window.

Close up, it revealed wooden ornaments of skiers, black bears, Canada geese, and assorted wildlife, all unique vintage collector items. Only the arguing voices coming from the bowels of the cottage prevented Agnes from exclaiming in delight.

Solicitously, Phil helped Sera to shed her ski jacket and was about to store it when the dispute rose to a pitch. His own belated call of "*Père!*" was drowned by a voice Agnes did not recognize.

"I'm acting on information received," it shouted. "If you think you can drive the price up by playing coy now, think again. Our offer is more than—"

"How often do you want me to repeat—I won't sell. To you or anyone."

The second yeller, a sonorous bass with a Quebecois accent, might be Robert. She associated a deep francophone voice with her memory of Jac's father. As Phil visibly cringed, she assumed to be correct.

"Why call Gino if you're not interested?" The first speaker's tone grew nastier.

Immediately, Agnes's ears pricked up. Wasn't that one of the similar sounding names Sera had mentioned last night?

"I did no such thing," blustered Robert. "In fact, I told the little weasel to get lost before I'd kick him out."

"Your son—"

The son clearly didn't want to be dragged in. Whether the cold turned his cheeks a deep red or his sire's inhospitable conduct, he shouted something in French, which Agnes failed to grasp. No matter its meaning, both adversaries stormed into the room and stood transfixed on seeing the guests.

Despite the brief acquaintance and the lapse of ten years, Jac's father was easy to identify by his indoor clothes. Dressed in a bulky, beige cable-knit sweater and broadly ribbed brown corduroys, Robert's face was as crimson as his heir's. Not surprising, given the emotional and actual room temperature. In no time, she'd be sweating in her thick fleece and the tense atmosphere, Agnes figured.

By comparison, the other male, in his mid-fifties, presented the air of a sleek, urban businessman. Perhaps aiming to appear unruffled, he stroked his clean-shaven chin and wished them a good afternoon. Only Sera responded promptly. As he strode to the door, he buttoned his black camel-hair coat, donned a silver-gray Karakul hat, and departed without a backward glance.

Aha, the prospective buyer, Agnes deduced. How convenient to stumble to the heart of the matter. The Gino in question must be the agent Jac had mentioned. Robert's threat to kick him out sounded like Jac's dad could well deal with harassment.

Agnes made a mental note to ask Sera later about this Gino, apparently one of the people in their log house. Shouldn't be hard to strike an acquaintance and learn more.

The rapid exchange in French between father and son distracted her. At least, it cleared the atmosphere sufficiently for them to refocus on their guests. With profuse apologies, Robert fussed over seating them comfortably and asked Phil to fetch refreshments from the kitchen.

Talk of the weather and the prospect of being marooned by a major dump if a blizzard developed, diverted from the altercation they'd witnessed. While listening with half an ear to the conversation, Agnes surreptitiously watched Robert. How could she guide the conversation to what she needed to find out for Jac and satisfy her own curiosity?

"What happens if you get blizzards?" she heard Polly ask. "I googled and saw pics of humongous snow drifts."

"Well, you might lose a day of skiing if the roads are impassable and the lifts close," admitted Robert. "We'd keep you entertained. Our snow-shoe and Nordic ski trails are groomed in no time. I have a three-hundred-acre property with an extensive trail network. Keeps you busy for a day or two." His laugh was heartier than warranted, it seemed to Agnes, whose mind conjured up power outages caused by inclement weather.

Phil's return interrupted her thoughts. He loomed large in a bulky sweater over jeans as he placed a tray on the tiled coffee table and distributed cups and small plates.

The brew proved hot, strong, and excellent. So was the assortment of sumptuous *petit fours* in various shapes, colors, and styles. Soon, everyone relaxed, Agnes was glad to see. While their chat about skiing at Tremblant held little interest for her, sampling the pastries did.

Just when Agnes wondered again how to introduce real estate investors, Polly jumped in at the deep end with a question about development and expansion in the area. Apparently, she'd noticed the building boom around Tremblant when she and Sera drove up from Montreal. Keen on the environment, as Agnes knew from their German encounter, Polly's interest was the encroachment and impact on the national park.

Shadows of the earlier spat soon spread.

At first, Robert answered reasonably enough. He pointed to the increase in condo developments around the resort and in the neighboring communities. Real estate values increased steadily, and an influx of second-home buyers from Montreal and Toronto drove prices up, he asserted.

"It benefits local homeowners and businesses to some extent, doesn't it?" said Sera.

"Sure. Values have doubled for many. The tourist industry means profits and jobs," said Robert. "But our youngsters can't afford their first home, and Quebecois seniors don't have a lot of money either. Rents shoot up. Why offer long-term leases to local folks if you can Airbnb for four times as much and more?"

"Won't your resort profit from the tourism boom? Seems fully booked, from what I can tell," said Polly.

"If we weren't during the holiday season, we'd be in serious trouble," said Phil, who'd been rather quiet throughout the exchange, though Agnes felt sure his hooded blue eyes didn't miss a thing. "Not so great during the off-season and even in summer. There's way too much competition."

"We've managed so far and continue," their host said.

To Agnes, who focused on listening intently, the flat tone appeared to hold a hidden message to his son.

If so, Phil ignored it. "C'mon, Dad. Times are tough. Airbnb and mega corps are killing us."

Turning to Sera, he explained, "The most difficult thing nowadays is to staff a place like this. College kids come up during their vacations to work in hospitality but want to be close to the action at Mont Tremblant. None of that on the north side. It's off the map. Without a car, nothing goes. We can't house the entire staff. Our overhead is huge, and—"

"I'm sure our guests didn't come to hear your tirade," interrupted his father, who'd been drumming his fingertips on the leather armrests. "All this is no reason for me to quit. No matter what you think."

34

Perhaps to distract Phil, Sera asked him, "Do you work at the lodge full-time or only during the season?"

"Hell, no," he said contemptuously. "I'd die out in the sticks. My own digs are in Montreal. I manage a bar in the old downtown core."

"And dreams of buying in," supplied his dad. The dismissive tone showed what he thought of his son's aspirations. With interest, Agnes realized her gut feeling was correct. The controversy had to do with the pub job.

"Why shouldn't I? At least the bar has a future." From Phil's tone, Agnes guessed it was a well-worn argument.

"So has this resort. If you would pull your weight—" Robert interrupted himself, maybe shocked at growing louder. He wiped his mouth with a white handkerchief and turned to Sera as though confiding made up for the social faux pas. "My son and daughter are part owners of the lodge. They inherited their mother's share. My wife passed away. Cancer."

Though Agnes recalled Madame Xavier's passing when Jac had been an undergrad doing a study abroad year in France, the sudden mentioning made her uncomfortable.

"I'm so sorry," said Sera and included Phil in her compassionate gaze. "A harrowing loss for all of you."

For a moment, Robert's eyes glazed over. "It was years ago. The youngsters were grown up," he replied, a little gruffly. "Now, each of my children has an equal part of their mother's half-share." He glared at his offspring. "I count myself lucky the wife insisted on the lawyers adding a codicil. We all must agree for the lodge and property to be sold. Otherwise, this young fool could force me out. He's trying hard enough as is. Over my dead body, sonny."

Sera shifted in her seat, clearly uneasy. Time to interfere, Agnes figured. Unless she brought up the laptop issue now, she'd lose her opportunity. A little too brightly, she said, "Oh, before I forget, er, Robert," feeling awkward addressing the angry man, "Jac asked me to show you something, uh, on the internet. When would be a good time?"

The fierce glance he bestowed on his heir made Agnes regret having spoken. His voice was calm enough when he said, "If it's quick, we could take a moment now. If you won't mind, Sera?"

"Go right ahead, please," her mom said graciously. "My daughter mentioned it earlier."

"Would you like to see photos of how this place has changed over the decades?" Robert asked. When Sera and Polly assured him they'd love to, he spoke as if his temper never had flared. "Phillipe, why don't you show Sera and Polly the album? My wife was keen on documenting how the resort grew. I've tried to add to her collection."

As she followed Robert, Agnes was glad she'd forewarned her mom. The den they entered was tiny, just a recliner in front of a TV, plus a small desk with a chair and an open laptop, its screen dark. Photos and memos, stabbed by thumbtacks, covered the walls.

"I'll just log in, and you can set up this fingerprinting thing Jacqueline insists on," Robert said and sat in front of the desk. The cramped space allowed Agnes to stand right behind him and glance over his shoulder. Ideal for testing if he used any precautions. Oblivious to her closeness, he typed awkwardly with his index finger. After he hit j, a, c, q, and u, she could have closed her eyes and still been sure of the password.

Yikes, so much for security. Causally, she asked, "Do you always work in here, or do you have another office where you take your laptop?"

Focused on waiting for Windows to load, Robert replied, "I take it with me to the office at the main lodge. That's the original building, you know," he said with pride. "We need this machine for planning and all kinds of day-to-day tasks. But it's set to go to sleep after ten minutes."

And anyone who ever watched you can wake it and log in, thought Agnes while she guided him to activate fingerprint access. Off-hand, she inquired, "You say, 'we.' How many people need to use the laptop? I'm just thinking in terms of us changing the access now. Will you need to share a new password with anyone? Say, like your son?"

Robert threw her a dark look. "I'm not sharing it. Philippe has no call to use my laptop. And the manager I employ only uses it in my presence."

Not wanting to offend her host further by probing questions and anxious about her mother waiting, Agnes briefly explained how to choose a secure password others wouldn't be able to guess at and recommended ways to keep it safe from prying eyes.

When they returned to the others moments later, Sera said, "Well, it was lovely to see what you made of a little hunting camp. Wonderful photos. We so appreciate you taking time from your busy holiday schedule."

Robert looked very pleased but said the resort needed a bit of work.

Sera assured him, "Your place is just lovely. The proximity to the park and all the lakes—simply stunning. A phenomenal area in any season, I find. Fall for hikes, summer canoeing, winter skiing. What more could one want?"

With a cheerful laugh, she qualified, "The black fly season, of course, puts a damper on things for a few weeks."

Like a wet cloth, Phil grumbled, "Not to mention the spring floods before the bloodsucker season. Never a dull moment."

As everyone grabbed their outerwear and thanked Robert for his hospitality, he said softly to Agnes, "It was good to see you. I know my little girl is very fond of you. Thanks for being such a good friend to her."

Agnes almost choked on her reply, thinking of the mission his little girl had tasked her with for the holidays.

"Enjoy the special Christmas dinner at our main restaurant tomorrow night. I reserved a table for the three of you. It's on the house," Robert said and waved off their gratitude.

Phil led them out into the blowing snow. No sign of Gabe.

Darkness had descended while they'd been huddling by the fire. Agnes glanced back at the twinkling lights behind the frosted windows. Backlit by the mellow indoor lights, their host stood in the open doorway, bulky and solid like a ship in its berth. A man who wouldn't budge or bow to pressure.

'Twas One Day Before Christmas...

CHAPTER 5

Morning of December 24

AGNES

"Ah, don't let them defeat you," a male voice said behind Agnes. Cheery early birds spouting platitudes, detestable at any time, were an insult when one struggled to wrestle recalcitrant skis from a roof rack, thought Agnes, not bothering to turn. Stationed in the parking lot at the North Face lift of Mont Tremblant, tons of people around her unloaded their equipment for a day's skiing.

"May I lend a hand?" the guy offered.

Of all the silly questions—she glanced over her shoulder and promptly lost her footing in the clunky ski boots. Before she could crash down from the Explorer's elevated sidebar, brawny arms lowered her gently to the slushy ground.

"So sorry to startle you," he said.

"No, all my fault. Thanks," she said, straightening up on safe ground. "Slippery soles."

"These boots aren't made for walking," he sang out and made her smile.

When he lifted his ski goggles, Agnes recognized him as the taller and more muscular of the two guys they'd encountered in the bistro two nights before.

"You are..."

"Greg—at your service." A mock salute and, one-handed, he hauled her skis off the SUV while she dived for her poles and helmet in the cargo space.

"I'm Agnes," she said as she twisted her unruly hair into a coil to squish it under the helmet. "Nice to meet you again." Of course, they'll be seeing lots of each other, given the proximity of the apartments in the log house.

"I hear you're a friend of Phil's sister."

Her involuntary "Oh?" prompted him to explain, "Phil's a friend of ours. He told us you'd be staying downstairs with your mom."

"Ah, I see." So, it was this Greg whom Phil intended to meet in the bar. Well, made sense for Jac's brother as a part owner to invite his friends for the holidays. But didn't Sera imply the people in the other apartments belonged to a large family party?

Before she could figure it out, Greg's face split into a broad grin. "There comes my better half with your friend Polly."

Following his glance, she caught sight of Polly and Greg's slim-built partner—was it Joe... Jack? Instead of joining Agnes, Polly waved to a petite female unloading a snowboard from the roof of a hatchback.

While Polly sauntered over to speak to the helmeted woman, Greg's partner sped on. "Hey, Agnes. How're you this morning?" he greeted her. "Your mom said to meet her at the lift. Sera's doing a quick warm-up run."

"I'm well. How about you? Oh, and thanks for telling me where she's got to." Everyone seemed to know more about her mother than her. "Sorry, didn't catch your name the other night."

"You sure looked bushed. Arriving at night is the pits, isn't it? I'm Josh. We've chatted with Polly and your mom a couple of times already. They always get up early, don't they?" His laugh sounded nice. "Phil told us to make sure you were comfortable and found your way around."

Next to Greg, Josh appeared much smaller than from afar, side by side with Polly. Not more than an inch above her own 5 ft 6, Agnes figured. The tight-fitting black ski garb accentuated his slim build. His broad-shouldered partner towered over him. Their fondness for each other spoke in every glance the guys shared.

"Your mother knows this place better than us, I bet," said Greg. "She

41

told us about skiing at Tremblant for ages, and how she saw the ski resort develop over the past thirty years and more. Just like my nonno."

"I've got some memories of skiing here as a kid," said Agnes. Not the most pleasant ones, she added in her mind. "Mostly sliding down the bunny run on my bum. The ski instructors despaired of me." Her laugh sounded forced to her own ears.

"Hey, don't say you don't love skiing," cried Josh, mouth wide open in mock outrage.

"Want the truth? It frightened the hell out of me as a kid. I gave it up entirely as a teenager. Something's wrong with my genes. The sporty ones didn't transmit, as you can see." She patted her hips self-consciously. If such predisposition were genetic at all, she thought, her unknown dad's must have been 100% couch potato.

"Oh dear," said Josh. "And Mom's a wizard on skis, is she? Your friend Polly has done Heli snowboarding in the Alps, from what she let on. Geez, not the best slope match for you." He looked so crestfallen; it made Agnes laugh.

"I guess I'll take lessons again and let them do the black runs."

"Hey, what's up, guys? Aren't we meeting Sera at the lift?" Polly called from ten yards away. "Let's get cracking. Nine o'clock already. Time's a wasting."

Speak of the daredevil, Agnes sighed as she watched the tiny Polly in a baggy outfit, helmet straps dangling, approach in a bouncing gait.

Beside Agnes, Greg reached over to relieve her of her skis.

"Here, let me carry them," he offered. "You'll get to lug them around often enough today."

As they walked towards the lift, Polly said, "Me and Maria are going boarding together this afternoon. Her hubby is too busy. Sounds like one of these workcation type of guys."

A quick glance passed between their male companions, Agnes noticed, but couldn't interpret it.

"You know people at this place?" asked Agnes. "I thought you've never been to Tremblant?" Secretive, or maybe fiercely private, as Polly had been already in Germany, she might know people here and elsewhere. In the summer, Agnes googled her with little success. Polly and Holt were too common to allow for an ID. After they'd left Bosum for Berlin, they discovered Polly had published a feature article in a very well-known German news magazine, but under a different name. Hard to determine how many pen names she used and what her real name might be, Agnes figured.

"Maria and Gino are in the other downstairs apartment. Talked to her for a bit in the great room last night. I couldn't sleep and watched TV there so as not to wake you and your mom."

Trust Polly to beat her in striking up an acquaintance. Well, apparently not with the guy but with his spouse. Agnes had noticed Polly's interest in the unhappy young couple arguing in the bistro. It only clicked when Agnes asked Sera the night before who Gino was. She didn't want to reveal her actual interest in the man or discuss Jac's family affairs with her mom, never mind with Polly, whose curiosity was insatiable.

"Eh, you know what?" Greg interrupted her thought. "We've got the perfect ski buddy for you, Agnes. My Aunt Bella. You'd never find a nicer person and gentler guide to skiing. She taught me as a kid. Just yesterday, she was saying she'll take it easy and stay mostly on green runs."

"Oh, I wouldn't want to impose—"

"She'd love to have your company, I'm sure. My Uncle Teo is too busy for skiing."

"I can't leave Sera—" As the words formed, Agnes realized it was quite ridiculous. If anything, her own clumsiness on the slopes would hamper her mom's enjoyment. They could do a run or two together in the morning. After that, she would take a lesson, or maybe, yes, she could at least meet Greg's Aunt Bella.

"I'm so sorry, Aggie," said Polly. "I figured you two would want to spend some quality time alone. So, when Maria said Gino won't go..."

"Don't worry about your mom skiing alone," put in Greg. "We've got the perfect partner for her, too. Haven't we, Josh? My nonno is the most expert skier of—"

"Hey, you won't believe this." Josh pointed with a gloved finger. "Look over there."

Ahead of them, at the end of the lift lineup, stood Sera in animated conversation with a man in an old-fashioned racing-style red and marine blue ski outfit. Unlike most skiers and snowboarders mingling about, he wore a matching wool beanie rather than a helmet.

The bright sunshine sparked off the narrow, silver reflection stripes on Sera's lapis blue ski jacket. Her mother had insisted on cycling and skiing helmets for as long as Agnes could remember. Safety first was her motto. Learn how to do things properly and then take calculated risks. Mostly, Agnes skipped the latter.

Her glance strayed toward the distant summit. From down here, only the dark green of trees against the white was visible. Above it, a brilliant blue sky. A long-forgotten yet familiar shiver prickled from her shoulder blades along her arms. Once on the lift, she'd have to ski down. Who'd want the total humiliation of descending alone like a failure on the chairlift, ogled and pitied by countless people on their way up?

Must be regressing to childhood, she thought. Grow up, darn it, she exhorted herself. If you don't like it, you can always go back to the lodge. And sulk. The last made her grin.

"Need help with your skis?" asked Josh when Greg lined them up for her to step into the bindings.

"I think I remember," said Agnes and promptly had them snap shut, with her boot slipping out sideways.

Josh went down on one knee, flipped the binding back again, and guided her toe and heel in. A couple of satisfying clicks and the skis were secure.

One foot strapped onto her snowboard, Polly scooted ahead to Sera.

"Let me introduce you to my nonno," said Greg. "He's quite a character, eh Josh?"

"Sure is. Can't hold the candle to Nonna. You've got to meet her, Agnes. She's the sweetest little old lady you've ever seen."

"Oh, is she skiing, too?" If grandparents brave the mountain, so can you, Agnes coaxed herself.

"Not her. Nonna's a homebody like Rosa. That's my mom," said Greg. "They don't venture out into the cold."

"Women after my heart." The guys grinned at her self-mocking sigh.

With Agnes pushing herself laboriously along with her ski poles, they'd finally reached the trio at the end of the lift line. To Agnes's practiced eye, Sera looked a little impatient to be on the lift again but masked it with a welcoming smile.

"Nonno, meet Agnes. This is my granddad, Matteo. Skis like the devil."

Under his dark blue hat, rimmed with two red stripes, the weathered features of the elderly gent creased into countless wrinkles as he saluted Agnes with a formal bow.

"I am delighted, signorina," he said. "Your mama told me how pleased she is to be skiing with you."

"Likewise," murmured Agnes, somewhat embarrassed after admitting to the guys how she felt about skiing. "Nice to meet you. Greg told me what a fantastic skier you are. I'm just an eternal beginner, I'm afraid. Not in my mom's league."

"It'll come back, dear," said Sera.

Nothing can come from nothing, Agnes wanted to say but swallowed the thought.

They fell in step, moving in line to the six-pack chairlift, with Sera and Matteo in the middle, Greg and Agnes on one side, and Polly with Josh on the other.

"Actually, I was thinking, Nonno, wouldn't it be nice for Bella if Agnes would spend a few hours with her on the green run? If you can spare her, Sera, I mean. Perhaps you could give Nonno a run for his money." Greg laughed disarmingly.

The grandfather's face beamed. "It would be an honor, signora. You see, my son and my wife don't ski. For very different reasons. These young yahoos," pointing his pole at Josh and Greg, "are just too reckless for me."

Josh shook his pole in the air as if rearing to conquer the slopes.

Greg rolled his eyes, "Yeah, right, Nonno," he said to Sera. "Why not meet up at the summit at lunchtime, say at one? You can talk it over among yourselves, and I'll text Bella to meet us up there."

Once they'd settled and closed the chair's safety bar, Greg reached into his pocket to pull out a mobile and held it out to Agnes. "Take my number and text me if you'd like to swap ski partners."

Not comfortable fishing out her phone while holding her poles, she dictated her number.

Huddled shoulder to shoulder on the chair for six, the ride to the summit passed quickly with bantering and ski anecdotes from Matteo and the guys. Wedged in between Greg and Josh, Agnes almost forgot about her fear of heights. The lift on this side of the mountain was not high off the ground. Or maybe, no longer being a small child, it didn't feel as scary.

Agnes didn't share her nightmarish childhood memories of a ski instructor frightening her to death with horror stories of naughty children not closing the safety bar and plunging from the lift. Or steel ropes of lifts failing. Another story was about skiers stuck on a lift during a power outage, dangling a hundred meters over a valley.

Icy ripples ran up her arms under the warm jacket. Was it last winter she'd seen online news of 150 people trapped in gondolas in the French Alps?

Now, she wondered why she'd never told her mother about the ghoulish instructor. Instead, she'd just howled when her mom dropped her off at the ski school. No recollection of what Sera had done about it. Probably remained calm but firm. The 'never cry wolf' syndrome of a daughter who threw too many tantrums.

"Tips up—ready to unload," Greg's cheerful voice broke into her dark thoughts. "Remember, we'll meet again at high noon."

"Smokin' guns and all," quipped Josh as they raised the safety bar a bit early for Agnes's liking.

Now came the true test, gliding off the chair without knocking into her neighbors and making their entire row tumble like dominoes.

CHAPTER 6

Afternoon of December 24

"Hey—look at 'em go," cried Polly Holt, out snowboarding the same afternoon with their apartment neighbor, Maria. Weight of the board shifted onto her free-dangling foot, she twisted around on the chairlift to follow the passage of two tykes zooming down the black run on teeny-weeny snowboards.

On the outer end of the seat beside her, Maria craned her neck, knocking her board against Polly's in the process. The couple on the other side remained mute and uninvolved—their faces inscrutable behind full face masks and goggles.

"Kids are so amazing," sighed Maria, delicate porcelain doll features dimpling.

The wistful tone prompted Polly to ask, "Got one at home?"

"I wish." With a timid giggle, she elaborated, "Three is my goal. Gino says to wait until he's making better money. Omigod, he's so busy. I hardly see him at home." Perhaps worried about sounding negative, she rushed on, "No, don't think I complain. With all the kiddies at work, I'm okay with it."

"Cool. What's your job then?"

"Daycare—I'm in ECE," said Maria—all five feet of her sitting erect in pride. "Early Childhood Education. I graduated with a college diploma two years ago. The little monsters keep me hopping, I can tell you."

The trilling laugh delighted Polly. "Is hubby also an educator?" she asked and caused a renewed ripple.

"Gino? You've got to be kidding. No, he's all business. A Bachelor of International Business and all."

"Sweet. Ah, you met at college, eh?"

"No way. His BBus is from university." Again, the pride came through loud and clear for Polly. "We met clubbing. Back in the day," her tone dreamy now.

"You can still do a lot more club hopping with no kids at home." Unless the dude prefers barhopping with his chums. The way he dumped Maria the other night without a backward glance smacked of habit.

"Not with Gino always out at night. I totally get it. Him needing to network, I mean. Like wine and dine prospects and that stuff. If only..." Her pal's sweet voice faded.

The hut at the top of the chairlift came into sight. Hm, thought Polly, working late, eh? Curiosity triggered, she slipped on her gloves and fished for more, "Ah, so tough on you stuck at home. What line of business is he in, then?"

"He's self-employed," Maria said, like it was a special achievement. Well, maybe it was. "Scouts for developers. When we first dated, he still worked for Matova."

"Ma—who?"

"You know—the huge family at the resort," said Maria, like any dummy ought to be better informed. "All of them belong to *Matova INC*. The Executive Board's annual meeting, they call it. Must be nice, the company paying for your ski hols." With this, she slid down the ramp.

Polly kicked like mad with her right foot to catch up.

Once they'd scooted along the top to a double black diamond run, the steepest and narrowest as far as Polly could tell, Maria beat her in strapping the left boot into the binding. Made one feel downright ancient, thought Polly, to watch this agile babe swoop down the hill.

She hastened to follow and promptly had to stop after a few hundred yards to adjust her binding. When she scanned the slope to see if Maria was waiting for her, Polly noticed angry voices wafting from farther down, near the trees along the side of the run. Two skiers, to judge by their stance. One leaned forward, braced by ski poles. The other waved a pole in the air for emphasis. Something about them struck a familiar chord. None of her business. Still rather interesting.

One eye searching the hill for her new friend, the other on the squabblers, Polly let a few moments pass before gliding in controlled speed in the latter's direction. Snowboarding along, facing uphill and downhill with equal necessity, enabled her to catch a good gander.

The male of the pair, his goggles pushed up onto his helmet, made identification easy. Matt from upstairs. Saw him at the bistro with the owner's son, Phil. Plus, she'd run into him almost literally this morning when peeking out their cottage's front door. Introduced herself, which gave him no choice but to do likewise. The pole-wielding female, Polly figured, might be his spouse. There was a certain intimacy of manner.

Seemed the cheer of the season led to a lot of domestic spats. Could get abusive. She'd covered enough domestics as a news hack when she started out at a small local rag.

C'mon, Pol. Chill out, she exhorted herself. You're on a holiday.

Not to embarrass these two, she pretended zero recognition and sped downhill to catch up with Maria.

CHAPTER 7

Still Afternoon of December 24

AGNES

"Terrific! You've nailed it," called Bella from a few yards lower down the slope.

The praise and brilliant smile filled Agnes with pure joy. Without a hitch, she stopped, not in the slightest danger of toppling over.

"The trick really worked. This time was so much easier," Agnes said as she panted from excitement as much as from the unaccustomed exercise.

When Greg introduced his aunt in the crowded eating area at the summit, Agnes immediately felt drawn to the serene woman, maybe 15 years her senior. With Bella, she felt she needn't be embarrassed about never having progressed beyond beginner level. Sera and Matteo couldn't wait to hit the slopes together. Well, Polly hardly stopped to eat lunch at all.

"Practice makes perfect," said Bella now.

"No, it's thanks to you," said Agnes. "You're a natural teacher."

Her companion erupted in delighted laughter. Elegant in a tailored black ski outfit—the jacket stepped in tiny diamond shapes instead of the popular puffer style, crowned by what Agnes feared to be real fox, Bella's expression grew wistful.

"I really should teach again. In my distant younger years, I used to. Elementary grades in a Catholic private school." With a hint of regret, she added, "Somehow, I never went back after my son was born."

Before Agnes could respond, Bella said, "How about playing truant for a while? Given what we've accomplished so far, we deserve a treat. The *Nansen-Bas* takes us straight to *Place Saint-Bernard*."

Agnes's, huh? elicited an apologetic smile. "The green run we are on leads to the central hub of the resort."

"Sorry, no clue of the whither and whence. I'm following you blindly without reading signs or the map. This morning, I made one disastrous attempt at the North Face with my mom and then joined the tyke brigade on the bunny hill. They were about my speed."

"Oh, you are doing wonderfully well. You've mastered the south side with flying colors, Agnes. The long run we did right after lunch is on the Sun Side. *Le Soleil* chairlift took us back to the top. This is the south-central side now. Once we're out of the trees, you'll see the resort town. You'll love the Express Gondola ride back up later."

"So, we're now going to Tremblant village?" asked Agnes.

"No, the old village is still a few kilometers away. The resort at the foot of the mountain dates back only to the early 1990s. A make-believe town solely devoted to hospitality services and commerce."

"I'd no idea."

"Let's go on and find a cozy coffee shop where we can chat at leisure," said her guide and pulled down rimless, rose-colored mirror goggles, shuttering the smiling eyes. "Your turn to go first."

With much more confidence, Agnes pushed herself off, using her poles. Under Bella's directions and teaching by example, she had learned to traverse the hill in gently descending diagonals. Initiating a turn proved no longer a nail-biting experience. Hard to bite them anyway when encased in bulky mittens, she supposed.

A paid instructor would intimidate her, Agnes figured. Taught by a nimble guy in his early twenties, she'd be two left feet, self-conscious and clumsy. Whereas a genuinely understanding and caring woman like Bella proved a tonic for an out-of-shape restarter.

As they continued at a slow, steady pace, Agnes surprised herself, wondering if she might tackle a blue run in a few days. For now, the last stretch of the green took up her full attention. Increasingly narrow, it tunneled between boulders on both sides, with houses crowding in on the right. Before she could panic, Bella coasted ahead. With a "follow me," she demonstrated how slowly the skis glided when not making any turns at all.

"What a fairytale village," cried Agnes as they came out into the open.

Covered in snow against an azure sky, sunlight sparkling, glimpses of wine-red, pewter, and slate-blue metal roofs tantalized the eye. A Mediterranean flair emanated from the beige and ochre houses—windows, balconies, dormers, and turrets whimsically outlined in contrasting or matching colors of the roofs. The architects of this complex clearly aimed for harmony in diversity. Each of the three-storied houses differed from its neighbor in some features and in size. Yet all contributed to the same design concept and overall palette.

"We can stroll through the streets if you like. Let's get rid of our skis first," said Bella, waving her pole at the numerous racks in front of the buildings. Reluctantly, Agnes tore her eyes from the view and propelled herself along the busy flat stretch. Snow enthusiasts came shooting down from the steeper slopes to perform snow-spraying, skidding stops at the lift lineups or ski racks.

On Bella's advice, Agnes stored the right and left rental skis in different racks to deter theft. Her companion secured her own expensive pair with a lock. They laughed when they said simultaneously, "Now for the washrooms." Bella pointed to a café right across from the Express Gondola.

Not long after—furnished with giant bowls of *café au lait* and sumptuous pastries—they conquered barstools at a ledge facing a widow. Bella removed her helmet and gave her head a shake. Lustrous black hair fell into a perfect short bob. Pays to have an expensive coiffeur, thought Agnes in envy as her own curls sprang out of their confinement every which way.

"*Cin, cin,*" toasted Bella, clinking her green mega cup against the gold rim of Agnes's. "To many more delightful runs."

"Right now, a little ski holiday appears an enjoyable prospect," said Agnes.

"Oh? Were you in doubt? Your mother and sister love it, don't they? At least, from my brief impression when we met at lunch."

"Polly's a fairly new friend, actually. Both are such experts. It must be painful to ski with a beginner like me."

"I feel out of my league when skiing with my son Matt and his wife, no matter how often he assures me they don't mind," said Bella with a sympathetic smile. "His nonno taught both of us. The Italian Alps daunted me, while my rubber-legged offspring did slalom around his dad and grandpa."

They grinned at one another.

"Do you ski with your spouse most days?" Agnes asked.

"With Teo? No, not usually. It's a business trip for him. The annual board meeting of our company." Hesitating, she added, "And plans for a new development command his energy. Besides, we all take turns staying with Nonna to keep her happy. Winter is not my mother-in-law's favorite season."

"Ah, Nonna sounds like my kind of person," said Agnes with a grin. With a vague hand sweep, she went on, "I'd love to hear more about Mont Tremblant. Such a wonderful toy town, isn't it?" Might get a more balanced view from the Xavier's yesterday.

Bella stirred her coffee. They both contemplated a family passing outside. The kids chomped on Beaver Tails. The long, flat, sugar-laden, flaky pastry half-wrapped in white paper was a Canadian specialty easily recognized from afar.

"Intra West built it from scratch. They developed and operated lots of North American ski resorts, like Steamboat in Colorado, and Whistler-Blackcomb and Panorama out in western Canada."

"Past tense," observed Agnes. "It's now an independent town, is it?"

"Not really. There are multiple corporate and private interests and ownerships. But Alterra owns and operates the Tremblant ski resort now," said Bella.

Agnes's sleuthing nose quivered. Quite casually, she asked, "How come you know so much about this?"

"Let's call it a business interest. We specialize in real estate development and property management. Matova INC is a family affair, you might say. Everyone serves as a board member. Except for Nonna. The

Company, as we call it, has holdings in several provinces, primarily in Ontario and Quebec."

Bingo, Agnes's mind produced a series of images and rapidly drew connections. Greg and Josh high-fived the elusive Gino at the bistro, who hastened after them to the bar. Phil and the tall man in a parka also went into the bar. Sera knew him as Matt from the apartment upstairs. And Bella and son, Matt, were on the board of the family firm.

So, they're all in it together? Agnes wondered and chewed her croissant to gain time.

Was Gino working for Matova?

Bella's spouse was too busy with a new project to go skiing. Was he the elegant, urban businessman in the shouting match with Jac's dad? The pricey attire matched Bella's.

Not something one could ask about without further ado, Agnes realized. Nor did she want to kill the enjoyable sense of instant rapport with Bella. Any display of her own interest might ruin things. Though wouldn't Greg and Josh have mentioned her being a friend of Robert's daughter?

She needed to figure this out without rushing into anything. Aloud, she said the first innocuous thing entering her mind, "How wonderful for loved ones to work so well together and celebrate the holidays in a spot like this."

"You sound wistful," smiled Bella.

"Do I? Maybe it's because I only have my mom."

"I'm sorry. Did your dad—"

"No idea who fathered me or if he's somewhere out there. Mom never told me." Confused about being so blunt, venting her pet peeve to someone she'd merely known for a few hours, Agnes's cheeks flushed. Uncanny how this woman's serene vibe prompted confidences.

"Well, families can be difficult," Bella commiserated. "Tensions arise from too much proximity. Fathers and children don't always agree. Especially with much at stake. Teo and Matt are a case in point. And so is Cheryl, er, my daughter-in-law."

The faraway expression of her companion stopped Agnes from speaking. Like an afterthought, Bella said, "She's hand in glove with her dad, though."

Lost, Agnes asked, "Who?"

"Oh, my goodness, I didn't realize." Bella's focus returned. Agnes suspected her companion hadn't been aware of voicing a thought. "My apologies. Lately, things worry me. Menopause?" She laughed unconvincingly. For a few seconds, she studied Agnes's face. "Sometimes, we need to trust our instincts. Mine tell me you are safe to talk to."

"Oh," muttered Agnes. Flattered, she admitted herself capable of keeping a confidence. In fact, professionally, she often had to, whether or not she wanted to.

As if reading her mind, Bella agreed, "Teachers are used to being dumped on, aren't they? Anyway, the place is rather public for a heart-to-heart. Only so much, my disquiet relates to the awkward position of my son's wife. Cheryl plays a key role in the Company's property acquisitions, but she also owns half of her dad's company."

"Is that a bad thing?" Her comment came in reflex while she grappled with the implications. Was there an ulterior motive for this unsolicited sharing? But Agnes felt sure no one knew about the mission Jac had tasked her with. To see how far Bella would go, she said, "Don't many people sit on multiple executive boards and hold interests in several outfits?"

"Sure. A conflict of interest arises if they compete for the same projects. A question of loyalties and insider knowledge. Unreasonable to expect a couple not to share information. Or a daughter and father. Where lies the stronger obligation?"

On cue, Bella's phone vibrated discreetly on the counter next to her empty bowl. With a glance at the incoming SMS, she sighed. "Time's up. We don't want to rush our last run down the *Versant Nord*."

"Ah, I'm so stiff," groaned Agnes, sliding off the barstool.

"Oh, you'll love the promised gondola ride," smiled Bella. "Then down *Petit Bonheur*. A 'Little Happiness' is the perfect way to end a glorious day."

CHAPTER 8

Evening of December 24

AGNES

By nine-thirty on Christmas Eve, Agnes felt exhausted and a little overwhelmed by all the good cheer at Nonno's party, as everyone seemed to call it. After skiing, when Sera relayed Matteo's invitation to a casual get-together at the chalet the Matova family rented, Agnes had welcomed the opportunity to find out more about the Company and its members.

It also proved a perfect morsel of information to relate to Jac in their phone call. Loath to spoil Jac's Christmas cheer by reporting the father and son spats and her own suspicion Phil might collude in siphoning unauthorized info, Agnes felt relieved Jac's mind was on revisiting Paris's famous Quartier Latin.

Agnes had even enjoyed the short walk over to Matova's place despite the blowing snow. Greg had lent an arm to Sera on one side and Agnes on the other, making them laugh by pretending to fight a much worse storm. Josh and Polly ducked close behind the frontrunners' backs and made a great show of using them as a windshield.

The wide-armed hug from Bella upon their arrival was a lovely welcome. The party turned out to be a casual open house affair for the first hour. People from the neighboring cottages popped by for a drink, spicy eggnog, or mulled wine. Some dropped in on their way to other evening engagements. The noise level didn't allow for meaningful conversations, and Agnes didn't catch most of the names. Hard to tell who was family beyond those she'd already met before.

Within the last ten minutes, the steady stream of drop-in guests had dwindled. Apparently, Matteo had invited Sera to join a card game, and Agnes didn't mind staying on but needed a moment of quiet after the din. The Christmas carols set at low volume created a soft backdrop.

Their own party included, over a dozen people still mingled in the Matova chalet's great room. She noticed Robert at the card table with Matteo, Sera, and another woman.

When did Jac's dad come in? Perhaps it explained why she hadn't seen the young couple from their own log house, Maria and Gino, Agnes mused. Even as the proprietor, Robert wouldn't show up if he'd run into the guy who pestered him. But if Matova INC was after buying the lodge property, and Robert refused to sell, why would he join their party? Agnes hadn't noticed Robert's antagonist, the urban businessman, this evening. He certainly wasn't here now. Not Bella's spouse, then.

"*Ah*, away from the maddening crowd," said a cultivated voice close beside her, interrupting her reflections.

As Agnes pivoted to see the speaker, he bowed. "Yours truly, Pierre Voltaire." One hand raised to forestall comment, he uttered a well-practiced refrain, "No—no relation of mine in this best of all possible worlds."

For a moment, she eyed him, speechless. His quoting his namesake, the eighteenth-century French writer, was par for the course. Her loss for words arose from pure aesthetic pleasure. The flawless skin, a rich mocha tone with a dash of cream, framed by raven close-cropped curls highlighted by silver streaks around the temples, accentuated the striking features. Regular workout toned muscles spanned chest and arms under a beige cashmere sweater over deep-indigo jeans that spilled onto dark brown Blundstone boots.

Only when his eyes and mouth crinkled appreciatively did she realize her stare. In hopeless confusion, she stuttered, "Oh, I wasn't ... I mean. Agnes—I'm Agnes." Furious heat prickled on her throat and cheeks.

In her embarrassment, she scanned the room, pretending she was expecting someone. Silly, of course.

"Seems you're stuck with me," said the gorgeous Adonis. The mental image brought a deeper burn to her face. "My apologies, I hope I didn't discomfit you. Sorry about my poor manners. Especially since Bella asked me to make you comfortable."

The mentioning of her new ski companion restored a sense of proportion. Agnes took a steadying breath and said, "Not to worry. I'm just trying to sort who's who before joining the fun again."

"How about I grab us some of the hot hors d'oeuvres the restaurant staff just delivered? Then we park ourselves over there." He pointed to a cozy window seat next to the tastefully decorated Christmas tree in ivory and gold, sparkling with mellow light chains and angel hair. "I take you for a sideline observer type like me rather than the center stage variety."

"Got me pegged, alright," grinned Agnes. "I'll save you a space." The tantalizing scents of appetizers wafted across the great room of Matova's place. Mouth-watering, though she'd already indulged in the profusion of canapés, prosciutto, olives, grapes, and nuts on display.

Installed now on the well-padded seat, concealed by the spruce tree's luscious branches, she inhaled the spicy resin scent of the branches and relaxed. From this vantage point, it was easy to appraise the gathering in the well-proportioned room. As in their own place, a soaring window wall extended to the upper story and into the rafters. A blazing fire overheated the space. Agnes was glad her hideaway was sheltered from the flames in an inglenook at the far side of the room.

Pierre returned with a tray of goodies. Saying, "Hold this for a sec," he placed it on her lap and fetched a pine bench to relieve her of it a moment later. "Here—serve yourself." He offered her a dessert-size plate and festive paper napkin.

Close up, the food smelled divine. Without hesitation, Agnes loaded up and popped a golden puffball into her mouth. As the melting gruyere hit her tastebuds, her eyes devoured already a Philo square oozing spinach and feta. A chuckle from her left brought her to her senses.

"Woman, you sure enjoy your food. A pleasure to behold these days when dieting reigns supreme." Pierre lounged against the sidewall to face her comfortably. "Tell me, have you met everyone yet? Should I give you a run-down on who's who?"

"Yes, please. New faces and how everyone's related still confuse me. To begin with, where do you fit in?" As soon as it was out, Agnes cringed at the ambiguity and hastened to explain, "I mean—"

"No worries, I get you. A black in an *Italo-Canadese* family is unlikely to be a natural offspring." His amused laugh lessened the sting. "My relations are two-fold. On the one hand, I'm married to the patriarch's daughter. Rosa over there," his hand waved at an attractive, well-rounded woman in her fifties Agnes had seen at the card table and now rejoined the players.

Surreptitiously, she glanced at Pierre. Must be a good ten years or more than the woman's junior. His dark eyes mellowed further as he gazed across the room at his full-figured, curvaceous spouse.

A smile still lingering, his face swiveled back to Agnes.

"On the other hand." He paused on a raised note. "A black guy looks good at the Company Board's table." Into her shocked silence, he said, "Don't think I mind. Suits me just fine. Their representation is an asset to my portfolio. I'm a lawyer, you see."

"Are you Quebecois?"

"Not me. My people hail from France. Rosalinda and I fell for each other on my home turf, the Big Apple. By then, she'd tired of roaming the States and yearned to return to the family fold—or Canada, I guess. Fine by me. A quiet spot like Toronto makes for an easier life."

"Hahah, not how us Torontonians view our mega city. You're right, though. Compared to New York City, it's downright provincial, I imagine." The evening promised to pay off after all if she could tap into Pierre's insider knowledge. Of course, a lawyer might be cagey. Still, worth a try. She rested her plate on the bench and prompted, "Now, on to the rest of the bunch. Unravel the mystery of their connections."

"Nothing mysterious, I assure you. You've met Nonno, I take it?" Agnes nodded. "Matteo II, the *paterfamilias*. The real ruler, of course, is our dear Nonna, the matriarch Valentina over there."

Somewhat incredulous, Agnes bent forward to seek the elderly woman by the fire, enthroned in a wing chair much too voluminous for such a small stature. Wrinkled like an apple doll with lily-white hair, she talked animatedly with Polly, who hunkered on a stool at her feet. Their chat appeared to involve a lot of gestures and laughter.

"Yes, a tiny personage. So was Napoleon, if you recall." His deep chuckle was rather sexy. "Granted, Nonna's a few inches shorter than the emperor."

"Not on the Company's executive board, is she? Bella mentioned it."

"Nope. Valentina rules the roost. A far more important power base."

While he spoke, raised voices on the other side of the room caught Nonna's and their own attention. A distinguished, elegantly clad man with well-groomed hair more silver than black stood abreast of a guy maybe half his age and evidently took him to task for something. The broad-shouldered young man gave back as good as he got. With shushing sounds, Bella hastened over to them.

"Ah, angel Annabella to the rescue," commented Pierre. By now, Agnes could guess, but Pierre confirmed for her, "Matt scolded again by his dad."

Though what with the fur-lined hat and heavy parka, she'd virtually seen nothing of Matt's face at the bistro. Bella's expressive features spoke of motherly love. Didn't take a Holmes to deduce the trio's relationship.

"Teo never learns to let him be," said Pierre quite conversationally. "In case you are wondering, the male Matovas are actually called Matteo, after the founding father of the Company, Matteo I, who emigrated from Italy in the wake of World War II."

Elegant and prone to shouting, he might well be, but this Teo was not the man who'd argued with Robert yesterday. One eye still on the trio, Agnes asked, "Is Teo the head of the Company?"

"Matteo is the president, Teo the CEO."

"Matt and spouse stay at our place. She's not here, though?" said Agnes, scanning the room for any female who might fit the bill.

"Um." Pierre fiddled with his empty glass. "Cheryl's with her dad, I assume. He arrived yesterday."

"Oh, my. How many of you are there? I'm losing count." Agnes masked her interest behind a humorous tone while her mind unraveled the threads. From what Bella said about Cheryl's father, it sounded like he had a competing firm. Was it farfetched to assume the man at Robert's had been Cheryl's dad?

"Her dad is not joining our party," said Pierre as though closing the subject.

"Ah, I see," said Agnes. It would sound odd to ask for a description of the dad to confirm her suspicion. Something she needed to follow up on in a different way. Another burning question would fit in far better now.

She hoped it didn't sound pointed. "Which reminds me, I'd been looking earlier for the other young couple from our place, er, Maria and Gino. I believe they're friends of Greg and Josh. You must know them too, then, as Greg's..."

Pierre chuckled. "Yep, technically, I'm a stepdad, I guess. Rosa and I only married a few years ago when Greg stood in no need of a dad. Not after doing very nicely without one for the first twenty-plus years of his life."

"Oh?" Her interest quickened. Anyone fatherless could count on her full sympathy.

"No reason to feel sorry. The young blighter makes no bones about preferring to be the center of his mom's universe." Pierre's ineffectual attempt at looking severe made Agnes laugh. Yet, she realized the lawyer was digressing from her intended point about Gino. "I'm not telling you a secret here. Rosa shares with all and sundry how she lit three candles when the guy packed his bags before finding out she was pregnant. Saved her all kinds of legal costs for custody battles."

A hollow bang interrupted, accompanied by a gust of icy air. All eyes swiveled to the door onto the front porch. Still swinging in the wind, admitting blowing snow, it evidently had thudded against the exposed log wall.

"Shut the damn door," yelled Teo.

The man, dusted in white, his face concealed by a fur-lined aviator hat and neck gaiter, propelled the woman, wrapped in a hooded *Canada Goose* parka, forward out of the draft. His foot shoved the door, banning the elements.

Comments on the brewing storm from all sides aimed to gloss over Teo's rudeness, Agnes thought as she herself remarked on the weather. Only to have Robert's resonant voice rise above the general babble, accosting the newcomers in French. Unable to catch the words, the lodge owner's puckered brow and tone as he approached the door alerted Agnes to his seething anger. From across the room, Josh hurried over.

Oh no, Agnes thought, not another scene. She didn't need to wait for the face revealed to recognize Phil now. Did he bring his girlfriend or partner? Jac hadn't mentioned one.

61

Next to her, Pierre gave an exaggerated sigh, "We're in for another son bashing."

Still following her thought, Agnes asked, "What is Robert yelling about? Who is—"

"Didn't you hear him? I assume you know his son, Philippe. The prima donna, shedding her garb so exquisitely—"

Whatever else he might have said was drowned by the woman's high-pitched screech, "Don't touch me, poofter!"

As if zapped by a live wire, Josh, who'd tried to catch the coat as it slid off her shoulders, jumped back.

A collective intake of breath preceded a momentary stunned silence. Then everything happened at once.

With a muttered, "Bitch," Pierre jumped up, leaving Agnes speechless at this family drama.

Then, a sweet voice called, "*Vieni dalla nonna, mio piccolo Giosuè,*" accompanied by dry, elderly hands clapping the armrests of the wing chair, eased the tension. It stopped both Greg and Pierre in their tracks and eased Josh's frozen features. Meeting him halfway, his spouse wrapped an arm around his upper back and led him to their grandma. Polly moved aside to make room for them.

As the elderly lady's arm reached up, pulling Josh close for a smacking kiss on the cheek, Agnes figured Nonna must have called for Josh to come and join her. Out of the corner of her eye, Agnes noticed Matt striding over to the woman who viewed the assembly, apparently pleased with the effect she'd caused. The gold-blonde mane freed from the hood tumbled over her shoulders, contrasting vividly with a shimmering black top.

Hm, Agnes thought, obviously Matt's spouse, Cheryl. Joining the party late with Phil. Interesting.

With a slight headshake, Bella made to follow her son but turned back and spoke to the sneering Teo. From Bella's stern expression, Agnes judged even an angel's patience had its limits.

Only now did Agnes think of her own mom, who still sat with Matteo and Rosa at the card table. The fourth chair, pushed back, stood empty. Robert's outburst had broken up their game. Nonno, dressed in a vintage brown sweater that sported an old-fashioned skier image embroidered on its front, half rose and fluttered his arm up and down like saying, no harm done.

Her mom, however, looked pale. Might be the lighting, Agnes thought. Still.

Pierre's glance followed hers as he asked, "Want to see how your mother's doing?"

As they passed by the fireplace, Polly made to join them. The movement caused Nonna to turn, her crinkled features lighting up. "Bella!"

Confused, Agnes told the elderly lady, "Sorry, no, I'm Agnes."

Pierre chortled. "Nonna means you're beautiful. She's got a good eye."

A familiar flush crept up Agnes's throat. She remained mute to Nonna Valentina's, "*Come stai?*"

"Say, '*va bene,*'" prompted her legal aid.

When Agnes proffered her hand and murmured, "How are you?" the little grandma rose to her full height of four-foot-eight and reached out for Agnes's hands. The dark eye twinkled.

"*Mascalzone, Pietro,*" Valentina wagged a finger at Pierre.

"Who's calling me a rascal? I'm your *avvocato*." He squeezed the tiny woman in a fond embrace.

With one arm around Josh's shoulder, Greg regarded his young stepdad indulgently. To Agnes, he said, "Are you coming out for first tracks tomorrow?"

"Um?" Neither the words nor the change of topic made sense to her. But better than dwelling on the shocking spectacle from a few moments ago.

"We expect tons of powder by morning," Greg explained. "They open early for season pass holders or if you pay for early admission."

"No worries, Aggie, I'll fill you in." Polly sidled up to her, looking tired and much older.

A stab of guilt for not having spent any time with their visitor, almost intentionally avoiding her, prompted Agnes to ask, "Are you okay, Polly?"

"Still jet-lagged, I guess," Polly smiled. "Gotta get up early to hit the slopes, don't we? What an exhausting day of fun all around."

While Polly bent over Nonna for a quick hug, Pierre said to Agnes, "Let's talk some more over coffee soon, if you like."

Agnes shot him a glance and waved 'goodnight' to Valentina and her grandsons. As a source of information, Pierre was ideal. As a man, he was all too attractive for his own and her good. Drop-dead gorgeous males were her downfall. A married one was a non-starter.

"Hm," she said non-committal and headed for her mom's table.

Pierre followed in her wake. "Woman, I'm not proposing to seduce you," he said with assumed offense.

"Is he flirting terribly with you?"

The melodious contralto prevented Agnes's response. A proprietary beringed hand hooking into her husband's arm, Rosa winked at Agnes. "Don't mind my Prince Charming; he can't help himself."

"Oh, he wasn't. I mean, he's just been..." Before she could stutter any more inanities, Agnes pulled herself together. "It's getting late. My mother probably is ready to call it a night."

Under other circumstances, she supposed, she might have liked this formidable lady who obviously was at ease with her voluptuous figure. The chestnut, chin-length, wavy hairstyle suited the discreetly made-up, heart-shaped face. The dark brown eyes sparkled with amusement as she watched Pierre air-kissing Agnes's cheeks.

"Tell her I'm safe to be let out for a coffee, Rosa darling," he joked. "And you never know when you might need a loyal lawyer friend, Agnes."

"By all means." His wife chortled. "Your mother is a delightful person, Agnes. A true card shark. She and Nonno beat Robert and me, hands down. Our family's antics spoil the evening's pleasure."

With Polly tagging along, they ventured over to the two remaining card players.

"Ah, *la filosofa*." Matteo got up to greet Agnes. He was slightly shorter than she. "Your *mamma* tells me you are a professor, young lady." With a bow, he shook her hand for the second time tonight.

"Thank you so much for having us. It was so kind to invite us on Christmas Eve, sir," said Agnes. "Mom, are you ready for bed? Polly's getting sleepy."

"*Mi scusi*," apologized Nonno and hastened to pull back Sera's chair as she got up. "My dear, I should not have kept you so long."

"It was my pleasure, Matteo," Sera assured him. "Our little game was most enjoyable."

Gallantly, the elderly gentleman took Sera's hand into both of his and bowed to air-kiss her fingers. Apparently, they really hit it off, Agnes deduced.

"Pierre, grab a coat and walk our friends home," instructed Rosa. Their assurance it was quite unnecessary for anyone to go out into the cold on their behalf was waved aside by the others.

As they went to say their goodbyes to Bella and Teo, Agnes noticed Matt and his spouse had left. So had Robert and son. She saw Josh help Valentina to a downstairs apartment.

A moment later, Josh, Greg, and Pierre reappeared in parkas and hats.

When Agnes, Sera, and Polly stood wrapped snugly in outerwear, the paterfamilias wished them a Merry Christmas and hoped to see them again soon.

"Ready to tackle the storm?" asked Pierre.

The blizzard certainly was ready for them as Pierre opened the door.

And A Merry Christmas to All...

CHAPTER 9

Dawn of December 25

POLLY

"Walking in a winter wonderland—Gone away is the bluebird," trilled Polly softly on Christmas morn as she skipped through the fluffy stuff towards the pond, or where she assumed it to be hiding under a thick white blanket.

Pre-dawn, the string of lights along pathways shone brightly, reflected by zillions of ice crystals. This was true Christmas magic. Nothing could have kept her in her cuddly sofa bed any longer. Without making a sound, she'd crept along on stocking feet, boots in hand, and let herself out into a transformed world.

Still an hour to go before Sera would be up, never mind be ready for first tracks. The guys from upstairs planned to join them. Too bad Aggie didn't feel up to it. Had no idea what she'd be missing. Must remember to leave the little present.

A figure emerging from the main path—now deeply covered in snow—interrupted her train of thought. Curious about what other early bird was up and around, she stopped to wait, masking her intention by throwing snowballs that scattered like dry powder.

"Maria?" For a moment, Polly wasn't quite certain. The familiar snowboarding jacket of the small figure, a neck warmer pulled up to the eyeballs with the hood drooping from above, allowed a guess.

When a gloved hand reached up to tug at the face-covering, it proved her right.

"You're up early," Polly said and immediately regretted the silly remark.

Her boarding buddy mumbled something like, "Couldn't sleep," and brushed past. Not before Polly caught the fear in eyes so wide the whites showed unnaturally. Perplexed, she stared at the retreating back and followed.

Not paying any heed, Maria went into their building and crossed the great room. Didn't bother to remove snow-covered moon boots and trailed white stuff across the pine floor. Polly kicked off her UGGs and spurted to catch her buddy before she disappeared.

Needn't have worried—Maria left the apartment door wide. An invitation to enter? Still, Polly hesitated. Didn't want to intrude. For all she knew, Gino might be up and about in his underwear. Or less.

Concern won out, and treading softly—ready to take flight at the slightest sign of life within—she sidled into the small living room, a mirror image of their own, outfitted almost identically.

In her jacket, hood still up, Maria sank onto the edge of the sofa and doubled over, her arms hugging her shins like in pain. A soft moaning muffled by the thick material of the collar.

Ears pricked for any sound from the bedroom or bath, Polly squatted in front of her.

"Maria, listen. Are you ill? Should I wake up Gino?"

At the last words, an agonized cry rose and subsided into sobbing. Polly slid onto the sofa and rocked Maria gently in her skinny arms, attempting to provide warmth and solace, yet painfully aware of them not quite reaching far enough around the other's baggy jacket.

When the sobs eased, she tried again. "Won't you tell me what's wrong? Maybe I can help."

"No!" And then quietly, "No one can help me."

"Are you in pain?"

A hysterical laugh turned into a hiccup. Polly jumped up and ran to get a glass of water from the kitchenette. With one arm around Maria's back, she urged her to drink. After several tries, she succeeded. The water stopped the hiccuping, and its coolness seemed to bring the distraught woman to her senses. She did not resist when Polly pulled off the mittens soaked in tears and carefully rubbed her icy fingers.

"Let's get rid of this coat and wrap you in a blanket. You'll feel better stretched out. Eases the diaphragm." Like a soft body doll with a porcelain face, Maria allowed herself to be arranged more comfortably on the sofa, cushions elevating her upper back and head.

"I'll make some coffee. Or better still, hot strong tea." Best remedy for whatever ails anyone—or so the Brits claim—Polly mentally chattered.

As she filled the small electric kettle and rummaged through the cabinet for mugs—at least having a twin setup over their way, she knew exactly where to find stuff—it suddenly hit her. The racket Maria had made was enough to wake the dead.

So why did Gino sleep through it? Hung over? Those two hadn't been at Nonno's Xmas Eve bash. Later, no one was in the great room or came out when they got back and yakked for a few minutes with Pierre, Greg, and Josh making plans for today.

Pensively, she removed wrappers from complimentary tea bags, unearthed creamers from the mini fridge, and grabbed sugar sachets from the counter. Back in the living room, she laced the stewing tea with sugar. Supposed to be good for shock and stuff, she figured.

"Milk in yours?" Getting a nod, she stirred it in and squatted to be eye-level with her reclining patient. "Careful. Pretty hot." After a couple of assisted sips, Maria grabbed the mug in both hands, showing she could manage.

Polly dumped a couple of fat cushions from a settee onto the floor so that she could be close yet face Maria. No point in asking again, she thought. Either the patient talks of her own accord or—so be it. Can't stay all that much longer. Sera will be up soon. Not sure what to do.

The sweet beverage must have done the trick. For resting the mug on a side table at the head of the sofa, Maria rushed into anxious speech.

"You must think me a total wimp to make such a fuss. About him not coming home one night, I mean." Face averted, the dimpled hands twisted and threaded the fleece blanket like trying to make a knot.

Ah, explains why the commotion fell on deaf ears, Polly deduced and resisted verbalizing her mental knee-jerk reaction. Bloody hell, I'd be beside myself if my spouse—if anyone ever was crazy enough to marry me in the first place—didn't come back during a blizzard out here.

Instead, she aimed for diplomacy. "Well, naturally, you would be a bit concerned. If it's unexpected, I mean." And t'was the night before Christmas—oh, that really sucks.

"I thought he might. He was so angry." Maria's hand swiped at her cheeks, smudging teardrops. Before Polly's glance could discover a box of tissues like the one on a shelf in their own room, Maria had used her sleeve to wipe her nose.

"Honestly, it wasn't my fault. He went on about how we didn't get invited because of me. Like I should be more friendly to Matt and his cousin. That's so not true."

"Heck, the party wasn't grand to begin with. You didn't miss—"

"Silly—it's not the party he cares about but business. Matt promised to talk to his dad, and Greg was to help."

"Sorry, you've lost me. What about? Why would he not come home then?"

The questions brought Maria up short. A wary glance assessed Polly and appeared to find her wanting.

"I think I need some sleep now." Lids closed like a door. Dismissed.

"Well, try not to worry too much." Inane advice, Polly told herself, never helped anyone. Defeated, she collected the empty mugs and carried them to the sink. A glance at the clock on the microwave sped her on.

Just when she eased the door shut, she heard Maria say, "See you tonight."

Perhaps not all was lost.

CHAPTER 10

Morning of December 25

Ten o'clock on Christmas morning found Agnes on the ski lift, going up the North Face of Mont Tremblant. No sight of Sera and Polly when she woke up all groggy an hour ago. Hard to relate to their enthusiasm for fresh powder. White stuff was white stuff, as far as she was concerned.

With a somewhat furtive glance, she turned to Pierre, her only fellow passenger. As arranged the night before, he'd picked her up at the apartment to drive her to the north base. "You really don't have to stay with me. Once we get to the top, I'm okay on my own." Brave words. The prospect daunted her.

"Woman, you break my heart. I was looking forward to a few hours of skiing in your company," the unflappable lawyer said. "Rosa and Bella are at church with Nonna and Nonno. I'm free until lunchtime."

Instead of revealing the soulful eyes she remembered so well from last night, the blue-toned goggles threw back a miniature of her own helmeted head when she twisted awkwardly on the lift bench to gauge Pierre's expression.

Fat flakes fell steadily from snow-laden clouds, running a gamut from silver to lead. No matter how often her mittens swiped, wet layers covered her thighs and jacket sleeves. Visibility decreased the higher they went.

Scary stuff. She hated the disconnect of poor vision. So easy to lose one's way on the vast terrain.

Into the muffled silence of the mountain, she said, "Are you sure? You'll find me dithering at every hump on the green and the slowest of the slow. If I'm not crossing my tips and topple over."

"No worries. I'll pick you up whenever you fall." His pole beat a tattoo on his ski. "How about one run before morning coffee at the summit?"

"My kind of skiing. It's a plan." Maybe she'd still discover the joy at a Christmassy winter wonderland if the clouds lifted.

Like hugging this thought to herself, she pulled the wooly-soft, azure-blue neck warmer over her nose. A present she'd found next to the coffeemaker with a note, "See ya at the summit for lunch—Santa's elf."

Warmed by a fuzzy feeling inside out, she wondered how Polly liked the green and red elf hat with a tiny golden bell at its jelly bag tip. To make sure Polly would find it under the Christmas tree, Agnes had sprinkled a paper trail of tiny notes to the gold-wrapped package while Polly was blissfully snoring on the sofa. The memory split her mouth in a wide grin, well hidden by the gaiter cuddling her cheeks.

Left well alone, the awkwardness between her and Polly might sort itself, she hoped. Or was that a cop-out? No matter. Right now, she had more immediate worries.

"Here we emerge from hibernation and ready ourselves for new adventures. Tips up—as they say," her ski buddy announced.

The warning came not a moment too soon. Together, they glided down the lift ramp. Already, while going up, Agnes had noticed far fewer people on the lift and slopes. Usually the busiest spot, the summit area wasn't crowded. Maybe everyone was still home, lingering over breakfast and opening gifts. Somehow, being out made Agnes feel virtuous.

"What's your favorite run?" Pierre waited patiently for her to slip her mittens through the pole straps, all the while drawing teeny Christmas trees in the snow with the tip of his own pole.

"Not sure I recall which is which to have any preference. The sunny side was nice when I went with Bella."

"As long as you don't mind a more exposed ride up. *Le Soleil* crosses a long open area, remember? Always chilly in weather like this. But you'll truly appreciate your coffee break after. Grab my pole end. I'll pull you along the flat stretch."

Her own poles dangling from her wrists, Agnes hung on tight for the next few yards until her skis gained momentum.

"Let go and do your turns," he instructed. A few vigorous skate kicks and Pierre skied ahead and, to Agnes's amazement, flipped around to ski backwards, watching and coaxing her on with praise and prompts.

Despite the unrelenting snowfall, she progressed well, too focused on her guide to worry about falling.

On the flat stretch at the bottom, he held out one pole behind him and catching on right away, she grabbed it with both mittens to let him pull her along. By the time they reached the lift line, she glowed with exhilaration and pride. Not a single tumble all the way.

The tiniest stab of being excluded marred her holiday spirit as Pierre bantered in French with the blond lift attendant who scanned their passes. Her high school exposure to the language had faded into nothingness long ago. Still, she could echo the woman's cheerful '*merci*.'

"Who says you're a slow skier? You were just amazing. I'm impressed," said her ski partner as soon as the lift swept them away. Again, they were the lone riders on the six-pack chair, huddled side-by-side in the middle to avoid tilting it. Well, she admitted to herself, one could sit at opposite ends to balance the weight.

As Pierre swiveled sideways to face her, she tugged the azure gaiter up to hide a rising blush. Its softness muffled her speech. "Thanks to your coaching, I didn't even notice how I got down. How come you ski so well?"

"You mean for a black guy?"

His mouth twitched for a moment as if in pain before twisting into a grin when she replied, somewhat offended, "I did not. What's color got to do with it?" Her mind provided the answer by conjuring images of the predominantly white and Asian ski population she'd seen thus far, here and in Ontario.

Saving her further embarrassment, he explained, "My parents ski and took me along from early on. Mostly Vermont, New Hampshire, and the Rockies, but also the French Alps. For a while, I competed in races as a kid, then lost interest in my teens." He lifted his goggles. "It is a white sport—in every sense of the word." The grin took out the sting.

Into minutes of contemplative silence, the lift cables groaned and clanked each time they passed a tower. In search of something innocuous to say, Agnes scanned the tree line to her right. As on cue, she noticed smoke lazily rising from among the trees.

"Is that a fire? Over there. See?" Her pole served as pointer.

"You didn't notice before? The *Refuge du Trappeur*. Never been there?"

"No. What is it?"

"A rustic café. Smoke's from the wood stove."

"*Ahh*—can we go there? I mean, for our coffee?"

"Sure. If you're up to trying a blue run."

For a moment, Agnes hesitated. The snow fell heavily, obscuring vision. What the hell, why not? Won't see the slope anyway if this keeps up, she told herself. Aloud, she said, "Let's try. With help, I might manage."

"Woman, it's a road of no return." The startled jerk of her head made him explain, "Once you're on the blue run, you've got to go all the way down. The only alternative is to switch over to a black run. Or slide down on your derriere."

"Hey, I'm good at that. Lots of practice," she joked, amazed at her sudden courage.

Ten minutes later, her legs were shaking. The momentum she gained on the steeper slope caught her by surprise. After a few awkward turns, facing her skis uphill and sliding backwards, only to topple over, Pierre stopped to announce, "I think I'd better tow you to the *Refuge*. Here, hang on to both my poles and hold tight. Give me your poles. They look too skimpy to use."

He extended his poles behind him, and once Agnes grabbed each securely, he slowly glided down the hill with her in tandem. Despite the low speed, she felt her jaw muscles clench.

Just when he called out, "We turn in here," they gained speed. The sudden snow plow he did to slow them again made her slide on. Losing her grip on the poles, her skis slipped through between his legs and knocked right into the V formed by the tips of his skis. The impact brought them both down, Pierre partly on top of her.

Evidently a man of fast reflexes, he rolled over to face her sideways.

"Are you alright? Did I hurt you?" One gloved hand reached out to wipe snow off her goggles while the other lifted his own shades onto his helmet. His velvety eyes were grave with concern.

"I'm so sorry—all my fault to make you fall," Agnes stammered. A giggle rose insuppressibly in her throat. "What a sight we must've—" Laughter choked off her words.

Joining in, Pierre bounced to his feet and stretched out a hand to haul her upright. "Here, let's kick off your skis and walk the last bit. It's only a few yards farther down."

A few minutes later, they leaned their skis against the weathered railing of the porch and clambered up the wooden steps. The sound of their boots clattered unnaturally hollow in the snowy stillness.

Warm, moist air mingled with wood smoke and coffee aroma when they entered. The dimness of the old log cabin blinded after the whiteness outside. Rough-hewn tables, some long with benches and a few smaller ones with chairs, filled the small room. Iron racks near the woodstove held mittens and other damp stuff the patrons wanted to speed-dry. Misted, narrow casement windows overlooked the porch facing the valley, Agnes assumed from what she'd glimpsed on the lift ride.

"The food's standard fare, unfortunately, and minimal options," Pierre said, steering her to a table a couple just vacated next to the porch door.

"Coffee is all I need," Agnes assured him and turned towards the serving counter.

"You save our seat while I grab it." Before she could answer, he handed her his helmet and gloves.

When he placed mugs, condiments, and chocolate croissants in front of her, she grinned her approval.

"You deserve a treat after what I've put you through. Don't rat on me to Annabella. She'd never forgive me if I scared you."

"Now that we are safely inside," she said. "I believe I enjoyed it. My legs went wobbly, and my heart was in my mouth. What a thrill. In retrospect."

"Glad to hear it. Because there's more to come." He shook off his jacket and stirred sugar into his coffee. "We've got plenty of time before I need to join the family's Christmas do. Speaking of the devil," he grinned disarmingly, "what did you think of the Matova folks yesterday?"

"Well, too early to form an opinion. Bella is wonderful. I'm sure they are all nice people." If one overlooks the conduct of some of them, her mind added. Here was an opportunity to revert to the question Pierre never answered last night. "So kind of Matteo to invite us. How come the other couple at our chalet wasn't there? Aren't Maria and Gino friends with you guys?"

"Him, we all know very well. The wife, not really."

"*Oh*? Sounds ominous, the way you say it."

"A bit of a rift, shall we say? Without being indiscreet, I can tell you what's public knowledge: Gino used to be associated with Matova as an acquisition specialist." Her questioning glance prompted more. "Land sourcing and prospecting."

"Hm. Sounds like the old gold rush. What does he do?" She kept her tone mildly interested, sure Pierre would explain.

"In layperson's terms, he used to scout on behalf of the Company and its clients for objects to buy and develop. The job involves finding the right properties, analyzing suitability, and putting out feelers to initiate negotiations. Then, one of the senior members takes over. Usually Teo."

"Ah, I get it. Gino no longer works for the Company." Scouts for the competition but hangs out with Matova's younger generation, her mind added.

"Sees himself as independent consultant. The Company disagrees. Anyway, he's good friends with Matt. And Greg and Josh, of course."

"Must make it a bit awkward socially. Especially being at the same resort and during the holiday season. Odd for him and Maria to pick the same place for a vacation. As a former employee and friend of the other guys, isn't Gino aware of Matova's tradition?"

"More than aware. It's not without reason everyone's here."

"Oh, I recall Bella mentioning the Company's business interests in

Tremblant." Confirmation of Phil playing the prospective buyers against each other would be useful. Not the kind of thing one could ask directly.

An oblique approach was in order. "I imagine," she said, "the guys find other times and places to hang out together away from family. Like we saw the cousins, Gino, and Phil home in on the bar the other night."

"No surprise there. Last week, I ran into them at a gay bar in downtown Toronto. Not my kind of hangout, but a client invited me for an after-dinner drink. Doesn't mean every patron is gay. Who knows, he might have had more in mind."

Given Pierre's gorgeous appearance, Agnes could well imagine both male and female clients hankering after his body rather than seeking only legal advice.

"Besides, though your friend Polly is gay, one wouldn't assume you are. In fact, I sense a different vibe." He grinned at catching her intense contemplation.

"People's sexual orientation is their private affair. But, yeah, I'm not. Nor even sure we are friends," Agnes muttered.

"Oh? How come?"

"Never mind, different story." To avoid his glance, she twisted around to the window—and stopped dead. "My god! We'll never make it down. Look how it blows. A blizzard."

"Not yet a storm. Well, time to brave the elements. Don't worry. You'll be fine. This time, you'll go in front, and I'll brake from the rear."

Only when they stood in the swirling snow did she realize he'd skillfully gone off on a tangent, avoiding what she actually wanted to find out.

CHAPTER 11

Early Afternoon of December 25

POLLY

Back from slopes with a long afternoon inside the apartment stretching ahead, Polly felt restless. The wind howled relentlessly. With blizzard conditions, they'd called it a day after a quick lunch at Le Grand Manitou on the summit. Its food court with a stone fireplace and panoramic view was a must stop and loiter. But not today.

The drive back had been dicey. No wonder Sera felt tired and opted for a nap after their early return.

Agnes had texted she'd drive back with Pierre. The morning ski with the sumptuous legal eagle must've been exciting, to judge by the healthy color on Aggie's cheeks ever since.

Polly sighed and made for the door into the great room. "Back in a tic," she called over her shoulder.

"Where're you off to?" Agnes's head poked around the entrance to the kitchenette.

"Wanna check on Maria. Make sure her migraine's letting up."

Nice euphemism, she silently added while crossing to the other apartment. Took three SMS to get a reply from Maria. Concerned about her brand-new pal's ability to cope, Polly had announced a quick visit.

When she tried the door, it yielded to her touch and swung open. The over-heated living room smelled stale. Whiffs of strong liquor fumes mingled with other undefinable odors, none of them pleasant. Closed blackout curtains and no lamps lit, the murky daylight stood no chance of penetrating.

Careful not to step on the discarded outerwear or the blanket littering the rug, Polly picked her way across. Something wet invaded her wool socks. Spilled booze, judging by the stench.

A snuffled snore guided her to Maria's head-end under the bulky duvet bunched in a heap on the sofa. After rousing herself sufficiently to text back and leave the door ajar, Maria must've passed out. The regular deep breathing, punctuated by intermittent snorts, was reassuring.

No sign of Gino. How could a guy abandon his wife on Christmas? Polly shook her head and regarded the vulnerable sleeper while she mulled it over. Did a fling with another woman keep him away? If he'd arranged for his bit on the side to join him during a vacation with his wife, he's got to be a creep. Maybe he'd gone for a visit to Montreal the night before. The current blizzard condition might make the two-hour drive back north to Tremblant impossible. But wouldn't any half-decent hubby give a sign of life? Even if he felt miffed?

Lost, whether to wake Maria or what else to do, Polly considered her duvet-swaddled buddy. Better to sleep it off than waking to a giant head and heartache. Tidy things a bit, in case her man comes back now, Polly figured. Most useful course of action. Plus, leave a couple of aspirin and water at the ready.

First, she cleared the booze bottle and glass away. With an armful of discarded clothes and a towel or two, the blanket trailing the floor, she went to stow things in the bedroom. Her search for painkillers struck lucky. A half-full bottle parked on the sink counter of the ensuite bathroom.

When she returned to the bedroom, she heard a noise.

Totally awkward if this was the errant husband's homecoming. Unsure about coughing or clearing her throat to draw his attention without startling him into a heart attack, she glanced into the living room.

A bulky figure in a parka and aviator-style hat stood bent over the desk, rummaging in its drawers. The outline did not resemble the slim, below-average height dude she'd seen having dinner with Maria the other night. Far too tall and much older to judge by posture and movement. A burglar?

Unlikely. Would take a lot of nerve to enter a fully occupied place on the off chance someone—silly, like her—left their door ajar. Nothing for it but to scare him off.

She cleared her throat loud enough to make him jump. But not retreat. Instead, he switched on the shaded desk lamp. Its dim glow illuminated his features. What was his name again? Matt's dad, something or other.

"Who are you?" Authoritative and belligerent, his tone left no doubt who was in charge. Yet, the volume appeared intended to let sleeping wives lie.

Undaunted, Polly walked in and placed a couple of aspirin and a glass of water on the coffee table within the sleeper's easy reach.

"Friend of Maria's. Her migraine's acting up," Polly said, matching his low volume. Closer to him now, she could see his mouth twist into a derisive grimace. The liquor stench told anyone what caused headaches here.

"Can I help you with anything? We should let Maria get some rest," she said.

His eyes returning to some papers partly pulled from the drawer, he waffled, "I was hoping to catch Gino. One of our employees. The door opened when I knocked. We don't stand on ceremony."

Could be true, admitted Polly to herself. To him, she said, "Sorry, but he's not in at present. Maybe try after the holidays?" After all, it's Christmas, dude. No time to bug people, employee or not, she mutely commented. "Just making sure Maria's got all she needs, and I'll be gone."

The reluctance to leave was obvious in the way he let go of the sheets he held and emphasized by the hesitation in shutting the drawer.

"Someone should clean up this pigsty," he said. "Disgraceful. A woman drunk in the middle of the day." With this parting shot, he aimed for the door.

Now, what was that all about? wondered Polly as she collected another booze bottle she saw lurking under the sofa. Dirty dishes and other debris removed, the place looked almost acceptable. Room service probably hadn't wanted to disturb the slumbering guest this morning.

After washing up the stuff in the kitchenette, Polly checked once more on the sleeper. Like Mother Goose, she tucked the duvet in to leave the face exposed and the mouth breathing freely. A deep sigh and a murmured "Gino" answered her ministrations.

Best to leave a note. The desk should hold the usual hotel stationery. Well, okay, she admitted grudgingly. Just dying to find out what the man was after.

The papers evidently pertained to some real estate inquiries. Surprised, she read the lodge's name and that of its owner. A tentative proposal from Vincenti Commercial Realty. Curious, Polly mused, the Matova geezer claims Gino works for him. Robert shouts he's got no intention of selling. Wow, didn't he threaten to throw Gino out? But, no, Gino wouldn't depart without wifey. Plus, you can't just evict people who've paid for their stay.

Puzzled and aware of breaking rules of trust, Polly dropped the sheets back and wrote a brief note to say she'll pop by again and to call or text anytime. With a last peek at the fragile porcelain face now puckered in a dreamland frown, she tiptoed to the door and closed it softly behind her.

Heavy treads on the stairs drew her attention. Greg came down, dressed to go out.

"Braving the storm again, are you?"

"Family festivity call and brook no refusal. We'd risk our lives and souls if we'd let Nonna down," he said, chuckling appreciatively. Then, his holler aimed at the upper floor, "Get a move on."

The outside door opened, instead, and let in a snow-covered Matt together with a blast of icy air.

On cue, Greg caroled, "Frosty the snowman was a jolly happy soul—" He broke off to say, "Not exactly jolly, are you, man?"

His cousin stamped his feet on the mat and showered the surrounding wooden planks with a white dusting. An unseasonable scowl furrowed his forehead when he pulled off his hat.

"Where've you been, mate? Time to enter the family fold," said Greg with a devious grin.

"Not until later. Cheryl and I meet her old man for lunch."

"Bugger for you."

"Did you see Gino?" Matt asked, frowning more furiously.

"No. Why? Didn't you?"

Polly held her peace.

Behind them, boots clattered down the stairs.

"Here comes the sun," intoned the musical Greg, grinning from ear to ear as he watched his partner descend the stairs all spiffy in tight black pants and a Canada Goose parka.

"What's up?" asked Josh and swung a mega-size Santa Claus gift bag from his hand.

"Seems cousin mislaid our mutual friend," said Greg.

"I thought you said earlier—"

"Mathew!" interrupted a strident voice from midway on the stairs.

Heads swung around at the sound.

"Sorry, Cheryl." Rather than look up, Matt contemplated his boots.

The wife holds the reins, thought Polly. The guys' expressions reminded her of little boys caught sharing a smoke behind the garden shed.

"You are late." Pointedly, Cheryl pushed back the wide sleeve of a silvery shimmering top to consult her wristwatch. "Dad expects us in exactly seventeen minutes." Favoring no one else with a glance, she reascended.

Fascinated by so much woman power, Polly surreptitiously watched the woman's tight buttocks move elegantly under the stretchy material of her skin-tight, charcoal pants. The high-heeled ankle boots emphasized her muscular calves.

Greg's laugh broke the spell. "In the doghouse again." He slapped his cousin's shoulder. "Wouldn't want to be in your shoes. Up you go. Atone for thy sins."

Matt swore and strode after his spouse.

"Show's over," said Greg to Polly's chagrin.

All frazzled, she stammered, "Jeez, I'm sorry. Didn't mean—"

"Hey, don't worry about a thing. You're more than welcome to join any of our family entertainments," said Greg. "It's us who should apologize. Dear Cheryl loves a stunning entrance. Gosh, they have their up and downs, like all of us. Poor guy ended up sleeping on our couch to avoid the fallout, didn't he, Josh?"

His partner merely muttered something under his breath.

Unsure why Greg would share such personal tidbits, Polly beat a strategic retreat.

"Well, enjoy your family festivities today," she said cheerily. "Your nonna's so sweet. I'd steal her any day. Say hi for me and *Buon Natale*. Gotta run. My friends are waiting too."

CHAPTER 12

Same Afternoon of December 25

AGNES

I n the semi-darkness of the twin bedroom, curtains tightly drawn, Agnes cuddled deeper under the covers. A little snooze would be heavenly before afternoon coffee and the Christmas dinner at the restaurant tonight. Her mind drifted back to Robert's parting words. "On the house." So kind of him.

The thought shook her right out of the cozy drowsiness. She should call Jac, who must be waiting for a progress report. Later, Sera would be up and Polly back too. No chance of privacy for a call to Paris without obviously closeting herself. Once Polly's curiosity was triggered, she'd be all ears. Agnes had no intention of disclosing her mission to either of them.

Not much to show with three days out of seven almost gone. Agnes sighed and reluctantly wriggled up against the headboard to grab her mobile from the nightstand. Without turning on any light, she punched Jac's name in favorites. The phone's brrr...brrr sounded like a lonely cry in the ether when no one answered. Dejected, she cut the connection and slid onto her back again.

When she plonked her mobile none too gently into its former place, it vibrated as if in protest. Jac's name appeared on the screen. Phone to her ear, she scrabbled half upright, not giving Jac a chance to speak. "Hey, there you are. I'd given up hope. *Joyeux Noël*, Jac."

"And a Merry Christmas to you, too, Agnes," came Jac's voice from afar. "Have you been practicing your French?"

It was so good to hear Jac all cheerful. A sudden feeling of longing for her friend's presence hit Agnes unexpectedly. Silly, she scoffed. You've just seen her a few days ago. But won't again for months to come. Irritated with getting emotional, Agnes sat straighter.

"So, how's it going in swinging Paris? Are you settled in? Had a good Christmas thus far?"

"It has been hectic, to say the least. Jet lag, of course, and my friends have arranged a full program for me. Visit after visit from the moment I arrived. In fact, you just caught me getting ready to go out again. They'll be waiting for me. I'm so sorry to keep this brief."

"Should I call back tomorrow or the day after?"

"First, tell me quickly how things are at the lodge. You saw Dad and Phil. Oh, and thanks for securing his laptop. I'm so glad that's solved."

The fingerprint login solved even less than a new lock after the family jewels got stolen, thought Agnes.

"Speaking of 'lodge.' Got to be the understatement of the year. You made me think I'd be going to some rustic little hunting camp. And here we are at this beautiful—"

"I'm glad you think it's nice. But Agnes, what's going on up there? I'm getting more worried about Dad. I called him in the morning, your time, and he sounded even angrier. Has anything happened?"

"Well, it's early days, Jac. Don't expect miracles."

"Please, Agnes," Jac's voice rose a few notes higher and rang in Agnes's ear. "I need your help with this. I feel so useless having gone away when Dad and Phil might do something stupid."

"Okay, okay. Calm down. I'll give you a quick rundown of the little I found out." Perhaps, she could evade premature tattletaling about the male Xaviers if she focused on the other players, thought Agnes. Without having a clear sense of what went on at the lodge spreading her impressions of father and son would do more harm than good. "First off, there are really two different parties interested in buying the property. One looks like your typical city businessman. I don't know him or even his name yet. Apparently, both he and his scout or prospector approached your dad, possibly with an aggressive sales pitch."

86

"Did you speak to this scout to get a sense if he is harassing Dad?"

"No, I only know he's young, late twenties, I guess, and called Gino. So far, no opportunity to chat him up." Agnes considered for a moment. Might as well say it. "You could ask Phil. They are friends, I heard. Which brings me to the other party involved. I'm punning here because they are actually an extended family. About a dozen of them. We got invited to their Christmas Eve party last night. Your dad and brother know them. Phil is chummy with the younger generation." As she spoke, Agnes felt quite smug about this bit of news. Then realized how ridiculous such feeling was. After all, the invitation was not her achievement.

"What are you saying about Phil? Is he playing these people against each other? Trying for the highest bid or something?"

"Frankly, Jac, I don't have an idea what your brother is up to. From what I gathered he wants to buy into a partnership at this Montreal pub he manages. At least, that's what your dad says. But going back to the family I mentioned, they are in real estate and property management. Matova INC, it's called. Most of them are really nice and caring. I've been skiing with them."

"My goodness, Agnes. You've been busy. I knew people would talk to you and share things they'd never tell me," said Jac, sounding satisfyingly impressed. "Are they pressuring Dad, too, like the others you mentioned?"

"I don't think so. Give me a few days to learn more. I've connected with the lawyer of the Company."

"You did what? Agnes, you can't call their lawyer—"

Jac's admonition broke off when Agnes erupted in laughter. "No worries, Jac. I'm more subtle than that. Nothing heavy handed. It all comes about quite naturally. Must be the season's spirit, or maybe the lodge's spirit here. It's an awesome place, Jac."

"I'm glad to hear it. So, how did you connect with their lawyer?"

"We skied together this morning. He gave me a beginner lesson. We even went on a blue run." No point telling Jac how that ended. Agnes suppressed a giggle at the memory of their spill. Well, the nail-biting descent to the base lodge in a snowstorm hadn't been funny. Yet, she'd survived, she acknowledged with a touch of pride. "My mom and Polly skied with the younger generation at the crack of dawn because of the powder."

"Ah, first tracks. Lovely. My favorite skiing. They open around eight, not quite an hour before general admission. Try it, Agnes."

"Yeah, well. Next time. Tons of snow's coming down as we speak. At least, I think it's still blowing." Agnes heard rapid-fire French in the background at Jac's end.

"You still there, Agnes?" asked Jac after a moment. "I'm afraid I need to let you go. Tomorrow, we're visiting friends of friends near Versailles. Should we say the day after?"

"Sounds good to me, Jac. Have a lovely evening. Hey, before I forget. Thanks so much for the Christmas dinner gift at the lodge restaurant. You really shouldn't have. But it's so sweet of you and your dad. We're greatly looking forward to it."

"Oh, nothing to do with me," said Jac airily. "Wish your mom and your friend Polly happy holidays for me. And a big hug for you. Enjoy your dinner tonight."

"Hug you too, Jac. I miss you."

When Agnes disconnected, she felt a pang of guilt. So much she hadn't touched on. Interesting that Jac suspected her brother of pitching the buyers against each other. Did Jac also share her own suspicion Phil might have accessed his dad's digital files and passed on information to prospective buyers?

CHAPTER 13

Evening of December 25

POLLY

W hen Polly entered the lobby of the main lodge, it was already ten minutes past seven p.m. on Christmas Day. Conscious of being covered in snow, she slipped out of her jacket and shook it, spraying wetness against the glass door. The young guy behind the reception desk pretended not to notice. She quickly folded the jacket inside out over her arm and rushed across to the restaurant, combing her spiky hair with her fingers along the way.

No time prettying up after the evening's sick visit. At least the patient had taken some broth.

A hostess approached and escorted her to the table Robert had reserved for them.

"There you are, dear," said Sera rather redundantly. "We told them to hold back the appetizers for a few minutes."

"I'm so sorry to keep you waiting. Wanted to make sure Maria would eat the soup I got from the bistro. She's on a liquid diet today." Better not mention what the girl guzzled. Instead, she slid into the vacant seat and draped her jacket over the backrest. "Her bloke still hasn't shown up."

"What do you mean? Isn't he here for Christmas?" asked Agnes. "Sounds unusual for her to be on her own when they came together."

"Not sure what he's up to," admitted Polly, surprised at Agnes's keen interest. She hesitated for a moment, unsure if it was okay to share. The burden felt too heavy for her as an outsider to this land. "Maria told me this morning hubby didn't come home last night. Well, home's not the right word, is it?"

"He is missing. Is that what you are saying?"

"I've no idea, Sera. Too confusing. First, Maria told me he stormed out last night, blaming her for not being invited to Nonno's party. Just now when I talked to her, she hinted he's with another woman."

"Here? At the lodge? Ugh, how low." Agnes's lips curled.

"Quite indiscreet," agreed Sera. "The staff would notice, one would expect. Much worse, however, if he were missing in weather like this."

"Couldn't agree more. Don't want to scare her," said Polly. "When I say she needs to tell someone at the resort, she clams up."

"Well, if she thinks he's safely cocooned with a mistress, you wouldn't want to broadcast—" Agnes broke off as a waiter leaned in with a tray.

As she eyed her appetizer, Polly noticed she'd absentmindedly crumbled baguette slices on her plate. Mind your manners, she urged herself as she buttered a sliver and chewed it thoughtfully. Fresh from the oven.

Aggie asked her to pass the *paté foie gras*. Her mind still on Maria, Polly sipped the *Côtes de Gascogne* the waiter decanted. It complemented the taste of the creamy goose liver paste.

For a few moments, they savored the *hors d'oeuvres* in companionable silence. As expected, the dining room was packed and hummed with conversation. One or two tables still waited for occupants. Like the adjacent one divided by narrow bamboo planters. None of the Matova crowd in sight. The festivities at the family's chalet must be an all-day affair, Polly guessed.

"Does the young woman seem capable of dealing with the situation?" asked Sera. "I'm sorry to be harking back to it. One doesn't want to meddle. Yet..."

"Yeah, exactly. Bothers the hell out of me. If he doesn't turn up by tomorrow—think I should have a word with a manager or someone? I mean, if Maria won't."

"So difficult to say. Interference in private affairs is intrusive. Still, Robert would be the one to talk to."

"Ah, not sure, Mom. We all heard Robert say he'd chuck Gino out. Maybe the guy went home." Agnes fiddled with her fork without lifting it to her mouth. "No, not without his spouse," she said. "Or would he?"

The server approached with their next course. A lime sorbet palate cleanser decorated with a sprig of mint. While she sampled it, Polly's mind churned on. Aggie was right. Maria hadn't mentioned Gino taking his gear. Shoot, should have checked the closet. Nay, two toothbrushes in the jar by the sink. Still, ratting to the resort owner won't do. An explosive type. His son might—

"Excuse me," a voice interrupted. The male of the couple at a table across from them got up to come over. "Your coat. My wife noticed..." With that, he bent down to retrieve Agnes's jacket from the floor behind her chair.

Polly added a polite smile when Agnes and Sera thanked him and his elegant companion, who gave a little wave. The icebreaker inevitably involved them in a cross-aisle chat about the storm outside and the need to bundle up.

Honeymooner from South Korea, the bespectacled guy announced proudly. Didn't have to travel all that far to ski up here as he worked as an intern at a Boston hospital. Their cabin was on the fringes of the resort. Jeong found the path to it roped with string lights, romantic. To Polly's surprise, his newlywed wife, in a pricy Euro-style après-ski outfit, nodded eagerly with a brilliant smile. Didn't look the type to like roughing it in the woods.

Sounds of chairs scraping in her rear made Polly glance around. Through the leafy bamboo planter dividing the tables, she spied Matt. Well, of all people, she thought when she recognized the spiffy man beside him. The yeller from Robert's place. Arm in arm with the stunning Cheryl. Must be her dad, then.

"May I remove your dish?" Their waiter distracted Polly when he whisked away the empties.

In his wake, a waitress served up the main course and wished them *bon appétit*. Salmon in flaky pastry for Agnes and traditional turkey with all the trimmings for Sera and Polly. Cross-aisle talk with the young Korean couple ceased.

From behind Polly, the newcomers' voices filtered through the palm screen. Sheer professional habit trying to catch a few words, she excused herself. A guilty sidelong glance confirmed Sera politely ignored the familiar voices. True, none of their business.

Why then did Agnes, who faced the awesome view outside the large windows onto the giant snowy Christmas tree, surreptitiously eye the newcomers' reflections in the polished glass? A foodie like Agnes absent-mindedly stabbing the innocent fish in its mantle while focused on their neighbors? Something's afoot, Polly deduced.

Behind her, the volume of the table talk increased a notch. If you had dog ears, you could turn them like radars, she thought as she wriggled against the back of her chair.

"Easy for you to say. I promised my family we'd be over tonight. We missed lunch already." Matt's voice rose and fell.

"I should think four hours this afternoon was plenty of family time. Dad flew out from Toronto to spend Christmas with me—with us. Is it too much to ask, spending occasionally a little time with *my* family? You can be all of Boxing Day with yours. I won't get in your way."

"My impression is you came out here on business, Vincent. I didn't expect you to have time to socialize. My family always spends Christmas—"

"Precisely my point, Mathew." The strident diva voice from last night cut him off. "I'm sure they'll understand if, for once, you join us instead."

"Give it a rest, pet." The dad's appeasing tone changed as he said, "Speaking of business, Matt, is your family poaching on my deals?"

"What do you mean?"

"Has my prospector switched sides again? A friend of yours, isn't he? I won't tolerate Matova's interference."

Matt's stammered reply was too low to make out. The spiffy Vincent was miffed at Gino. In absence, Maria's spouse loomed large everywhere. No getting away from him.

"Earth to Polly. Hello—oh?" Aggie's voice cut in. "Are you listening? Mom asked you something."

Well, yeah, listening—but to the wrong side.

'Twas One Day After Christmas...

CHAPTER 14

Morning of December 26

AGNES

A t 8:30 a.m. on Boxing Day, Agnes padded into the living room, rubbing sleepy eyes. From the larger bedroom came faint bursts of Sera's voice but no responses. Must be on the phone, Agnes figured. The sofa showed no signs of its overnight purpose. Another early riser on the go.

Just when Agnes turned to the kitchenette, the apartment door burst open, and Polly danced in, glowing from cold and evident delight.

With perfect aim, she tossed her jacket onto a hook by the door, chanting, "Yay, hurrah, we're snowed in." UGGS dumped onto the plastic boot tray, she prattled on, "Staff say roads aren't cleared yet. Ah, can't wait to hit the slopes."

Not able to handle so much enthusiasm before breakfast, Agnes mumbled, "How nice," thinking, hope plowing takes until noon or so. Couldn't expect Bella or Pierre to play instructors again. "Want a coffee?"

"No, thanks. Just a shower to warm up. Unless you need the bathroom."

"All yours."

A minute later, the sweet voice drifted from behind the closed bathroom door, "*Let it snow, let it snow, let...*" growing fainter until the sound of rushing water drowned it out.

Agnes ripped open a portion pack of coffee grounds and was filling the reservoir when she heard a rat-a-tat on the outside door.

"Never get a coffee at this rate," she muttered and stopped at the mirror next to the entrance to stroke back her sleep-messy hair. Her Santa-red, long-sleeved night t-shirt and green flannel bottoms sporting countless Rudolphs seemed childish now. So what? she thought. We're on holidays.

Outside stood Josh, not much advanced in the dress department. His black outfit, a hoody over white sweatpants, showed the University of Toronto logo prominently on the front and side panels. Unkempt, short brown hair stood up in tufts. Unshaved, to judge by the dark stubble.

"Good morning, Agnes. Brekky's ready in five," he greeted her with morning lark cheer. "Nah, say in twenty-five minutes."

When her eyes went wide, he laughed. "Hey, it's still Christmas, isn't it? Greg and I ordered for the house. Self-serve buffet in the great room. Tell your mom and Polly while I raise lazy Gino and Maria."

"Oh?" Is he back? she wanted to ask but stopped, unsure about raising the topic of the guy's recent absence. Though, as close friends, Josh and spouse likely knew more than Polly or even Gino's wife. Time to devise to plan a subtle approach of pumping the philandering scout's buddies.

Things fell into place last night when she'd learned the identity of the argumentative urban businessman. Matt's father-in-law, as she'd already suspected. A communal breakfast might yield an opportunity to connect with Cheryl and discover details about the two competing buyer parties.

"Did I come too late? You ladies had breakfast already?" Josh's face creased in disappointment.

"Sorry, my mind drifted. Thanks a lot, we'd love to join you. Sweet of you to include us."

"Phew." He wiped his brow in mock relief. "Thought we'd be stuck with enough bacon and eggs to last us a week. See ya shortly."

Twenty minutes later, delectable scents hit Agnes when she ventured out ostensibly to check on the weather. Her keen eye took in the buffet spread from afar. Staff were unearthing all kinds of goodies from portable containers and arranging warmer dishes on a couple of folding tables probably kept in the broom closet for such occasions.

The female server smiled and called a friendly *bonjour*. When the other staff turned to greet Agnes, she recognized him at once.

"Hey, Gabe, nice to see you again. They keep you busy around here." Just the man she wanted to quiz. Not in front of his colleague, though.

As Agnes gazed out at the swirling snow, Gabe came over to greet her. "Hi, Dr. Taylor. They're short-staffed today because of the weather. Only a few of us who stay in the staff quarters are on site until the roads get cleared."

"How long will it take to dig us out?" Perfect opportunity for chatting up people marooned at the snowbound lodge. Less skiing, too, she smiled to herself.

"Just a few hours at most." Gabe dashed her hopes in their infancy. "Sorry, I've got another delivery waiting. Most patrons order in when it's blowing like this. I'll be plowing paths and blazing trails for the rest of today." He grinned at Agnes. "Being outside is more my kind of thing when I'm not writing."

Agnes laughed. "Better you out there than me. Maybe we might chat sometime? I'd like to hear more about your plans for an author career and your grad studies." And about Robert's unctuous manager whom they'd encountered as the restaurant's maître d' the night before. She'd disliked the man at first sight.

Gabe's eyes lit up. "Would you really? That'll be awesome. Thanks."

The staffers packed up and headed out. Their ATV sported a plow attached to the front, and a little trailer hitched to the back. Agnes noticed the path it had forged was already blurred by the relentless snow. A day made for comfort food and cozy fireside chats.

"Hi-ya, Agnes. How's it going?" Greg rushed down the stairs, Josh in his wake. "Sera and Polly coming to help us devour this feast?"

"Oh, hi, Greg. They'll be out in a moment." The guys cast wolfish looks at the table, as reluctant as she was to be the first to lift the lids from the serving dishes.

"Good morning," she heard her mother's cheerful voice. "What a lovely surprise. Thanks so much for this treat." Sera crossed the room and admired the offerings.

Polly joined them a moment later. "Hey, guys. Awesome. I'm famished." She reached for a paper plate but stepped back and looked abashed.

Greg dispelled the awkwardness by asking if he might help Sera to some bacon and eggs. A moment later, everyone was digging in.

"You've ordered enough for a whole army," said Agnes to Josh, who held up the lid of the pancake platter for her. "Are the others coming to join us?"

"Not sure. No answer at Gino's," he said. Agnes noticed Polly listening, the serving spoon of the hash browns aloft. "Matt should be down shortly."

Without Cheryl? Agnes wondered, but thinking of the scene on Christmas Eve didn't want to ask Josh. Presumably, Josh and Matt's wife encountered each other often enough, though. Horrible if they also worked together. Maybe they didn't always clash so dramatically.

"Do you and Greg work for the Company?" she asked, following her own train of thought.

"I'm a freelance interior designer. They hire me sometimes. Greg is fully involved. For better or worse," Josh said. "A kind of marriage."

His laugh sounded good-natured, not like a job-jealous spouse, thought Agnes, and bit into a cranberry muffin with streusel topping before tackling her pancakes doused in maple syrup. Greg's the extrovert but unlikely to share company secrets. Try Josh first, she figured.

After swigging from the paper cup to unglue her palate, she swallowed the rest of the muffin, wondering why the dough sticks to one's molars.

Aloud, she said, "With you guys being in Toronto and Phil based in Montreal, do you get a chance to hang out much?" While she spoke, Josh's eyes narrowed. She hastened on, "So nice catching up with good friends and relatives over the holidays, isn't it?"

"Depends on who you're talking about," said Josh, then laughed as if it had been a joke. Was he thinking of the in-law cousin? Or of Phil?

"My own folks are in Manitoba. Greg's family won the holiday roulette."

"Aw, yours must miss you. Maybe next year," she said, unsure how to reintroduce the elusive Phil topic.

"Yep. There's hoping." He stared into his coffee cup as if to read the future in the dregs. He lifted it, saying, "Excuse me. Need a refill."

Ouch, her interrogation skills were slipping, she silently admitted. Now, how to tackle Greg? Bemused, she tackled the pancakes instead.

Someone, maybe Gabe, had lit a fire in the grate. The apple wood crackled merrily and scented the air. Its warmth warded off the chill from the snow-crusted window wall.

"There comes cousin," announced Greg, imitating a trumpet fanfare.

Matt descended with slow, heavy steps like a man exhausted or lacking sleep. Feet clad in thick wool socks and sheepskin slippers, he wore a flannel check shirt in different shades of brown and ochre over blue jeans. A listless 'hi' addressed no one in particular.

When Sera politely inquired about his spouse, he replied Cheryl rarely ate in the morning and preferred tea in bed.

Not my lucky day, thought Agnes. The man himself scowled. Too grumpy for a morning chat.

"Save a blueberry yogurt for me to take up," Matt told Greg.

His cousin paid no attention. Both thumbs texted furiously before he looked up to announce, "Hey, everyone, Rosa says Pierre's coming over with Bella."

For no reason—or so she insisted to herself—a blush creeped up Agnes's neck into her cheeks.

Strangely quiet after the earlier exuberance, Polly now asked, "Who's Rosa, then?"

"Greg's mom," said Agnes.

"Rosa never liked me to call her 'mom.'" Greg chuckled. "She's my best friend—"

"Ahem," came Josh's exaggerated interruption.

"Oops—after my better half." Fingers of both hands shot up as if to protect his face from an imaginary attack.

"I'm willing to share the place of honor with my dear mother-in-law," said Josh. A grin undermined the magnanimous flutter of his hand. "She's a darling."

"Didn't get a chance to meet her the other day," said Polly. "Is she joining us?"

"Rosa? In this weather? Not on your life," laughed Greg. "She takes after Nonna. Winter is for hibernation unless they can spend it in Florida or in the Bahamas. Mom preferably poolside with a cocktail shaker nearby."

Just then, the outer door opened. Two snowy figures, bundled up to the eyes, stamped their boots and kicked them off on the mat. Josh and Greg hastened to relieve them of jackets, scarves, and hats.

Unwrapped, a smiling Bella came to hug Agnes, who'd moved to meet her halfway. Dressed in tailored, vintage-style, black stirrup ski pants and a matching Norwegian jacquard sweater with an elaborate star pattern around the neck and shoulders, she looked stunning.

Self-conscious about the jeans and humdrum fleece she'd grabbed in haste, Agnes said, "Sorry. Didn't have time to get ready when Josh announced breakfast."

"It's us who are intruding. Come, let me say hello to your mother."

Glad of an excuse to stay away from Pierre, Agnes followed in tow. Her mom rose from the couch to greet the newcomer. A fuzzy, warm sense of pride suffused Agnes at her mother's stylish attire of slim dark wool pants and turtleneck sweater. The short hair, lavishly shot through with silver, looked so good on her.

Josh sauntered over with a mug for his aunt-in-law and received a peck on both cheeks in thanks. The two women, perched in wing chairs by the fire, leaned in for a chat. Glad to see them together, Agnes offered to get Bella some goodies to go with her coffee.

Her back to the room, while filling a plate with fruit and mini chocolate and almond croissants, a voice at her shoulder startled her.

"Woman, are you avoiding me?"

She whipped around, plate extended to ward off an embrace.

"Don't drop that. Here, let me carry it." A devilish grin, and he relieved her of the sweet load. "Where do you want to sit?"

"Oh, no." She cleared her throat. "It's for Bella."

"Then come along. I've got some announcements for you."

Uncertain, Agnes followed, a little nervous about what he might have to say.

After greeting her mother, who seemed much taken by Pierre's charm, he addressed the room at large. "Ahem. Listen up, folks. You too, Matt," he called when the latter made for upstairs.

Grumbling, Matt turned back but remained on the lowest step and leaned against the banister.

"Here's some bad and some good news." They all stopped talking as the lawyer spoke. "The bad news: the bridge has collapsed."

"What?" shouted Greg. "Are you kidding?"

Josh walked closer to his spouse before asking Pierre, "When the heck did it happen? The guy from staff didn't say a word."

"Didn't I say so?" said Agnes, nudging Polly, who'd come up beside her. "Now we're stuck."

No response from Polly, who stared at Pierre, mouth slightly open. In a low murmur, Sera was conferring with Bella.

"Sorry, I'm not joking," said Pierre. "It happened within the last hour. They've called in a roadwork crew to assess the damage. We won't know for a while what will happen."

"Isn't there another means of access?" Of course, her mom posed the practical question. She sounded calm and matter-of-fact, to Agnes's relief.

"Not what you would call accessible," said Pierre. "I asked a grounds guy. Apparently, the resort property borders on the river on two sides and merges with extensive forests on the other sides. There are some logging roads farther out, but not cleared this time of year and not connected to the Xavier property."

They all looked at each other and tried to digest this tidbit.

"Now, it's no reason to worry. We're completely safe here and well looked after by the staff. Remember, I promised you some good news, too. Here it is. Phil is organizing an outing for us in the afternoon." Pierre continued, unfazed by their grumblings of disbelief, "The forecast calls for sun before noon. With snowmobiles, they'll have some trails groomed in a couple of hours. Whoever wants to come along on Nordic skis or snow-shoes is most welcome."

"Yay, awesome," said Polly. "Thought we'd be stuck inside all day."

"Phil is sorting things, and the lodge provides some rentals free of charge today."

While he spoke, Agnes's heart sank. Cross-country skiing on narrow skis was more treacherous than alpine, she knew from abortive experience. Snowshoeing, she'd tried once as a kid. The huge wooden type tripped her every few steps until she gave up altogether.

Around her, everyone seemed to speak at once. Into the chatter of comments, Pierre's voice came close to her ear. "You're joining the fun, aren't you? Bella is eager to go. She's just convincing your mom, I think."

"Sera needs no persuasion. She's born to ski. Unlike me. I'd fall over my own feet on either mode of transportation." Her laugh didn't deceive herself. Yet, she went on, "A perfect clod. Better stay home instead of slowing everyone down."

"No, you're not. You'll be in my group. Snowshoeing is easy. Can't come to harm on those things."

"Try me," Agnes said. "I'll manage to break a leg or something."

CHAPTER 15

Afternoon of December 26

POLLY

P olly trudged along, doing her best to match her strides to her
companions'. Long-legged Pierre on the far side had a harder
time adjusting to Agnes's snail's pace.

"I'm surprised Matt's wife didn't come along. She looks so sporty,"
she heard Agnes say. Why the heck was Aggie hankering for the drama
queen's company?

"Eh? Appearances deceive," said Pierre. "Cheryl rarely joins the boys. I
imagine she's spending the afternoon with her dad."

"Must be a little awkward for Cheryl. Like musical chairs, with her
and Matt in our place, the in-laws in the Matova chalet, and her dad... Is
he in another log house? I can't see a cityfied person like him roughing
it?"

Why the hell is Agnes so interested in those people? Not her type at
all, thought Polly.

"Oh? Have you met Vincent?" Pierre asked.

"Not to say hello," Aggie said, oh so airily. Not sharing about the
dude's shouting match with the proprietor, is she?

"You're right. It's not his turf at all, I should think," the lawyer agreed.
"He's got a suite in the main lodge, with direct access to the restaurant and
bar without getting his feet wet."

Bored out of her mind by the idle chat and crawling pace, it took all of

102

Polly's willpower not to jog in giant steps, turning snowshoes into seven-league boots like in the fairytale.

Could be zooming along on skis with the fast set, her mind grumbled, and tuned out of her companion's talk. In envy, she gazed at the frontrunners a few hundred yards ahead.

Sure, Aggie had begged—okay, merely asked nicely—to stay with her. The reluctance for a *tête-à-tête* with gorgeous Pierre had dissipated within minutes on the trail. Well, the guy's personality, admittedly, was as attractive as his exterior. Beside them, Polly felt insignificant and redundant.

At least she'd convinced Maria to let her in for a quick visit. With the breakfast party gone, she'd harvested the remainder of the feast set aside by the staff. A plate loaded with goodies served as a votive offering.

A prearranged signal tapping on the door gained her entry. Made some tea for the sufferer and coaxed her to finish half a cranberry muffin and a handful of berries. Best of all, she convinced Maria to talk to Phil if hubby remained AWOL by late afternoon.

Think of the devil. Far in the distance, Phil stopped as though her thoughts had reached him. Looked like he and Matt were having a spat. Josh and Greg forged ahead, not giving a hoot.

Hundred yards behind the arguers, the other skiing trio came to a halt. Nonno, flanked by Sera and Bella, did a full-body turn to glance back at the snowshoeing stragglers.

Perfect excuse for Polly to wave and call "wait up" and fall into a trot. Hell, jogging on snowshoes ought to count for some aerobic brownie points.

"You hop like a bunny," joked the elderly gentleman, his face creasing into countless wrinkles. "*La filosofa* and Piero are much too slow for you. He is a great talker, our *avvocato*."

The older women exchanged a quick glance—Sera's expression serious, while Pierre's sister-in-law smiled enigmatically.

The sound of raised voices recalled Polly's attention to the men further ahead. Aiming for a casual tone, she said, "Yep. Need more exercise. I'll mosey on and catch up with Josh and Greg. See ya." A quick wave and she was off again.

When she approached Matt and Phil, she faked being out of breath. Chat them up and pump for info on Gino's whereabouts. Sure to brag to his bar cronies if he was taking off with a girlfriend on the side. Them arguing now was interesting too.

Pace slowing, she pressed her right hand below her left rib, ready to mime side stitches. Bent over slightly, she pretended to be too self-absorbed to listen.

Needn't have bothered. The two were oblivious of her. She slowed further and snatched a few sentences.

"Easy for you to say! I'm going nuts with worry." Without looking up, she recognized Matt speaking. Voice lowered now; Phil tried to calm him.

"C'mon, man. Get a grip. No cause for panic."

"If she finds out, I—"

"She won't, I tell you. It's all under control and—"

"You don't know my dad. He's gonna—"

"Hey, cool it," Phil grunted. And then, with artificial cheer, "Oh, hi there. Are you alright, Polly? Snowshoeing is hard work, isn't it?"

Looking up like totally surprised to find them there, Polly said, suitably breathlessly, "Oh, man, is it ever? Way tougher than snowboarding."

Out of the corner of her eye, she noticed Matt forcing himself to smile.

"No worries," said Phil, "I was just suggesting to Matt here that we should head back soon. Snow's going to come down hard again."

The weather was the last thing on her mind, but even a dud could see the storm clouds gathering behind them, she admitted.

Just then, something else appeared on the horizon towards the lodge. A faint droning noise vibrated in the still afternoon air.

"A copter," said Phil. "I wonder..."

"Are they inspecting the bridge?" asked Polly.

"Could be. Well, let's head back then. By the time we get home, the storm will hit. Heads up," he warned before putting two fingers into his mouth to issue a shrill whistle.

All heads spun around. Ski pole raised high, he pointed to the sky. Unclear if he aimed at the black clouds or the helicopter now descending.

CHAPTER 16

Later in the Afternoon of December 26

AGNES

D rops of sweat mingled with melting snowflakes and dripped from the tip of Agnes's nose. Under the warm jacket, her long-sleeved t-shirt below a merino sweater stuck damp to her skin. Her breath came panting and in gasps. Still, she persevered, legs throbbing from the exertion.

"Let's rest for a moment, Agnes. No need for us to rush."

Wiping her nose with the back of her glove, Agnes turned to Bella, who'd come to a stop, leaning elegantly on her right ski pole. The others were far ahead, much closer to the lodge already.

"I'm so sorry to slow you down, Bella," said Agnes as she sucked in icy air, grateful for any brief respite. "You could be home free roasting marsh-mallows," she added with a grin.

An intense whirring and droning disturbed the stillness. The heli-copter rose like a dragonfly right above the lodge compound. In the distance, Agnes saw their companions halt, a ski pole waving in the air as if in farewell. With a sideward swipe, the heli disappeared toward the threat-ening clouds. As it became smaller and smaller, it swayed over to the southwest. Headed for Montreal, she suspected.

"Somehow, I doubt the toasty fire romantic for today," Bella said dryly. "Something's up."

Maybe the bridge repair was a major affair, and the heli brought fresh supplies, Agnes thought full of hope. Her legs would refuse to ski for days after this torture.

Driven by curiosity, they both moved forward, Agnes in awkward fits and bursts on snowshoes. Next to her, Bella glided along on skis with graceful ease.

The group had stayed together for a while on their way home. When Phil and his buddies increased their speed, Bella had said a few words to Pierre in rapid French, prompting him to hurry after their guide. It amazed Agnes how he could jog on those unwieldy aluminum contraptions. Polly even kept up with Nonno and Sera despite their advantage on skis. Yet, Agnes rather resented the others leaving her behind.

As they trudged along, Bella matching her glide to Agnes's lumbering gait, silence descended with the twilight. They fell farther and farther behind the lead. For the umptieth time this afternoon, Agnes cursed herself for joining this grueling and pointless outing. Her hope of chatting up the guys to learn more and being introduced to Matt's spouse was dashed as soon as she realized how far she'd be behind everyone else.

Much more sensible to have remained at the lodge and devised a means of connecting with Cheryl and her dad. Though what she might say to these people eluded her. If she quizzed them about their interest in the Xavier property, they'd clam up. Her interference and presumptuousness would outrage Robert if it came to his ears. Jac had landed her with another mission impossible.

Relieved, she noticed the trail widening. In the distance, she could make out smoke curling from chimneys. An end was in sight. With a ragged breath, Agnes renewed her efforts. All she could think of was a hot bubble bath. Every muscle in her body ached ferociously.

Another fifteen minutes brought them to the *Va au Diable* resort. No sight of Phil or Pierre. Nor did Agnes see Polly anywhere. Nonno strode toward them, skis carried on his shoulder. The smile he directed at Agnes appeared forced. After inquiring in mere politeness if their outing had been too tiring, he turned to Bella in a torrent of Italian. Both their faces grew serious. Interjections by Bella unleashed a flood of words accompanied by flurried gesticulation.

Visibly shaken, the elderly man apologized to Agnes and, with a final '*arrivederci*,' hastened away.

"So sorry, Agnes, but I'll have to go with him to calm him down. Excitement is not good for his heart," said Bella and kicked off her skis. "I'm sure your mother knows more than I and will explain." She hugged Agnes, shouldered her skis, and followed Matteo.

Dazed with tiredness, Agnes glanced around and saw Sera in deep conversation with the man they'd met at dinner the night before. What was his name again? An intern at a Boston hospital, he'd said. A doctor. She'd been trying so hard to snatch fragments of the neighboring conversation she'd missed much of Sera's chat with the honeymooning couple.

Soaked with sweat, she shivered now as the wind picked up. Did she really want explanations rather than hasten straight for the bathtub? Resigned, Agnes lumbered the last steps to join her mom.

"You remember Jeong?"

Agnes mustered all her resources to respond with a friendly greeting.

Sera continued in a subdued tone, "Robert called him in when they found the body."

"The what? Whose?" asked Agnes, too exhausted for Sera's words to compute.

"Didn't Matteo tell you? The young man next door. Maria's husband, Gino."

"He's dead? Oh, my God! The poor girl." And after he took off on her. At Christmas time. But maybe he'd not stayed away voluntarily. Did he get caught in the blizzard? Horrible if no one looked for him. They'd just assumed he was with his mistress.

Shaking now, she asked, "But how did he die so suddenly?"

When Jeong made to answer, Sera laid a light hand on his forearm. "Maybe better not stay out here. Would you come by our apartment? My daughter needs to get out of the cold. The shocking news after being chilled…"

The young doctor regarded Agnes, whose teeth were chattering uncontrollably. "I agree. You need to warm up. If you don't mind, I would like to go and reassure my wife. There was no time to explain."

"Of course. Please ask her if she would care to come along too. Say, in half an hour, if that suits you? You'll find us right there," she pointed to their log house. "We're in number two on the main floor."

Grateful for her mom's arm around her shoulder, Agnes still shivered as she walked with Sera along the plowed path to their front door. As much as she wanted to know what happened to Gino, she dreaded finding out their collective negligence had killed him.

CHAPTER 17

Early Evening of December 26

POLLY

A sharp jolt shot up her benumbed arm when Polly knocked on the apartment door. The boots tucked under her other arm dripped melting slush. Despite the mittens, her hands had lost sensation.

Dog-tired, she closed her eyes and almost fell forward when the door opened.

"Polly, where have you been?" Agnes's voice reverberated in Polly's brain like a shout in a tunnel.

"Did you find her?" Sera came up behind Agnes. They both stepped back to make room for Polly to pass through the narrow vestibule.

In a throwback to her childhood habits, Polly's gloved hands shot up to cover her ears and shut out questions. It took a moment for the unconscious reaction to register and her hands to slide under the elf hat like its removal was the intention all along. The tiny bell tinkled as the hat hit the floor.

Agnes reached for it, saying, "It's covered in icicles. Polly, you must be freezing cold. Let's get you inside."

An odd sense of unreality, a feeling of being a helpless child, weakened Polly's aching body as Sera peeled off the jacket and led her to the sofa. Only, she had no memory of such caring from a distant childhood.

"No. No luck. I searched everywhere," she mumbled a belated answer.

"Are they quite sure Maria didn't go with the air ambulance?" asked Agnes, hunkering onto the edge of the sofa seat. "Wouldn't they want the spouse to be there when they flew him out?"

"They couldn't wait any longer, Jeong said. With the storm moving in, they had to leave," said Sera. "Let's hope the others locate her before nightfall. You need a hot drink, Polly. The kettle is on a boil. A shot of brandy in your tea won't go amiss. Jeong is coming over and should be here any minute."

The heat of the small living room felt overpowering after hours out in the cold. Through half-closed eyes, Polly saw Agnes's forehead pucker in a frown. Aggie must've taken a shower or bath, what with her hair still damp.

Like a mind reader, Agnes rose. "Polly. You're shaking with cold. Should I run you a warm bath?"

Hot pinpricks stabbed Polly's fingers as some sensation returned. Wincing, she shook her head. "Not yet."

"Then we wrap you in a blanket. You'll catch your death of hypothermia if we don't get you warmed up." Agnes already grabbed a fleece throw from an armchair, and Polly felt herself swaddled like a chick under wings, protected and clucked over by the mother hen. Agnes's arm supported Polly's shivering body while the other hand reached for the mug Sera held out.

A giggle bubbled up in Polly's chest. The irony of having Aggie minister to her now, as she herself had done to Maria, was just too much for her frayed nerves.

"Oh, I'm so glad," she heard Agnes's murmur close to her ear. "If you can still laugh, you're very much alive. I'm sure the guys have found Maria by now."

When Polly twisted to smile her thanks, she saw worry in Agnes's gaze. They both realized, Polly suspected, the news would have reached them if Maria were back.

A hesitant tapping on the door saved her from stating the obvious.

"That'll be Jeong," said Sera and went to answer.

"Ta, Aggie, I think I can manage now," Polly said and scrambled upright. Her hand reached for the mug Agnes still held aloft. A couple of deep drafts of the hot toddy restored her senses. Her other hand pulled the fleecy blanket tightly over her skinny frame.

"A St. Bernhard couldn't have done a better rescue job," she said. "Hey, I'm not calling you a doggy." The grin made her face ache. Maybe it hurt from the temperature shock of so much heat after the long exposure to frigid air. What really ached was her heart, she thought, as Aggie's arm hugged her close before releasing her.

Should've stayed with Maria, she lashed out at herself. What kind of friend are you? You always run off when someone needs you...

Sera walking in with the medico mercifully stopped her mind's tirade.

As Sera took his parka and offered tea, Polly's introspection-loathing reporter mind reasserted itself. Dispassionately, it registered the newcomer's appearance and demeanor. Black hair, short and straight, almond-shaped intelligent and alert eyes that wouldn't miss a thing, she figured. Calm enough, yet not at ease, he stood clutching his long-boned hands until Sera sat and invited him to take the other armchair. At the restaurant, he had shown no social anxieties. You'd expect a doc to be used to sudden death. Yet, he hung on to his tea mug as if it were a lifesaver.

"We're rather worried about Maria," said Agnes, leaning forward. "Did you hear if they found her, Jeong?"

"I'm afraid I did not." He sounded terribly apologetic to Polly. Like he'd failed Maria somehow. "However, I made sure to give Robert my cellular number. If the young woman has spent all this time outdoors, she might require medical assistance once she returns."

"Who's out looking for Maria, then?" asked Agnes, glancing from one to the other.

"My impression was the young men skiing with you this afternoon formed a search party. The ground staff went out on snowmobiles, too," said Jeong.

"Were you with the guys, Polly?"

"Nah, Aggie. Went on me own soon as I heard from the doc here, she didn't go with the heli." Polly groaned under the weight of having failed Maria yet again today.

Aggie's head swiveled around, eyebrows shooting up. The medico's perceptive glance felt kind of like an x-ray.

Polly huddled back on the sofa, legs tucked up under the blanket, arms hugged tightly around her knees.

"When we spoke earlier, Jeong. I sensed there was something more on your mind," said Sera. "Please, don't feel you need to share. But if it's of any help, we'll gladly listen."

Now, it was the doc's turn to shift uneasily in his seat. Polly guessed he had second thoughts about coming by.

Maybe Agnes figured he needed time, for she said, "Mom only told me the bare fact that someone found Gino in a snowdrift, and they got you to assist until the paramedics arrived."

"Yes," said Sera. "My daughter was so exhausted and chilled, a hot bath seemed best until your return."

"Would help me, too, to understand what happened. I got to know Maria a bit and feel really bad and worried about it all," Polly said.

He focused on Agnes when he spoke. "As I told your mother, the lodge owner sent an employee to my cabin to fetch me. It was lucky that my wife and I had stayed in after a brief walk. The young man told me there had been an accident and his boss, Robert, was anxious for me to come. I always keep a small emergency kit on hand, especially on a vacation like this. Second nature for a doctor."

He glanced towards the entrance and smiled nervously, like they'd think him odd.

"How very fortunate," said Sera. "I noticed the little rucksack you brought along. An excellent habit, I'm sure."

"Yes, I'm on call, you might say, just in case the young woman needs attention when she returns. This afternoon, however, my aid came too late." He cleared his throat. "The man was dead. Anyone could tell the body was long frozen."

Next to her, Polly felt Agnes shudder.

The doc must've noticed. "I'm so sorry to shock you."

"No, I'm okay. Please go on," said Agnes.

"There was nothing I could do except examine him superficially. We heard the Airmedic land, and Robert went to fetch them. A police officer came in the helicopter with two paramedics. They conversed in French. The officer then asked me in English to confirm the man's death. He noted down my name and contact information and told me I was no longer needed."

Easy to tell the doc wasn't happy at being dismissed. "And you left it at that?" Polly made it sound rhetorical.

The medico hesitated and shot a glance at Sera.

"If you feel you can trust me, Jeong," said Sera, "I vouch for my daughter and our friend Polly's discretion."

The last bit made Polly cringe and avoid checking Agnes's expression, yet heard her inhaling sharply.

Across from them, Jeong fought his own inner battle. Two fingers pinching the skin above his nose, he spoke. "I feel it is my duty to share my concerns with someone here in Canada. We're heading back to Boston tomorrow. In short, neither the officer nor Robert wanted to listen to me. They consulted in French, which I do not speak or understand."

"But what were you trying to tell them?" asked Agnes.

"You see, I'm not sure how the man died."

"Didn't you say it was an accident?" Agnes persisted and shuddered when she added, "He froze to death?"

"The resort employee called it an accident," said the medico. "When he showed me the body, Robert alleged the man wandered outside drunk and fell into a snowbank. The blizzard buried him."

"How horrible," murmured Agnes.

"It doesn't bear thinking of. His poor young wife," said Sera. "Her husband dying of exposure, and no one looking for him."

"Please don't upset yourself. No, I don't believe he did," said Jeong.

"If Gino's body was in a snowdrift," said Agnes, all pensive now, "it was out there since the night before Christmas when the blizzard was at its worst. Don't you think? Didn't he go missing already that night?"

"Robert did not mention the man had been missing," said Jeong, and looked even more unhappy. "This increases my concern."

Polly's instincts went on high alert. Time to state the obvious. "It wasn't an accident, was it, Doctor Jeong?"

None of them hurried him when he steepled his hands in front of his face. Maybe he was weighing professional confidentiality against his need to share.

Then his words came slowly, a slight shake of his head emphasizing the uncertainly. "I just...I can't be sure. You see, I only had a short time to examine the deceased while Robert was away. I briefly surveyed the surrounding area."

"Something didn't add up, you think?" Agnes asked.

His hand fingered his chin before he continued. "There was evidence of a deep skull fracture."

"Isn't that consistent with an accident? If he was drunk and fell, he could have struck his head and passed out. The snowstorm would have done the rest."

Trust Agnes to point out a reasonable explanation, thought Polly.

Jeong shook his head. "If he struck his head, it wasn't where he fell. I pointed this out to the officer and Robert."

Before getting into things, Polly looked at Sera. The older woman sat attentively, bent forward, taking in every word. Time to get involved, Polly decided. She needed certainty to protect Maria.

"Doctor, would you mind describing exactly how the body was situated when they called you in and what your findings were? If you believe some action is required, getting the details down might help."

Beside her, Agnes nodded emphatic agreement.

"A prudent suggestion, Jeong," Sera said. "Going over the facts might clarify things. Just tell us as verbatim as you can. It might even ease your concerns."

When Jeong nodded and made to speak, Polly interrupted, "Do you mind if I record it on my phone? From what you've already said, I get the impression you'd like to put things on record." Her hand already fumbled for her phone under the fleecy throw.

But Agnes interrupted, "Polly, I think his own or my mom's phone would be best if Jeong wants to record himself."

The distrust cut into Polly's heart. She's right, her mind shouted. You don't deserve their trust.

CHAPTER 18

Report of Dr. Jeong Han, MD

DR. JEONG HAN, MD — AUDIO
RECORDING — DECEMBER 26

For the record, I will provide an informal account of how I came to be called in to view a body at the *Va au Diable* resort in Mont Tremblant, Quebec. My name is Jeong Han, and I am a visitor to this resort.

Let me first say that my memory is highly developed. I believe I can give a reliable account of what happened this afternoon.

My wife, Su-Jin, and I returned from a walk to our cabin on the far side of the pond. I lit a fire in the wood stove, and we were settling in for a cozy afternoon when someone knocked loudly and called, "Dr. Han, are you there?" The cabin door is rather thin, I fear.

When I opened the door, I saw at once that it was a staff member. The outdoor employees wear the same black coats and hats with a red devil emblem, as you will have noticed. The young man appeared serious but also excited. A snowmobile with the engine still running sat on the path. We had not paid attention to the noise before. The snowblowers came by so often today. One gets used to the sound. But I digress.

"Dr. Han," the young man said, "My boss sent me. Would you come with me, please? There's been an accident."

Of course, I agreed to help. I told Su to stay warm and quickly dressed in outerwear. My bag always sits ready at the door. Force of habit, you might say. My father is also a doctor. Back home, he still does house calls.

The snowmobile was too noisy to ask questions. We reached our destination on the perimeter, perhaps a mile out from the main building. But my sense of distance is not very accurate, I must add. The spot is isolated. As far as I could see, there is only a small cabin in a clearing of the pine forest. A man stood beside a snowbank, maybe twenty or thirty yards from the cabin. He leaned against one of the snowblowers they use to plow the paths.

We stopped some way off and walked up. As the man turned, I recognized the proprietor, Robert. My wife and I met him on our arrival and had spoken to him briefly twice since.

He came toward us and immediately said, "Sorry, Doc, for ruining your afternoon with this. I've called the Airmedic service. Their helicopter will be here soon. No ambulance can get through with the bridge down."

I assured him I didn't mind at all and asked what had happened.

"Fool partied a bit too much. Got drunk and lost his bearings. Wandered outside, I guess, and passed out. The blizzard did for him."

At first, I didn't see the body. The snowblower obstructed my view. Robert pointed to it, saying, "Gabe here found him."

My driver nodded but kept his face averted. He hadn't raised the helmet shield since we arrived.

Behind the plow lay—I'm sorry—a denuded male body in nothing but the briefest of underwear. He was lying face down. His feet were still buried in the snowbank.

My immediate concern was to establish if anything could be done. The person was dead. One arm was twisted and damaged. Lack of bleeding indicated the injury occurred postmortem, presumably inflicted by the blade of the plow.

Gabriel confirmed that when I asked. He made the gruesome discovery while widening the path. After the heavy snowfall, and expecting far more tonight, he wanted to make room. Then, he saw the arm and uncovered the body sufficiently to determine the man was beyond help. Understandably, the sight sickened him, as I later noticed by the evidence not far off.

Be that as it may, Robert asked me to establish death. While I examined the body, as far as was possible under the circumstances, I could hear the noise of a helicopter. It surprised me how little time it took them. But I realized I did not know how long ago Gabriel had discovered the body.

Robert left with the snowmobile to bring in the paramedics. Gabriel stood at a distance. He evidently felt badly shaken, and I offered to attend to him, which he declined.

I won't confuse you with the medical details. Just this much. The body was lying face down, head toward the cabin. At the base of the skull, I discovered a contusion deep enough to show a fracture. By its shape, I inferred something like a square bar had caused it. There was nothing in the vicinity that matched. It seemed unlikely for him to have damaged the back of his head falling forward.

When I had freed his feet from the snow, I turned the body sufficiently to check for evidence of an animal attack before resting him again in place. I noticed that the undamaged arm showed signs of vertically aligned scrapes caused after death. There was no blood as you expect with such scrapes when a person is still alive.

Did it look like drag marks, Jeong?

A good question, Agnes. It is not inconsistent with the body being dragged over the icy ground to where it lay. But only if it had been lying on a heavy blanket because the rest of the body showed no obvious marks. I don't wish to speculate. Only a postmortem and forensic testing could establish this kind of thing.

It occurred to me that the man might have fallen closer to the cabin and hit his head. He might have stumbled on. I examined the area as far as possible. But there were no signs of any steel bars or fences. In fact, snow covered the entire area. Of course, I could not say what might lie beneath its cover.

Next, I consulted Gabriel. He assured me the space around the cabin consists of grass and a path lined with wood chips. Asked whether the cabin is among the rentals, he told me it belongs to Robert's son, Philippe, who often lends it to friends. Apparently, everyone on staff (and presumably the son's friends) knows a key is kept in a decorative mailbox outside the door. There is nothing to steal, the young man said.

At that point, we heard the engines of several snowmobiles. Robert returned with the paramedics and a police officer. Since all of them conversed in French, and Robert did not translate for me, I cannot tell you what they said.

When I walked up to them, the officer ordered me to step back and continued to talk to the proprietor. After the paramedics had lifted the body into a body bag, the officer and Robert came over to where I stood with Gabriel.

He took my personal information. I handed him my card, which he pocketed without a glance at it. He cut short any attempt to tell him my observations. All he wanted me to confirm was that death had occurred at least twenty-four hours, but more likely even longer, before I was called in. When I tried to insist on informing him of my concerns, he assured me that Quebec has excellent pathologists who are better equipped to determine the cause of death than a mere hospital intern. Since this was obviously true, I did not press my case.

Again, he consulted with Robert in French. Robert thanked me and apologized for the inconvenience. He then asked me if I would mind attending to the dead man's wife. She had not yet been told of the accident, as he insisted on calling it. Gabriel was to drive me back. Robert and the officer would follow as soon as they could. At that point, they told me that the dead man was called Gino—I'm sorry, I don't recall the Italian-sounding last name. His wife is called Maria.

I would have liked to stay and speak with the paramedics who attended to the removal of the body. But that was not to be.

As you already know, the wife was not in their apartment. Robert sent out some of his staff to look for her in the main lodge and elsewhere. But they had not located her by the time the helicopter had to leave. Gabriel, who stayed with me, said that the pilot was worried about waiting any longer because of the storm moving in. Maybe it also explains why the officer was so impatient to remove the body.

This is all that I can tell you. I hope there will be a postmortem and the pathologists will either confirm or disconfirm my findings.

CHAPTER 19

Still Early Evening of December 26

AGNES

While Jeong related his observations, Agnes suppressed an urgent need to discuss the implications. No good blurting out the connections her mind drew. She didn't want to influence Jeong's clinical perspective or worry her mother. Nor spook Polly, who'd fidgeted, threading the tassels of a sofa cushion and darting glances at the outer door. The worry about Maria was palpable and contagious.

Horrific in every way if Jeong's suspicions proved right. Though not stated explicitly, he must assume foul play. If Maria believed Gino spent Christmas Eve with another woman, as Polly had said last night, a tryst in the secluded cabin was a likely scenario. Could a lover's quarrel result in such a fatality? Robert claimed Gino was drunk, which wasn't farfetched. A drunken brawl? Why would he go out into a blizzard clad only in briefs?

Her mom's voice interrupted her musings.

"I don't know the procedures in cases of accidental death, Jeong, but I assume the authorities will investigate thoroughly."

Agnes frowned at the rather vague statement for someone of Sera's practical disposition. Yet, she felt guilty of equal cluelessness about Quebec's legal system and law enforcement.

Their guest still looked ill at ease as he passed back Sera's mobile.

"As a foreigner," he said, "one prefers not to get involved in an inquest. But the uncertainty about the true cause is disturbing. And medically dissatisfying." His hands rose, dismissing his last point.

"Jeong, I'm a close friend of Robert's daughter, Jacqueline," Agnes said to reassure him. "If there's an investigation, I'll hear of it and can let you know. Though the police will contact you if anything transpires from a postmortem, wouldn't they? I'll give you my number."

"Here is my card, Agnes," said Jeong and dug in a pocket for a wallet.

Faint voices reached them from the common area. In one swoop, Polly rose, shedding the blanket. She navigated the coffee table and ran to the door.

A moment later, she called, "Jeong, quickly. It's Maria."

All three followed the summons. Agnes saw Pierre about to lower a figure wrapped in a blanket onto the sofa by the great room's fireplace. Polly hovered close. In the center of the room stood Philippe, looking dazed. Snow melted from his clothes in rivulets and formed puddles around his boots.

"Please move Maria into their bedroom, Pierre, so the doctor can look after her," said Sera. "Jeong, just tell me what you need. Polly, you know Maria, and it will comfort her to have you there. Agnes, please get tea for the men. They must be chilled after hours outdoors. Take off your wet coats and warm up by the fire."

When Agnes brought the tea mugs to them, both Pierre and Phil hunkered down near the fireplace, still in their coats and hats. Pierre accepted the hot drink with a grateful smile, while Phil ignored the offering and continued to stare at the fire. Cradling her own mug, Agnes balanced on the edge of a hassock.

When neither of them spoke, she asked, "Where did you find Maria? Is she hurt?"

"Not physically, I think," Pierre said. "It would be more accurate to say she found us." Into Agnes's puzzled frown, he explained, "We were heading back to reconnoiter when she came out of the woods. The headlights caught her just in time for Phil to slam on the brakes. She stumbled and collapsed right in front of the skidoo."

"Damn lucky I was going slow. Could have run her over," muttered Phil, without taking his eyes off the flames.

"But where has she been all this time?"

"No idea, Agnes."

His hollow tone caused Agnes to glance closely at Pierre. Beneath the beanie he must have worn under the helmet, his face appeared drawn and tired. Her heart reached out to him.

Perhaps sensing her concern, his fingertip lightly tapped her wrist. "It's been a long day."

For a few moments, they sat in silence. The doctor's account of the discovery replayed in a loop in Agnes's mind. What a nightmare for a young wife to wake up to once she regained consciousness.

Bits and pieces Polly mentioned resurfaced. Did Maria already know her spouse was dead? Was it the reason she hid in the forest for hours? No, it made little sense. She'd been gone when the doctor sought her at this place. Or did the news leak out when Gabe alerted Robert? What a horror for Gabe finding a body! No number for contacting him now, Agnes thought. She must check on the poor guy tomorrow. If she could find him.

By random association, she asked without thinking, "Phil, did you lend your cabin to Gino?"

The man's head came up with a jerk, the facial expression inscrutable. Exhaustion or exasperation? Annoyance?

"None of my business. Sorry." Heat rising to her cheeks, Agnes cursed her unguarded speech. She'd never get answers if she blurted out whatever crossed her mind. The habit got her into serious trouble before.

In a barrage of French, Phil jabbered to Pierre. A mumbled "thanks for the tea" as he zipped his parka and left.

"He's in a rush to tell the staff Maria's back safely. Hard on him and Robert if anyone else got hurt scouring the woods at night. One fatal accident is bad enough. Apart from being tragic, it's not good for business."

"If it was an accident."

"Eh? What's that?"

The sharpness of Pierre's question alerted Agnes. She'd done it yet again. "Oh, nothing. Forget it."

"Woman, don't try to fool me. What put that idea into your head?"

Suddenly, Agnes felt uneasily aware of the public space. Where were the others?

"Are Greg and Josh still out looking? And Matt?" She realized she'd no idea if Cheryl and Matt were upstairs.

"Agnes, what got into you? You're jumpy like a rabbit." Something in her anxious glance softened his tone. "I realize it's upsetting for you. The guys said they'll grab some dinner when I texted to say we'd found her. Not sure where Matt and Cheryl might hang out if they aren't here. He made for this place when the paramedics airlifted the... Gino."

Agnes nodded to gain time. Her mind raced. Should she tell Pierre of Jeong's suspicion? After all, if Gino had died from a head injury, and if the injury wasn't caused by falling onto some steel bar or fence, then someone dealt him a fatal blow. Of course, all this might be nonsense. If true, however, whom could she trust?

CHAPTER 20

Evening of December 26

POLLY

P olly eased the door to Maria's apartment shut, though the sleeper in the bedroom wouldn't hear the click, anyway.

The doc shouldered his compact little backpack, a black one like tradition demanded of a doctor's bag. Then, her glance connected with the expectant faces of the two waiting by the fireplace. So, Pierre had stayed behind.

"How is she, Jeong?" asked Agnes, stroking the dark curls that swished her face when she rose. Her cheeks, Polly noticed, were crimson from proximity to the fire or...whatever.

"She is asleep now," said the doctor. "I administered a sedative. There is no injury, but I would be happier if we could get her to a hospital."

"Doesn't look like the storm's letting up," put in Pierre. "They'd have a hard time bringing in a chopper."

"An airlift would not be warranted, I admit. Her condition only requires observation. Her state of mind gives rise to concern. Understandably."

"Do you think she knows about Gino?"

"Difficult to say, Agnes. Without having met the patient before, one cannot hazard a guess. All I can say is her mind seems in turmoil." A slight shake of his head as he slipped on his jacket and pulled up its hood.

"Expect me early tomorrow morning. But please call me anytime if needed. I am a light sleeper."

"You're just awesome," said Polly sincerely.

As the three of them saw him out, she felt grateful for not being alone. The doc declined Pierre's offer to accompany him to his cabin. What a busman's holiday for a hardworking medico, she thought.

"Should I relieve Mom now? You'd better take a hot shower, Polly. Warm up thoroughly," said Agnes, hugging her close.

"Nah. Sera says to order in some soup or stuff. She wants to stay with Maria for the first couple of hours."

"Rosa and Bella are ready to come over to take turns for the night shift," said Pierre, while his thumbs kept busy texting.

"Thanks a million, but no need tonight," Polly said. "I'll camp on their sofa tonight. Wanna be close by if Maria wakes. She'll sleep through, Jeong thinks. Tomorrow, we'll figure out what's best after he's seen her."

"Good. What about supper? I'll phone in an order for you," Pierre offered.

"By morning, Robert or the police will have contacted Maria's family," said Agnes. "Let's head for our place and check the room service menu. Very callous of me, but I'm starved. My mom needs something too. I hope she's not overdoing it. Better bring her some fresh tea and biscuits now."

"No worry, Aggie, already made it over at Maria's, plus found protein bars in their kitchen."

Back in their own living room, Aggie grabbed the menu flyer the maid replaced daily and announced the *soup du jour*, Lobster Bisque and French Onion. The foodie picked options for all of them. Assorted mini sandwiches, like vegetarian choices of watercress and cucumber, plus smoked salmon on cream cheese. No need for beverages. Courtesy of the maid, the apartment's bar fridge miraculously refilled itself with spirits and water bottles, sparkling and the natural spring variety.

"Now, my duty as your *chef de cuisine* is done, I'd better make myself scarce."

"Don't go, Pierre. I mean, of course, you must. Your wife's anxious." Aggie got all flustered and flushed to the roots of her hair.

The man just grinned. Give him his due. He's drop-dead gorgeous for anyone so inclined, Polly thought. He'd discarded his hat and jacket by the door and stood at ease in stockinged feet, slim black hiking pants with the tartan flannel lining showing at the cuffs, topped by a half-zipped charcoal fleece top. His sensitive, long fingers combed through his close-cropped curls.

"Nice to be in demand. My wife okayed a leave of absence." He laughed softly, then grew somber. "No, seriously. Rosa and Bella asked me to make sure you're okay. I'll hang around until Greg and Josh come home. In fact, I intended to wait for them by the fire out there."

"You don't expect more bad news?" Came out like a question, Polly realized as she spoke.

"Um, no. Not to worry."

But the glance he and Aggie exchanged put her on alert. "What is it?"

"Okay, guys." Aggie ushered them to the table. "What would you like to drink? We're all flooded with tea. Time for a change. Or do you want to take a quick shower, Polly, while we wait for the food?"

Polly took the hint, nodded, and reluctantly withdrew.

CHAPTER 21

Later on the Evening of December 26

AGNES

Agnes leaned back contentedly. A warm and fuzzy drowsiness suffused her. Her eyelids drooped. Wine and good company were a tonic for mind and body. Worries would keep for tomorrow. Like what to say when Jac called.

"Hey, Aggie, don't fall asleep on us."

"Just resting my wind-weary eyes," Agnes muttered and straightened up.

"I should let you get some sleep," said Pierre, gazing at her with kind concern.

"Not at all," she said, glancing at the display on her mobile. "It's far too early for bed. I'll get coffee in a minute. Just want to check in with my mom."

His anecdotes, straight from the labors of a legal eagle—his words—had entertained them throughout their meal. At first, Polly appeared too distracted to listen, her glance turned inward. She barely touched the food. A little later, their male companion's curious tales triggered her impish curiosity. An experienced lawyer, he obviously knew how to intrigue. Though, Agnes suspected the stories to be generic rather than indiscretions.

While Pierre and Polly removed soup bowls and plates, Agnes got busy texting.

"My mother says she'll stay another hour. Maria is peacefully asleep," she reported a minute later. "We'll pop the soup in the microwave when Mom returns."

She replaced the plastic domes over the still plentiful sandwich collection to store them in the fridge and brew some coffee.

The mechanical task of filling the machine and watching it drip and gush freed Agnes's mental flow and set synapses firing.

Jac's gift horse proved to be the Trojan type. The death of the property scout was a game changer. If Jeong was right, did it throw a more sinister light on the squabble over selling the lodge? No, eliminating a scout was pointless. Unless the scout enraged the unwilling prospective seller beyond endurance.

A vision of Robert's solid figure, backlit by his cozy living room, replayed before her mind's eye. He might have a temper, as Jac claimed, but didn't look like a man who strikes a helpless drunk half his size or, more accurately, half his circumference.

The machine issued a frantic gurgle as it spewed the last burst of black brew. A wonderful aroma permeated the narrow galley kitchen. Now, the biggest question, she fretted, was to tell or not to tell.

Her spontaneous decision to take Pierre into her confidence, sharing the gist of Jeong's account, might come to haunt her. The lawyer in him had immediately questioned the doctor's wisdom of voicing suspicions formed on shaky ground, though he gallantly asserted Jeong meant well. Of course, she'd requested an assurance of lawyer-client confidentiality. But should she loop in Polly?

Agnes rolled her eyes at her blurry image in the microwave's tinted glass door. Why did she attract such deadly messes?

Two cups of coffee later, and sure she'd be standing upright in her bed all night wired by caffeine, she decided. It's now or never.

"Ahem," she cut into the enthusiasts' skiing and snowboarding lore. "Oh, Polly, before I forget, I meant to tell you earlier," she waffled, her eyes seeking Pierre's. "While you took a shower, I told Pierre about Jeong's visit."

Polly turned on her with unexpected vehemence. "How could you? We promised the doc."

"Wait. Pierre assured me of confidentiality as my legal adviser."

"What is said in this room stays in this room," said her lawyer. "If I feel there is a conflict of interest for me, I'll tell you and leave."

"What are you two talking about?" The elfish features puckered anxiously.

"Surely, you must have wondered about the implications of Jeong's concerns, Polly?" Agnes raised a questioning eyebrow. "If Gino died of a skull fracture not incurred by a fall, someone must have struck him. If the body was moved and buried in the snowbank, it shows intent to cover up a crime. Sorry, didn't mean to pun."

"All these ifs don't mean a thing. The doc had a few minutes and jumped to conclusions." Polly's worried eyes belied the dismissive tone.

Why is she taking it so personally? Agnes wondered. "I merely suggest erring on the side of caution."

"You what?"

"You're over-tired, Polly, or you'd have drawn the same inference long ago. I'm not saying the man was murdered. Maybe someone lashed out in anger with no intent. No. Makes no sense."

"Aggie! You talk in riddles. What the heck do you mean?"

"A strike from behind implies malicious intent? Well, not necessarily," said Pierre. Throughout the exchange, Agnes had been conscious of his intelligent, close attention.

"How come?" she asked.

"Think about it, Agnes. Say he had a drunken argument and angered the other person. Gino tries to escape, either to cut the dispute or in fear of aggression, and then staggers outside—"

"In his state of undress, wouldn't the shock of freezing cold have sobered him right then and there?" said Agnes.

"Drunks do weird things, Aggie." Polly nodded at Pierre. "You figure the angry dude ran after him and whacked him from behind? Left with a corpse out in the middle of nowhere, the perp hides it and sneaks off."

Again, the image of Robert intruded. Impatient with herself, Agnes shook her head and pointed out, "Still, it hardly precludes premeditation, does it?"

"How so, Watson?"

Agnes grinned despite the gruesomeness of it all. The reminder of their Holmes and Watson stint last summer now didn't feel half as bad. They were friends back then. Sort of. For a week. Polly Holmes had a nice ring to it. Inspired confidence. After all, in Germany, Polly had figured out who'd done it. Maybe she'd do it again in Quebec.

Wishful thinking, Agnes chided herself. Use your own brain.

"Picture it," she told her listeners, "Our infuriated X sees Gino escape and runs after him. Is that your scenario?" She let it sink in for a moment. "No way. First, X needs to stop to find a handy steel bar or something. Surely, a sign of intent to do harm. Isn't it, legal eagle?"

"Um. Possibly. You may have a point." He raised his hands, further weakening the judgment. "Our information is too sketchy to pronounce on the matter."

"Yeah, trust a lawyer to hedge his bets," said Polly. "What if your X grabbed the blunt instrument before?"

Agnes realized they'd embarked on a game of Clue. Perhaps it helped to keep the horror of death at bay. She'd gladly play along if it brought results.

Aloud, she said, "Really, Holmes. Put on your critical thinking cap. If the aggressor already held some iron bar during an angry dispute, it proves prior intent."

"Hold it," interrupted Pierre. "We're arguing here ahead of any facts. (a), the non-accidental nature of Gino's death is unproven. And (b), there is no evidence of the presence of a second person. It's futile to speculate about this fictitious person's state of mind or emotions. In short, it might be a mare's nest."

"Don't dismiss my X so lightly, Pierre. From what you said last night, Polly, I very much doubt Gino was alone." The wary expression on Pierre's face and Polly's fidgeting puzzled Agnes enough to break off.

"Let's leave it, Aggie. Was just some wild speculation." The small hands fluttered dismissively. "Groundless ramblings."

"Sounded pretty convincing to—"

Loud clatter and voices startled them out of their seats. Pierre held Agnes back and preceded them into the great room.

The entrance door had swung against the log wall. Icy air and drifting snow gusted in. Half across the room headed for the stairs, Greg and Josh propped up a staggering figure clad in a hooded parka. All three dripped melting snow onto the pine-planked floor.

"Oh my God," said Agnes. "Not another one.

Her companions stood speechless.

The spell broke when Greg called, "C'mon, Pierre, give us a hand." Hoisting the drooping burden, he muttered, "Damn you, Matt, you're such a sack of potato."

Agnes shushed him to no avail.

In an instant, Pierre came to their aid, relieving Josh, who struggled under the larger man's weight. The change of hands, or supporting arms, caused Matt to raise a wet face. Its contorted expression appalled Agnes. The eyes, bloodshot and bleary, remained unfocused. Then, the soggy hood shrouded the visage.

Josh stood by as the other guys lumbered up the stairs. Concerned in case the commotion had disturbed her mother, Agnes checked her phone display. Better text her, she figured, and dashed off a couple of lines, saying the guys were back.

Next to her, Josh said, "Pray the devil of a wife doesn't come back for a while."

"What do you mean?" Agnes asked, her eyes on Sera's response, glad Maria slept through the commotion.

"Sorry for venting. You've met Matt's wife. He's no match for her. If she caught him out, he'd be in deep sh... doodoo." Josh pulled off his hat, shedding more drops. His fingers brushed back strands of damp hair that clung to his brow. It left his face oddly naked and sad. "We'll keep him at our place for a few hours and sober him up with a gallon of coffee."

"A rough day for everyone," said Agnes lamely. "You guys must be exhausted after skiing and searching for Maria." Though she didn't smell booze on Josh, she assumed they'd hung out at the bar. Matt clearly couldn't hold his liquor. Or indulged more than his cousins.

"Oh, yeah, how's she doing, anyway?" The off-hand question did not speak of a sincere interest in Maria's well-being.

"The doctor gave her a sedative," said Polly, who'd been staring at the stairs. "Sera's with her. Aggie, tell your mom I'll be over in a tick. Just wanna grab my PJs. Ta." Already dashing off, she waved. "See ya, Josh."

"Bye, Polly." To Agnes, he added softly, "She's a sweetie. Guess I'd better give my partner a hand with our friend up there. Talk to you tomorrow."

His gait as he climbed the stairs matched a granddad's. But not one like Nonno, she thought. This day had got them all down.

The realization came with a vengeance, driving her hand to clutch her forehead. How unbelievably insensitive. She groaned at her thoughtlessness. The guys lost their friend. What a horrible way for a friend to die. No wonder they went to drown their sorrow.

'Twas Two Days After Christmas...

CHAPTER 22

Morning of December 27

POLLY

The next morning, Polly cast a glance at the bathroom mirror, grimacing at the creases the sofa pillow had embossed on her left cheek and the tufts of hair standing on end. Still in yesterday's fleecy pants and oversized sweater, now the worse for wear after the night watch, she sure looked a sight for sore eyes. Never donned the PJs. What with getting up every couple of hours, there'd been no point.

Cautious to avoid creaking, Polly eased open the bedroom door and peeked in. As she tiptoed to the king-size bed, she heard a soft keening muffled by the fluffy duvet. Concerned the cover might impede breathing, her fingers reached to reveal the face. In response, Maria's head rose in a startled jerk from the pillow, staring in terror, yet unseeing. The keening broke off.

Polly realized the sleeper had not woken. Slight body spasms and whimpering told of nightmares.

Down on her knees at eye-level with the fragile features almost as white as the sheets, Polly breathed calming 'psssst' and murmured soothing sweet nothings, hoping to reach the tortured mind. After a while, there was a deep sigh, and the furrowed brows relaxed. The breath grew regular and deepened.

A sudden vibration in her back pocket startled Polly. She'd been in danger of dozing off, too. Bum first, she inched backward in a crouch,

134

afraid of disturbing Maria's slumber. With infinite care, she stood up, shut the door, and pulled out her iPhone.

Her lips twitched and curved up when she read the SMS.

AGNES

Awake sleepyhead?

POLLY

You bet. Doc's due soon.

AGNES

How is she?

POLLY

Still asleep

AGNES

Breakfast in 5.

After shooting off a smiley, Polly pocketed her phone, started packing away the blankets, and puffed up the cushions strewn on the sofa. Hadn't even bothered to open it into a bed. Too worried about going comatose and Maria waking in the middle of the night frightened and alone.

Twice during the small hours, her cell's vibration right next to her ear caught her catnapping. Aggie checking all was well. Did old Watson reckon some killer was on the loose? Imagined the red devil skipped out of the logo and wandered the compound in the dead of the night or what?

With a tiny shake of her head, Polly pulled a face at her own wild imagery. True, last night's talk of blunt instruments had freaked her. Nah, who would want to off Maria's dude? Not your ideal hubby, but didn't look like a bloody drug pusher or mafiosi with mortal enemies. The doc was overreacting.

Her eyes wandered to the bedroom door, remembering the terrorized stare. Get with it, Poll, she exhorted herself. Don't you go fanciful. Focus on the mundane now. Like tidy up. Place's not fit for company.

She'd barely time to straighten things when a faint tapping on the hall door summoned her. Morphed into a friggin' model housekeeper, she muttered, taking a quick gander. All shipshape. Hell, neither Aggie nor the doc would give a hoot.

"Hey, pal," she greeted the gift bearer and grabbed the coffee mugs from the lopsided tray before they could topple. "Our patient's sleeping like a log." She led the way to the table at the window, away from the bedroom door. "Safe to chat quietly here."

Aggie's voice dropped, anyway. "Did you give her more of the sedative, like Jeong instructed?"

"Just the one dose during the night. Fretted a bit with bad dreams, I think. Now, she's settled down."

"I'm glad. Morpheus is a wonderful healer. You don't look too spritely yourself. Try the pastries. Best I could do for now. They smell delicious." Agnes lowered the cardboard tray and ripped open the bag. "The staff is frazzled this morning, Gabe says. He supplied us unasked while doing the breakfast runs. Seems few people braved the snowdrifts to the main lodge."

"Oh, yeah? Snowed in, are we?" Curious, Polly reached over to drag back the nearest curtain panel. The window, thickly rimmed with the white stuff, fogged up when the room's warmth hit the icy panels. She used her sleeve to swipe. "Wow! Up to the porch railing. Man, and us stuck here with the bridge down."

As soon as it was out, she bit down on her teeth. "Sheet, me thinking of hitting the slopes with her going to pieces when she finds out he's gone."

"Don't be down on yourself, Polly. You're doing so much to help." Agnes put down the half-eaten Danish. "It really is terrible. Poor Gabe kept on working yesterday and today. I asked him. Of course, he was in a hurry now, but you could tell it affected him badly. Seems he stayed up most of the night writing. Well, no surprise there. I'm sure you can relate. He wants to be a writer of some kind, too."

"True. Might be therapeutic. Do you know him well?"

"Not really. Just like any student. They come and go. For a while, there's a close rapport, at least with the ones who love philosophy and are eager to chat outside of class. Gabe's one of the keenest." Agnes studied the content of her mug.

Must be empty by now, Polly thought. "You figure he'll be alright?" she asked.

"Hard to say. While we're here, I'll keep in touch. He can't leave for home, anyway, with the bridge down. Probably better to keep busy than moping in his room." Agnes sighed. "Yikes, I don't want to seem ghoulish. Still, I'd like to hear his account of what he found at the cabin."

"Give it a rest, Aggie. An accident's bad enough." Polly clapped her hand over her mouth and glanced guiltily at the bedroom door, expecting the widow to stand right there listening. The door remained firmly shut.

Instead, Agnes's glance assessed her. "It's not like you, Polly Holmes, to be incurious, is it? Are you worried she is involved?" Agnes's chin jutted toward the sleeper.

For a moment, Polly felt tempted to shout. The mirroring of her suppressed thoughts was too much. Nails dug into her palms, she gritted her teeth. Then, she said, as quietly as she could, "We shouldn't talk here. Jeong said to be careful, didn't he?" she added, pushing the blame on Agnes.

"Sorry. Well, I'll be curious for both of us then." Agnes flattened the bakery bag and folded it smaller and smaller

To Polly's relief, her phone vibrated. "Ah, here's the doc." Her eyes on the display, she jumped up, eager for action, escaping the perceptive eyes. "He's out front."

In woolly socks, she skittered through the common space and opened the outer door. A snowman, swaddled in a hooded parka and calf-high, fur-lined boots, stamped his feet on the wooden deck. The little black backpack shook in unison.

Once unwrapped, the doc extended his hand. "Good morning, Polly. From your earlier message, I presume the night was uneventful?"

"Howdy, Jeong. She's still in dreamland. I checked every couple of hours." In case it mattered for the diagnosis, she added, "Seems to have nightmares."

"To be expected. You are a very conscientious night nurse." He nodded approvingly and removed his boots. "The young woman is in excellent hands."

As they entered the apartment, Agnes's voice rang out, "Jeong, quickly!"

The living room was empty, and the door to the bedroom was wide open. Agonized crying, interrupted by a high-pitched staccato of incoherent words, met them. In between, Agnes's strained voice tried to instill calm.

A moment later, the doc got things under control. His soft but firm voice immediately acted as a sedative on the patient and on Aggie, who had retreated from the vicinity of the bed. Polly ran to the bathroom and soaked a couple of hand towels. Asking Jeong's permission, she gently dabbed Maria's sweating brow.

When Agnes returned with the tea he'd asked for, he helped Maria to sit against the bunched-up pillows and coaxed her to drink. In an aside to Agnes, he said to order chicken broth and reheat it as needed. Later, he'd leave a list of what else to give his patient.

"But first," he said gently to Maria, "you need another hour or two of quiet rest. Once you've finished your tea, I'd like to give you a mild sedative to make you more comfortable. Is that all right with you?"

Maria nodded wearily.

Somewhat later, when the patient had dozed off again, the three of them stood outside the apartment door, where they could speak more freely. The doctor flexed his hands, his face creased in unease.

Polly felt a stab to her stomach. "Is she gonna be alright?" she asked, aware of how anxious it came out.

"She's young and overall healthy. They usually bounce back fairly quickly. Naturally, I'm concerned about treating someone under circumstances as these. A grave responsibility for a foreigner." In the bright light reflected from the white winter wonderland outside, he seemed awfully young and vulnerable to Polly.

"You're doing a wonderful job," said Agnes and reached out to touch his sleeve.

"Yes, Jeong, we thought last night how darn lucky you're here. Impossible to cope without you." And it's totally true, Polly thought. Just knowing the doc was on call made it all bearable.

"Thank you both for your kind words. I shall drop by in the early afternoon. Who is going to stay with Maria?"

"I'm taking the next shift," Agnes said. "The women from Matova have volunteered to take turns later in the morning."

"Hm... Not too many new faces, please. It might upset our patient."

"Oh, Bella and Rosa know Maria. Her spouse, I mean, Gino, worked for the Company."

"Very good. Please remind everyone not to mention what happened until I can determine the patient is ready to be informed. I would prefer Maria be told of her husband's death in my presence."

"Doc, are you sure she doesn't know yet?"

"Until she is ready to speak, no one can say either way, Polly. It is better to be on the safe side."

He shook hands with Agnes, who returned to guard Maria.

Polly went along to see him out. He shrugged into his parka and shouldered his backpack. "If she wakes and shows signs of agitation, please call me right away. Take another of my cards and leave it handy. You must instruct anyone staying with her to take this seriously."

"No worries, doc. We sure will."

"Thank you, Polly. Su and I will stay close to the lodge. The weather is not forecast to let up for the next hours."

Like proving him right, the wind howled and swirled miniature tornados on the porch when Polly waved him goodbye.

With a regretful sigh at all this wasted powder, Polly shut out the heavenly wrath.

On her way to Maria's, she glanced up at the stairs' landing and stopped in her tracks. Dressed in sleek, shimmering, midnight blue loungewear, towered Matt's wife. Their eyes met. The woman acknowledged her with a graceful little wave.

"How is Maria?" she asked from above.

"As well as expected," said Polly.

"Give her my best." The stunning blonde retreated, hip-swinging on two-inch heels.

Jeong's right thought Polly, everyone's staying put today. So much for merry Xmas holidays. With a regretful glance out the giant windows, she went to instruct Agnes for the next shift.

CHAPTER 23

Still Morning of December 27

AGNES

A fter Polly left to play in the snow, as she'd joked on the way out, Agnes paced forth and back in the small space, her tread silenced by thick wool socks. The couch and chairs hampered her movement. At first, she peeked in on Maria every ten minutes, but the sedative was working well. The breathing calmed.

Tired from a restless night and her aimless wandering, Agnes sank into one of the two wing chair imitations. Covered in dark rosé chintz with a pale gold leaf pattern, the upholstery was unyielding, designed for show rather than comfort. All the better in preventing her from falling asleep, she figured.

Earlier, she'd texted Jac to postpone their call until late afternoon without mentioning the fatality at the lodge. Now she fretted if Phil or Robert might spring it on Jac. Unlikely, she thought. They were too protective of Jac to worry her. What a mess, she thought and suppressed a groan.

To distract herself and while away the minutes that dragged unbearably, she browsed news sites on her phone but couldn't settle on reading more than a few paragraphs. Her unruly mind drifted.

Useless of Pierre saying they lacked factual data to form any type of theory about what might have happened to Gino. Used to speculative thinking, she could not have stopped herself even if she'd seriously tried. Thoughts floated in willy-nilly.

A lover might well resent the degrading position Gino put her in. Sure, she must have agreed to the arrangement. Jealousy would fester anyway. Furious at being in a mere cabin while his wife lived in style.

As she entered the kept woman's mind, Agnes could feel her hackles rise. How debasing. Add alcohol to the mix, and a spark sufficed to ignite the smoldering heap of the woman's pride. Brained him in a fit of temper?

But why was he outside in his underwear?

Well, he ran for his life when she came at him with a steel bar.

Agnes sighed. Her imagination was the one running here.

Police usually put the spouse at the top of the suspect list. Or do they only claim that in fiction? The cheated, rather than the cheater, has far more cause for anger. Say Maria caught them in the act, and the lover fled. Unlikely. Where would she flee to?

To stop her thoughts from chasing each other in circles, Agnes reverted to scrolling on her phone. Her hyperactive brain wasn't fooled and picked up the scent again like a terrier trailing a rat. Was she turning into a crime junkie? She grimaced as her intellect barged on.

What if the mistress was another guest? There was no reason to assume Gino kept her hidden in Phil's cottage. Far more likely, they only met there for a few hours when they could get away. Maybe this mysterious mistress had already left for her own quarters, and Maria found Gino alone.

A sound ripped her out of her thoughts. How long since she'd checked on Maria? Was she cooped up here with a sleeping killer?

Before her imagination could run riot, she swung her legs from the armrest and stood up resolutely. Quietly, she moved to the bedroom door that stood slightly ajar and took another peek at the bed. The fragility of the features on the white pillow made a mockery of her wild speculations. Someone so petite could hardly brain anyone.

Or could they? After all, the young woman was a snowboarder, which presumably built some muscle strength. And the man had been drunk like a skunk, Agnes's mind supplied unbidden. Not that the smelly animals imbibed.

Lost in thought, Agnes stepped a little closer. The skinny figure vaguely outlined under the duvet was a mere girl. Well, girls have been known to kill.

Now, there definitely was a light clatter. It came from the living room. Perhaps Bella or Rosa came early on duty. Soundlessly, Agnes retraced her steps and slipped around the bedroom door, anxious nothing should wake her charge.

And stopped dead.

Instead of her new friend, Bella, a tall and bulky male in a dark coat and hat picked his cautious way across the room, furtively glancing over his shoulder toward the entrance.

The killer! Agnes's mind screamed. Wishing she had something like a cast iron frying pan handy, she considered locking herself in with Maria. But what if Gino's wife had killed him?

Then her sane self kicked in and told her to get a grip. The whole killer idea was mere speculation. Broad daylight—outside, at least, banned by the half-drawn curtains—and a fancy lodge were neither time nor place for stalking killers. Or even for burglars.

With a will, she pulled herself together. Mindful of the sleeper, she spoke softly. "Are you looking for someone?"

The man spun around just before reaching the opposite side. The milky light slanting in between the curtain panels fell on his face long enough for her to recognize him. Bella's husband. Then, his wife wouldn't be far behind. Almost laughing aloud at having imagined furtive glances, she now realized he'd probably just wondered where Bella got to. A perfectly harmless fellow. Teo, wasn't it?

Slowly, she expelled her breath. "Ah, you came with Bella. Does she want to take over already?"

He stared at her, his eyes scrunched up in a puzzled frown. Then he stumbled into disconnected speech. "No, no...That is, a little later...No, I just happened to drop by. How are things going?"

Wary of his odd behavior, Agnes hesitated. Still, no point in holding back. He'd find out from his spouse, anyway. Might as well gauge his reaction. If she played her cards right and questioned him cautiously, Matova's CEO might slip a thing or two about the Company's interest in the lodge. Not here and now, though.

"Kind of you to take an interest," she said in her friendliest tone. "The doctor's keeping her under sedation for a little longer. She's resting and hopefully will feel stronger when she wakes."

"Good. Good. Just the thing. Mustn't disturb the poor little woman."

Rather than leave, he moved closer to the desk next to the window.

"I'll grab some papers here and get out of your hair. Business stuff, you know, Gino and I have been working on. A matter of some urgency. He'd want me to proceed after all the effort he put in."

While he spoke, Agnes went on alert. Something was wrong here. Gino had quit Matova's. Or had he played both sides? Hadn't Cheryl's father implied something like that when they argued at the restaurant on Christmas? Either way, she couldn't allow anyone to snoop while she was in charge, and hence responsible.

Used to assuming professorial authority in college classrooms, no matter how big some guys from athletic programs were, she stepped between Teo and the desk.

"I'm afraid you'll have to wait until Maria can consent. I'm sure you can work it out and take possession of whatever you believe is yours."

"Well, of all the nerve," he hissed. Despite the bluster, he was anxious to keep his voice down, Agnes noticed and felt confirmed in her interference. "The little woman has no clue about our work. Who are you to—"

The sentence remained unfinished as his eyes darted past her to the outside door. Lowering his voice further, he mumbled, "My lawyer and I will be back," and brushed past her.

At the door, he nearly collided with a woman entering. His annoyed, "You?" as he stormed out, was answered by a sarcastic, "I should have guessed."

Fascinated by this curt exchange, Agnes watched Matt's wife Cheryl glide in gracefully. Adorned in a most becoming après-ski outfit, white fluffy angora crew neck with skiers gamboling in a circular pattern at shoulder level, and sleek, black slim-line pants accented by pointed red pumps, Cheryl exuded confidence. Long, silky, golden-blond locks curled onto her back. When a ray of light hit the emerald-green eyes, Agnes wondered if nature produced such startling beauty or if it was owing to the artifice of contact lenses.

"Mind if I drop in for a chat? How's darling Maria? I thought I'd come down and relieve you for a while."

The voice was so sweet and solicitous, Agnes hardly trusted her recollection of the shrill insult hurled on Christmas Eve. If Cheryl was in a mellow mood this morning, what a perfect opportunity to connect. The mission assigned by Jac no longer was at the forefront. Still, Teo's hunt for business papers intrigued her. Either way, best to proceed cautiously, Agnes figured.

"So very kind of you," she said. "For now, we're good. Bella and Rosa volunteered to take their turn. The doctor is worried about too many nurses, so to speak. But great to meet you, Cheryl."

"It's so wonderful how everyone rallies around sweet Maria. Of course, I'm much closer to her than my mother-in-law and Rosalinda."

When Agnes's eyebrows twitched up, the emerald eyes sparkled amused. "She and I are of an age. You know, Gino worked for my dad. We girls hung out and bonded. She's such a sweetheart." Cheryl smiled like the memory gave her great pleasure.

"Mind if I sit?" Not waiting for a response, she slipped off her shoes and curled up on the sofa, legs tugged under her sideways. A picture of elegance at ease.

In her baggy sweats and pilling wool socks, hair still stringy in need of a brush, Agnes felt dumpy and gauche. Before her earlier sense of competence and authority might shrivel to nothingness, she perched on the armrest of the wing chair, taking advantage of the higher position to smile down on the visitor.

"I'm so glad of a chance to chat, Agnes," said Cheryl, entirely unruffled. "Philippe mentioned you are friends with his little sister. What a thrill for you to get such a lovely Christmas present. A week's stay for you and your family. My, that was generous, wasn't it? She must think the world of you."

Taken aback, Agnes shifted, digging her nails into the chair's upholstery. "Ahem, yes, Jac is extremely kind." A fierce blush rose to her cheeks. Reduced to the status of a poor relative dependent on handouts, she fumed and tried not to glower at the young woman. "I hear your dad actually wants to buy the whole place," she blurted out and instantly regretted the blunt approach.

Cheryl merely flicked a speck of dust from her pants with bright red nails that matched her pumps. "A passing interest. He might pick it up.

It's rather run-down, isn't it? The Xaviers don't invest in modernization, and it's not exactly a prime location."

"Well, I think it's very impressive and a beautiful place. Far grander than I ever expected," said Agnes, irked on Jac's behalf. Then she realized Cheryl might intend to launch an indirect attempt to drive the price down. Bloody cheek. So, she countered, "Well, your father is not the only one keen to buy the lodge."

Argh, no! Agnes's mental monitor kicked in. Shouldn't have let on. But then Matt's spouse was dancing at two weddings and knew all about Matova's interest. To be fair, Cheryl can't have an easy time with it. Yikes, a low blow to lash out at her like this. If she's a friend of Maria, and Gino worked for her dad, she must feel his death too.

"I'm sorry, it's a tough situation for you all." She wanted to send the younger woman a sympathetic smile. But Cheryl was busy contemplating glossy red nails, hands palm up on her black-clad thighs, fingers bent inward at the knuckles. So, Agnes carried on. "You saw a lot of Gino through the business connection and privately, didn't you? And as a close friend—"

The intense greenness of the irises amazed Agnes anew when Cheryl's head shot up, lips pursed. "Bah. Just between us girls, don't let on, I told you." Cheryl leaned in to whisper, "Maria is a little naïve where her dear Gino is concerned. She worshipped him."

"Oh?"

"You didn't think he'd spent the night alone in that cabin, did you?" Amusement flashed across Cheryl's face.

Did everyone at the lodge know about the guy's mistress? How awful for Maria. Her expression must betray her, for Cheryl confided, "Honest to God, if Gino hadn't been such a useful asset, my dad would have fired him. As far as the business is concerned, we're better off without him."

"Wasn't Gino working for Teo again?" Agnes asked.

"For Matt's dad? Whatever gave you that idea?" Despite the offhand tone, a sharp furrow appeared above Cheryl's pretty nose, making her eyebrows meet. It disappeared just as quickly. "I see. My father-in-law says so?"

"Kind of. From what your dad and Robert mentioned the other day, Gino's connection with Matova is history." No need to drag in Pierre.

"For a perfect stranger, you're quite involved in our family affairs."
The arch tone left no doubt in Agnes's mind that she had exceeded
prudence. As did the calculating glance Cheryl shot her now. "Or did you
know my in-laws before? Like, met Pierre in Toronto?"

Offended, Agnes rose from her perch. Sure, she was determined to
find out about Matova's aims. But the other remark insinuated an illicit
personal connection, which she resented on Rosa's behalf. Well, and as a
personal insult. The woman clearly had outstayed her welcome here.

With dignity, Agnes said, "You'll excuse me. I need to check on
Maria."

"Of course. I'm sure we all appreciate your help." Uncurling long,
well-toned legs, Cheryl gazed at her. The smile seemed so guileless, Agnes
thought she might have just imagined a jibe. "Give her my love when she
wakes. I'll be back after lunch to sit with her." Without a backward glance,
she departed.

Oh God, thought Agnes, hastening to the bedroom, if Maria woke up
and heard us—Jeez, of all the stupid things.

CHAPTER 24

Noon of December 27

POLLY

Refreshed by a hot shower after a long, restful nap in Agnes's darkened bedroom, Polly gulped down a third cup of the coffee Sera had made for her. She used her hands to sweep muffin crumbs from the table by the living room window and glanced at Agnes's mom at the desk.

"I'll just pop over to Maria's. You don't mind, do you?"

"Of course not, dear," said Sera. She raised her eyes from the laptop. "I'm glad to see you look less peaky now despite a restless night. Are you feeling alright?"

"Yep, lack of sleep doesn't bother me. Yesterday was tough on you, er..."

"Because I'm elderly?" Sera finished for her. "It's curious, Polly. I never think of myself in terms of age. Perhaps death does not affect us quite as much as we reach our last quarter. One feels terrible for the widow. And she's so young. Truly saddening."

Not a thought Polly wanted to visit right now. So, she switched topics. "Will you be sketching this morning?" From their summer acquaintance, she knew Sera always had a sketch pad somewhere close.

"Maybe later. Gwen and I are meeting on Skype in a few moments. Once we chat, there's no end to it." Her eyes crinkled in a mischievous smile. "We're no better than teenagers, I often think." One hand went up, fingers spread to comb through her short-cropped hair that gleamed more silver than black in the desk lamp's beam.

"Maybe we can brave the elements later and mosey over to the Bistro for lunch? I'm getting kind of antsy being cooped up inside," said Polly.

"Cabin fever already? After being out all day yesterday? You're even more of an outdoor enthusiast than I am," said Sera. Her tinkling laugh brought a fond grin to Polly's face. It sounded so like those tiny silver bells on Christmas trees.

"Nah, it's the nomad in me. Restlessness grabs me rather badly off and on." The banter distracted from deeper worries.

"Don't you ever wish you could settle in a favorite place, Polly?"

"Me? Not on your life. Can't stand routine and the same old sh—I mean, it's just stifling. Guess it's what you grow used to. Lived nowhere for long."

Sera regarded her thoughtfully but did not buttonhole her with probing questions. It's what's so lovely about Aggie's mom, thought Polly.

A few minutes later, Aggie let her into Maria's place.

"Did she wake?" Polly whispered.

"Not yet. Sleeps like a log." Agnes said softly as they moved to the bedroom door. "Just checked a few minutes ago."

Easing the bedroom door open, Polly peeked in. The dim light of the curtained room showed a ghostly pale face framed by dark hair that contrasted with the whiteness of the pillow. Softly, she stole closer. The fragility of the bones under the porcelain skin tore at her heartstrings. Awakens one's protective instincts, she thought in self-mockery as she withdrew to the other room.

She joined Agnes on the far side. One of the wing chairs now faced the window's snow-shrouded vista. A desk chair waited right next to it.

"This way, we won't disturb her if we talk quietly," Agnes said, echoing Polly's own injunction. "It's been quite a zoo in here this morning."

"What do you mean?"

"People coming by uninvited." When Polly raised a questioning eyebrow, Agnes continued, "First Teo. Then Cheryl—Hang on—" Thumbing her phone, she got busy texting. "Sorry. Rosa and Pierre are here now. I'll tell you later about my interesting morning."

So, the nosey old geezer had been back. Interesting.

The eagerness with which Aggie jumped up distracted Polly. With a sigh, she followed and saw Pierre brush Agnes's cheeks with his lips. Customary French greeting. Italian too.

When Rosa made to fold her into voluminous arms, Polly stiffened. Voluptuous, forceful women intimidated her. She caught Pierre's amused glance.

"Rosa, darling. Don't crush her." He raised his hand for a high five. Polly cracked a grin as her fingers met his.

"So, what's happening, ladies?" he asked.

"Agnes can instruct me for my shift," said his wife, "and then you all go for a nice lunch. Agnes, your mother must hate being cooped up. She's such an active person. I envy her."

"No, you don't. You love curling up inside on a day like this," said her spouse, smiling fondly.

A deep chuckle shook Rosalinda's ample chest. "Right you are, my pet."

"Sera's busy Skyping with her friend," said Polly. "I think I'll go for a little walk. Can meet you guys for lunch at the Bistro later, okay?" Won't play third wheel on a bike again, she added silently.

To her surprise, Agnes suggested, "I'd like a walk with you. Would you get my gear, too, and tell my mom we'll be back in an hour? Rosa, I'll quickly show you the way around and how to contact Doctor Jeong when Maria wakes."

"I'll wait for you out here," said Pierre. "A walk will do me good."

When Polly got back shortly after, the others were already waiting near the outer door.

Bundled into her jacket with Pierre's ready aid, Agnes said, "Let's stroll by Phil's cabin. If it's accessible, that is."

149

"Hadn't taken you for a ghoul. What's the idea?" The lawyer eyed Agnes speculatively.

Though Polly wanted to check out the joint herself, she hadn't bargained for company.

"Tell you on the way," said Agnes, while her gloved hand yanked at the door handle in unprecedented eagerness to be outdoors, it seemed to Polly.

Snow was coming down hard and accumulated fast on the plowed path. Icy flakes stung Polly's cheeks. Against her usual love of the cold, she shivered and buried her nose deeper into the high collar of her snow-boarding jacket. She reached back with one mittened hand and pulled the hood over the elfin hat.

As they entered the wider main path to the lodge, Pierre came up from behind and linked arms with them.

"Do we know where his cabin is?" he asked.

Stopped Agnes in her tracks. "I thought you would. Aren't you friends with him?"

"Not me. Of course, we're well acquainted, but not to that extent."

"We can ask—"

"No need," Polly told them. "I can lead you there. We turn off here. A shortcut through the woods." Polly felt cagey about sharing how she'd found out. When searching for Maria last night, the place where Gino died seemed obvious to start with. Tempted fate to admit even to herself, never mind say it out loud, why Maria might go there. Besides, hadn't found Maria, had she? So, no need to explain.

As Polly led them single file through deeper and deeper snow, she heard Pierre call from the rear, "You still didn't say why we're doing this. We could be cozy by the fire in the bar, woman."

"I've been thinking," announced Agnes.

The lawyer growled like a wolf. "Not recommended on an empty stomach."

Close behind Polly, Agnes laughed. "You're worse than me about food deprivation."

"Okay. Spill your cunning cogitations," he said.

"Might as well wait until we're out of the woods, Aggie. The trail's really narrow through the forest here. Gotta watch where you go," said

Polly. Not a good idea shouting wild ideas for anyone to hear, she thought.

After a slow trudge, they came out into a clearing. The cabin and surrounding area impressed Polly as lifeless and abandoned. Buried in white powder, a smokeless chimney, no light shining from the casement window... Well, not in daytime, anyway, Polly corrected her fanciful imagery of what a Hänsel and Gretel's hut in the wintery woods ought to look like.

The grin died on her lips when her eyes fell on the snowbank off to one side. You couldn't miss the break even with its outline now blurred by new snow. Caused when they dug out the body, she knew. Not only Jeong's narrative had made that clear. She'd seen it when searching for Maria.

Rooted to the spot, she watched Agnes and Pierre approach the cabin.

"Aren't you coming?"

"Be there in a tick, Aggie."

She watched them enter without need to unlock. Nothing to steal, Jeong had said.

For a few moments, Polly contemplated the lay of the land. She imagined sitting out here on a warm summer night, watching deer graze in the clearing. A death sure changed your perception, she thought. Made the scene kind of eerie. She shuddered and went to join the others.

The one-room hut boasted little furniture for comfort. A French bed, bedding and quilt bunched up in a heap, took up one wall. Across, under the window, stood a plain table with three scuffed Windsor chairs in dark wood. A few half-empty booze bottles, open bags spilling potato chips and pretzels, plus a couple of empty tumblers littered the tabletop. A rickety couch in grungy dark green sat against the third wall. Next to it, a single-panel louvered door. Probably a bathroom in the lean-to she'd noticed at the back last night.

She crossed the room to peek in and proved herself right. A smelly composting toilet, tiny washbasin, and a cheap shower stall where you'd knock your elbows when you scrubbed your back, she imagined.

The whole place oozed a stale smell of unwashed bedding, liquor, and something unpleasant and undefinable.

From his perch on the corner of the table, Pierre watched them. Aggie had walked over to the potbellied wood stove on a flagstone hearth strewn with ashes and seemed to scrutinize it intently. Does she want to light a fire? wondered Polly. How absurd.

When Agnes bent to study the fireplace utensils, a light lit up in Polly's brain.

Pierre stood rubbing the back of his thigh where the table edge must have dug in.

"Would one of you enlighten me? What's the big plan?"

CHAPTER 25

Midday of December 27

AGNES

Agnes pushed her hands deep into her jacket pocket and wished the dismal cabin wasn't so clammy cold. She turned her back on the uncooperative wood stove and regarded the disgustingly messy room.

"No plan yet," she admitted in answer to Pierre's question. "One thing's for sure, no woman stayed here for the holidays. Or, more precisely, not for more than a brief tryst."

"How do you make that out?"

"Use your eyes, Pierre."

"Squalor is just a male thing, is it? Aren't we being sexist?"

"No, I mean it differently. Say, Gino's lover came to stay over Christmas. Surely, she'd bring a bunch of clothes and stuff, like for a romantic weekend. Candles and things to create some atmosphere. Rather than merely for...you know what."

"Sure. I guess so. When she leaves, she packs it up and departs. Hence, it's no longer here. Maybe she goes in for oil lamp romance." He pointed to the dented metal one dangling from a hook in the ceiling. "No mystery involved," he added.

"Your tale doesn't fit," said Agnes.

"Why?"

"She means the stuff on the table," put in Polly.

"Are you contending a woman wouldn't leave a mess behind?" Pierre sounded like the lawyer he was.

"You both misunderstand." Time to spell it out, Agnes decided. "What I'm driving at is this. If Gino's lover had planned to stay here for two or three days, she would have brought some luggage. Agreed?"

Her listeners nodded reluctantly, the lawyer somewhat unwilling to commit himself.

"Then, instead of enjoying a romantic night, they fight, and she clobbers him over the head and—"

"Which night, Aggie?"

Surprised at Polly's anxious interruption, Agnes explained, "Didn't you tell me Maria and Gino argued on Christmas Eve, and he left and never returned?"

"T'was the night before Christmas, when all through the house not a creature was stirring," recited Pierre, but then continued seriously, "We don't know when he died. You said the doc wasn't sure because of the exposure."

Concerned about the imp's strange—almost frightened—expression, Agnes hesitated. "For my hypothesis, it doesn't matter which night we postulate. If they fought and the lover killed him in anger, I don't see her stopping to pack her bags so carefully she didn't miss a single item she'd brought along. Also, even if she was so cold-blooded to pack systematically after slaying her lover in anger, she could hardly leave with luggage during the blizzard on Christmas night. The roads were impassable."

When she stopped to let that sink in, Agnes noticed the elfin features relax. Puzzled, she picked up the thread. "Well, and the next night, it was even worse. They used skidoos for the main track to the cabin, even on Boxing Day. And the bridge came down. No way out."

"Where does that leave us? An accident, after all?" Pierre asked. "In my humble opinion, the most reasonable hypothesis anyway."

"Not necessarily. There are other options," Agnes pointed out. "Say Gino's lover has other accommodations at the resort. Or she works here. Or..."

"Or what, Aggie? Why do you look at me like that? I didn't do it."

"Of course you didn't, Polly. But you might not like me to be blunt about who could have."

"Eh?" Pierre regarded them, perplexed.

"The most obvious culprit is always the spouse," Agnes said with conviction.

"You gotta be kiddin'. Maria? No bloody way!"

"Polly, thou protests too much. Are you playing ostrich? You've only met the woman a few days ago." Love at first sight, Agnes thought, might do funny things with you. It wasn't the first time she'd witnessed Polly hopelessly in love.

"Call it gut instinct. Intuition. Maria wouldn't smash in Gino's head." The imp was vehement when roused.

"Your assumption is actually mistaken, Agnes." The lawyer's calm tone effectively ended the standoff.

"About Maria?" Agnes asked.

"No, about the most obvious culprit."

"Oh? Why's that?"

"According to our crime stats of solved cases," he lectured, arms crossed and feet apart, "casual acquaintances account for the largest number of perpetrators in homicides. Most importantly, for our purpose here, the number of legally wedded wives murdering their husbands is miniscule. I recall, for several years in a row, only one or two such cases per annum are recorded as opposed to 150 killed by acquaintances."

Polly's eyes shone. "So, you're saying it's not merely my gut feeling, but statistically, Maria is highly unlikely to have offed Gino?"

"With the caveat: she could be the one case," said Pierre. The quick smile made amends for the unwelcome reminder. "Of course, there are just as many cases with no relationship where the accused is a stranger. Or there's a criminal connection, or where no known connection exists. In short, the field is wide open."

Fond of stats, Agnes listened to Pierre with great interest. Yet, the stove tools mesmerized her.

"What are you staring at, woman?"

When Agnes did not respond, he came closer. All three now stood by the potbellied wood stove as though seeking warmth from its icy-cold metal. Sudden understanding dawned on Pierre's face. He hunkered on his haunches and scrutinized the poker without touching it.

"Our modus operandi?"

"Jeong believes something like a square bar caused the contusion. I'd say our exhibit A fits nicely. Must be antique to have this rough square iron shape—or perhaps a reproduction made to look old. Handy for bashing someone's head in."

"Smart of you to spot, woman."

Agnes raised a sarcastic brow. "Kind of you to say so."

"What do we do with it? If we leave it, the killer might come back and remove it," said Polly.

Instead of answering, Pierre took out his phone and shot pictures.

"Better not touch it," Agnes said. "It's safer where it is. Obviously, the killer thought so. If it's gone, they'll go on alert and destroy other possible evidence police might still secure—provided we can ever convince the cops."

"Right you are," said Pierre. "Forensic testing may reveal trace evidence. DNA, blood—"

"Not likely. Jeong only found a contusion indicating a skull fracture, no bleeding."

Polly nodded to this and crouched, nose close to the blunt instrument, as Agnes's mind dubbed the deadly thing. "They probably wrapped some cloth around it before hitting him. Or the edge would have broken the skin."

"Malice aforethought. At least a certain degree of premeditation," said Pierre, giving the nod to Agnes. "With luck, they tossed whatever they used. A search might discover it. Slim chance, but you never know."

"You'd assume they had a fire going. Fabric is easy to incinerate," Agnes said.

"Too true," he conceded and stretched, perhaps stiff from the damp cold. With a glance around the room, he said, "Time to leave. Wait for me by the door while I take more photos of everything in situ. We should head back. Your mother will wonder what happened to the promised lunch date."

"Jeez." Agnes yanked her mobile from the jacket pocket. "Look at the time. Poor Mom."

"Nah, don't worry, Aggie. Sera's having a good heart-to-heart with Gwen."

A momentary resentment bubbled up at Polly assuming the privilege of knowing Sera better than her daughter did. Then Agnes relaxed. So what? Tons of people must have grown close to Sera over the past decades.

While they watched the lawyer at work, Agnes put an arm around the skinny elfin shoulders. "You alright, Holmes? Not at the height of your sleuthing form today, are you? Anything bugging you?"

The little person wrapped her arm around Agnes's waist, or as far as it would go. "Got this gut feeling something's gonna happen." An uneasy chuckle. "Look at me. Hope I'm not going psychic."

For Agnes, it brought back disturbing summer memories of imp-type forebodings.

CHAPTER 26

Early Afternoon of December 27

POLLY

A t the bistro, Polly felt her patience stretched to the limit by the time they were ready to order coffee. Two-fifteen. Lunch lasted already over an hour. She yearned to hit the Nordic trails. Get some sweat-inducing exercise to calm her mind stressed out since last night.

Her hands shredded the paper napkin. Too bad she didn't have scissors to cut snowflakes while listening to Pierre and Sera trade notes on New York's MoMA arts exhibits.

Aggie got that faraway look, spaced out. Maybe they both wondered how their patient was faring with the next nurse on rota. Oh, man, why couldn't one just say, gotta go now? Not polite. Polly heaved a deep sigh. Earned her a commiserating glance from Aggie.

Polly's answering grin died when she spotted Pierre's voluptuous wife sail through the bistro entrance and bear down on them like a schooner in full mast, shawls billowing. Please, no more Italian greetings, prayed Polly, eyes supplicating the ceiling.

"Why, Rosa," exclaimed Pierre, who'd jumped up. "I was going to walk you home in half an hour."

"I know, sweetheart. The mood took me to surprise you."

Did she mean catch hubby gallivanting with Agnes?

"So unlike you venturing out in this weather a step farther than necessity demands, my dear." Pierre's fond smile and loving embrace showed no sign of a guilty conscience.

As he let her go, Rosa swooped over Sera, hands stretched out in an enthusiastic greeting. "How lovely to meet again, Sera. No need to ask how you are. You look the picture of health and bonhomie."

"Good to see you, Rosa," said Agnes's mom with just the right amount of geniality. "Would you join us for coffee?"

The solicitous hubby motioned to a waitress while he helped his wife unwrap layer upon layer. Before Rosa sank into the chair Pierre requisitioned from a neighboring table, she bent to squeeze Agnes's shoulders. "Don't you look lovely, *cara mia*," which brought a blush to Aggie's cheeks.

"Thanks, Rosa. Is Bella staying with Maria?" Agnes asked, a little breathless, maybe from the tight squeeze. "Did Jeong come by?"

"Goodness, yes. What a sweet man. *Amore mio*." Rosa gave her husband's wrist a playful slap, making him grin in amusement, "Why on earth didn't you mention what an attractive chap he is?"

Pierre laughed in genuine merriment. "Maybe I thought it irrelevant to his doctoring, love."

"Men." Rosa dismissed him and focused her chocolate brown gaze on Agnes.

But Aggie stuck to the topic. "Was Maria awake? Did Jeong say anything?"

"Yes, dear. The pet is doing well," Rosa said, leaving Polly to wonder if she referred to the doc or his patient.

"Rosa, darling, I believe Agnes would like to hear the doctor's diagnosis. And so would the rest of us," Pierre said. Sounds like he's used to wifey's meandering ways, thought Polly.

"Oh? The doctor could not possibly share his patient's medical condition with me, sweetie. I'm not related," said Rosa like they all were a little dense.

Sera nodded. "I'm sure Maria is in excellent hands with Jeong. A most conscientious person, I thought. By now, Maria's family will have been informed and might already be in touch."

The exchange only increased Polly's desire to jump up and run to check for herself. A glance at Aggie showed a similar dissatisfaction puckering the dark brows.

"The girl certainly attracts more attention when ill than when well," said Rosa, a puzzled shake of her head swaying the double chins and ample bosom. Her chubby, dimpled hand reached for Pierre's elegantly crossed knee. "You know, even Teo popped in to see how the poor mite is getting on."

Agnes sat up at that. "What? Again? He already came by when I was there."

"Twice a day shows dedication," said Pierre. His frown did not match the affable tone, Polly noticed.

So, she said, "Make that trice. Dropped in on my watch, too."

"Did he look for anything in particular?" Agnes asked.

This is getting weird, thought Polly, and raising an unobtrusive finger to her lips, she nudged Agnes's foot under the table.

Pierre shot her a glance but only stretched. "Under the circumstances, it's only natural for everyone to be concerned. Even my brother-in-law." He emphasized the last bit. "Are we ready to strike out again? Methinks I see sunshine on the horizon."

While all eyes veered to the window where a milky sun peeked through thick gray clouds, Polly saw Agnes's cheeks blush and eyes widen like somehow startled.

"Awesome. Ski time." A tad of enthusiasm to distract from Aggie's sudden discomfiture. "Anyone wanna come along?" Not that she wanted company.

Got her an indulgent smile from Rosa. Aggie did an eyeroll. "Count me out."

"You'd be lucky to find any skis left. They still offer them free of charge for today," Pierre said and grinned wickedly. "There are always snowshoes."

"That'll do fine to work off lunch." Raring to go, Polly wriggled in her seat.

"Well, duty calls," said Pierre. "My meeting with the Matova CEO won't wait. May I walk you ladies back? Your place is on the way to ours."

As they got up to settle their bill, Polly heard Agnes say to Rosa, "Since I'm not an outdoor enthusiast, I might as well relieve Bella."

"You're off the hook, dear. Bella is not there yet," said Rosa. "Didn't I say? My niece-in-law is taking her turn. Which is why I could leave early and join you for coffee. Wasn't that nice of her?"

When Agnes raised an eyebrow, Rosa added, "Cheryl said you and she arranged it, and she would let Bella know."

"I guess she mentioned it," said Agnes, but her brow furrowed so furiously Polly doubted it.

"Are we ready?" asked Pierre, holding the door for them to file out.

"You go on without me," said Agnes. "I'll follow with Polly."

"Hey, changed your mind? Can't live without a bit of snowshoeing?" Polly joked as the others were out of earshot.

"We'll see," said Agnes and led the way across the lodge's grand foyer.

CHAPTER 27

Still Early Afternoon of December 27

AGNES

A gnes stood, shoulders hunched, huddled into her jacket. Next to her, Polly kicked at the salt pebbles littering the forecourt of the main lodge. Silently, they watched the retreating backs of the others, Pierre and Rosa arm in arm, Sera disengaged at the other woman's side.

He hadn't glanced back once. Well, why should he? Angry at the stray thought, Agnes averted her eyes.

"Can we go now? I really want to get skis. Or snowshoes," said Polly. "Can't stand all this dawdling today."

"Yes, of course. Sorry. Just two things before you go," said Agnes. "One, what did Teo really want this morning? Two, would you pop by the apartment on your way to the trails and check on Maria?"

Polly's foot stopped scrabbling at the grit, and her head came up to peek at Agnes from under the elfin hat covering her eyebrows.

"Eh? Meant to check, anyway." Polly pushed the hat back a fraction. "How about you tell me what he was after the second time around?"

"Fair enough. He came for some business papers. Something he and Gino were working on. Or so Teo claimed."

"You didn't let him take the stuff," said Polly, matter of fact.

"Oh, how do you know?" Agnes asked.

"Elementary." The impish grin was so disarming Agnes grinned back.

"First off, wouldn't have come around again on Rosa's shift if he got it, would he? Plus, your conscience interfered, right? The dude can't take stuff without Maria's say so."

"True. Did you tell him on his first try? What cheek to keep asking for the papers." In retrospect, Agnes gave herself kudos for resisting the man's bullying.

"Bah. The guy never asked. Caught him with his fingers in the drawer. I'm not joking. He backed off. You saw the papers," asserted Polly matter-of-fact.

"No, I didn't. Okay, I was tempted, but no chance with people barging in one after the other. My guess is, it's real estate files from when Gino worked for Matova. Some dodgy deal Teo wants to keep under wraps?"

"Dodgy's the word for trying to steal the docs," said Polly.

"Hm, he feels entitled to his company's paperwork, I guess."

"Nah, it's not their stuff at all. If I hadn't surprised him, he'd have stolen the competition's offer to buy this place. Call it corporate espionage," said Polly, rolling her eyes in mock drama. "An offer from Vincenti Real Estate."

"What?" Frustrated that Polly beat her to the discovery, Agnes stated the obvious, "Cheryl's dad is called Vincent."

"Yep, the sleek guy arguing with Robert the other day."

"How much is he offering?" A specific figure was a juicy tidbit for the call with Jac later.

"No idea. They left it blank. More negotiations needed. Our Vincent is bound to wait until he can beat the competition if the Teo dude is also after this place." Polly's wistful little face swiveled toward the sun breaking through a chink in the clouds.

"Okay, off you go for your ski. We'll talk later. But not when my mom's around. She worries so."

With a gurgling laugh, Polly skipped away toward the sign announcing rentals at the side of the building. They both knew who the worrier in the Taylor family was.

Agnes checked her phone and found a text from Gabe suggesting meeting up in front of the staff's accommodation. She'd messaged him earlier, and he seemed eager for a chat during his break. Nothing philo-sophical today, she thought with a rueful smile.

A couple of minutes later, she found him bent over a skidoo, fiddling with its engine. His head jerked up when the reluctant sun cast Agnes's shadow over him.

"Sorry, Gabe. Didn't mean to startle you. How's it going? Is this an awkward time to interrupt you?"

He wiped oil-stained fingers on a cloth dangling from his work pants' pocket and pushed back the black beanie with the lodge's logo at the front.

The little red devil is everywhere, Agnes thought as she contemplated the larger clubfooted incarnation gamboling on the front cover of the shiny black snowmobile. Quite effective marketing if more people would see it. Like online.

"I'm ready for a break. Where would you like to go?" he asked shyly. "We're not supposed to hang out with the guests. But it's different. I know you as a professor."

"Sure is," Agnes said, not convinced it was. "I wouldn't want to get you into trouble. Maybe you can show me around the resort. Say I asked you for a tour?" Brave the cold for a good cause.

As they meandered along snow-covered pathways, nodding to other guests out for a stroll, Agnes's mind sought a natural way to introduce the topic she really wanted to discuss with her former student.

When the sun lit up the glass in front of an impressive chalet, she said, "Funny, when my friend Jac mentioned her dad's lodge over the years, I always envisioned some rustic hunting camp. This place bowled me over. It's so nice." She stole a glance at her guide. "You know your boss's daugh-ter, Jacqueline, don't you?"

"Not personally. But, yeah, Phil mentioned his sister." Gabe stood still and swiveled in a half circle like someone seeing the place for the first time. "You know, they've developed only the smallest part of the property. Monsieur Xavier doesn't like to book to capacity. The apartments sleep four to six, and the chalets up to a dozen, but I heard him tell Phil people come here for peace and quiet. They don't want a rowdy, overcrowded place with kids partying. Phil's always talking about Facebook and Google marketing campaigns like he runs for the pub in the city." Perhaps embarrassed by his long speech or about committing an indiscretion, Gabe started walking again.

To put him at ease and extract further revelations, she said, "No worries, Gabe. Jac told me her brother and dad don't see eye to eye about the business." Better not mention the feud about selling, she reckoned. Might set staff tongues wagging and cause serious harm.

"Staff always knows," he said with the wisdom of ages. "Phil wants to be shot of the place, but the boss won't hear of selling." He scratched the hairline at his prominent forehead with the bulky work glove and dislodged his hat.

As he crouched to pick it out of a snow heap, she saw his expression. The kid appeared far more worried than the sale of a place he merely jobbed at over the holidays would warrant. His blue eyes under the thatch of blond hair, darkened from sweat, seemed to plead with her.

After years of teaching, Agnes recognized a mute cry for help when it confronted her.

"Gabe, you had a dreadful experience yesterday. Such things are traumatizing. Is there someone at home you can talk to? Or your university's counseling services?" While she was talking, the young guy shook his head, leaving Agnes unsure whether he had no one or rejected the idea. So, she suggested, "Why not talk to the doctor here? Jeong's a kindly guy. He'd listen."

"I'll be okay, Dr. Taylor. I promise I will. If you don't mind, it's you I wanted to talk to."

"Just call me Agnes. No need for formality." She smiled to ease the tension. "You can tell me anything you like." As she spoke, an idea made her stiffen. What if he confessed to killing Gino? Didn't police always suspect the finders of bodies?

Unconsciously, her steps had slowed. She regarded the tall figure surreptitiously. Strong and solidly built, the features seemed guileless and trustworthy. Yet, her judgment of people, especially of the male of the species, proved wrong at times. Several disastrous relationships came to mind.

Nervously, she watched Gabe pull off one glove with his teeth, unzip his work coat, and slip in the ungloved hand. A ridiculous vision of the kid brandishing a gun or a poker flashed through her brain.

Oblivious to her wild imagination, he extracted a sheaf of papers. Oh, no, he'd absconded the documents. Vincent's offer of purchase and sale the CEO was after. Even while the notion formed, Agnes recognized its absurdity.

When Gabe handed her the sheets, rolled up lengthwise, she hesitated only for a second. Her mittens proved too bulky to unroll the scroll, covered in crabby ink handwriting. A horrible sense of déjà vu grabbed her. Not again! The last time she'd laid her hands on a student's scribbled opus, it had ended badly.

"Would you read it? Please, professor. I mean, Agnes. I wrote it last night when I couldn't sleep. They say writing helps one cope." Gabe's speech grew faster and more urgent. "And you taught us about Aristotle on catharsis through drama. Sorry, it's not typed."

"Of course, I'll read it, Gabe. I'm touched you'd like me to. It's only natural for an aspiring author to resort to writing as therapy." She glanced around uncertainly. He regarded her with such eagerness. Did he expect her to read here and now? Her fingers went stiff at the thought of leaving their warm shell to clutch the sheets in the freezing cold.

"It's a little chilly, though," she said, glancing at the cottages and cabins, so cute with frilly powdery dressings, thanks to mother nature. Soon, the string lights would come aglow and spread post-Boxing Day holiday spirit. She longed to be back in her log house with a mug of cocoa in front of the great room's fireplace. A few gingerbread cookies too. Couldn't take Gabe there. Bound to get back to his boss if he'd fraternized in their place.

"There's a sort of office in the back of the garage." Gabe pointed to an outbuilding not far off among a copse of tall pines they were passing. "Stores the machinery, and we use it to warm up. It'll be empty in the afternoon. I need to fuel up the snowmobiles after my break, anyway."

"Sure. Why not?" said Agnes, though she could think of a few reasons against it. "You can show me the wheels that make the lodge tick."

CHAPTER 28

Afternoon of December 27

AGNES

A few moments later, Agnes shed her mittens and woolly hat and sat, jacket unzipped, in an office chair that had seen better days ages ago. The tiny space, stuffed with metal shelving spilling assorted hardware and spare parts, was overheated and reeked of motor oil and gasoline.

Gabe withdrew to the main garage housing anything from lawn tractors to snowblowers and skidoos, plus ladders and other maintenance equipment. Agnes sighed, resigned to reading yet another student's emotional outpouring. A diary of some sort, she supposed. Upsetting not merely for the writer.

She unfurled the sheaves and glanced at the top page. The title made her heart speed up.

The Cabin by Gabriel Gagnon

Agnes caught her breath and read on.

A clearing blanketed in fresh powder snow opened as Gabriel emerged from the shelter of the pine forest. Out here, the snow came down thickly in tiny flakes. Forty yards ahead, the cabin sat in silence—deserted. No smoke curled from its chimney. No sound broke the stillness.

Gabriel slapped his fleece-lined work gloves together to boost his circulation after dawdling in the freezing cold on his walk over from the main lodge. Not using the skidoo gave him extra time by himself. He loved being out after a heavy snowfall, making fresh tracks. The mandatory steel-toe work boots, part of the resort staff's outfit, weren't meant for hiking. Bound to cause blisters again. Reluctant to disturb the virgin white vista, Gabe allowed another minute to laze by.

Better get on with the snowplowing job the boss's son Phil had assigned him to....

... Like an old man, he scrambled to his feet and stumbled away into the clearing. His stomach heaved and disgorged all it held. Weakened, he sank to his knees.

When she came to the last words, Agnes's mouth felt dry, like the sheets clutched in her fingers.

A sound from behind recalled her to the present. She pivoted in the screeching chair to see Gabe standing in the doorway, his expression apprehensive.

"My goodness, Gabe," said Agnes. "Not at all what I'd expected."

His face fell. "That bad?" Hand rubbing his cheek, he looked crestfallen. "I guess I should have waited. They say a writer needs a certain distance from events."

"No, the writing is great. I didn't think you'd fictionalize an account of, you know, finding the body."

"True crime is what I want to write. But, yeah, fictionalized. Not plain documentary."

The implication hit her with a two-second delay. "Crime? You think it wasn't an accident?" Were she and Jeong, and possibly Pierre and Polly, not the only ones suspecting foul play? Did staff gossip about it?

Gabe shifted his weight from one foot to the other. He glanced over his shoulder as if to ensure they were still alone. "You'll probably think I'm dramatizing. When I found him, my gut instinct screamed someone killed him. Later, the doctor asked me to describe what was under the snow cover. I realized he tried to figure out if the guy could have hit his head on something. But then the corpse wouldn't lie face down, and the snow would've cushioned the fall."

Without meaning to, Agnes nodded along while Gabe explained. Encouraged, he went on, "When the doctor tried to tell the boss and the officer, they wouldn't listen." He squeezed his gloves between his hands. "Doesn't sound like much, does it?"

"It's not for me to say," said Agnes, to gain time. How should she react? Confirm his suspicions? Pooh-pooh them? Surely not. Neither choice would do.

"When I drove him back, and we looked for Maria, the doctor asked me who Gino was. I only said a guest." Again, Gabe glanced at her anxiously. Another nod encouraged him to share what he had withheld from Jeong. "I didn't mention I saw Gino arguing with people here."

This was getting awkward, thought Agnes, but too interesting to pass up. "Oh?" She played with the zipper of her jacket. "Well, it's okay to tell me. I heard about some squabbles."

"It probably means nothing. I'm just not sure what to make of it."

"Okay. Shoot," said Agnes and leaned back in the creaking chair. "I'd say, make yourself comfortable, but you guys only have one seat."

Gabe dragged a large metal chest marked 'Tools' that protested with an earsplitting shriek. He plunked down and dropped his coat on the floor.

"I'll try to be systematic," he said and ticked off the first item by hitting his left thumb with his right forefinger. "A few days ago, on the 23rd, I overheard Gino talking to an older man. I was clearing the snow out front at reception. They'd just come outside, and the man grabbed Gino by the arm. Gino pulled back and shouted he was his own boss and could work for whoever he wanted. The other guy, he's the dad of Phil's friend Matt, called Gino a little runt and said he'd finish him."

Gabe, his face red from the stifling heat, took a deep breath and reached over to a scuffed cooler box. He extracted a water bottle and offered it to Agnes. "Want some?" She shook her head and watched him unscrew and tip the bottle against his lips.

So Gino was at odds with Teo. Stood to reason. The Matova CEO would bully anyone, she suspected.

Lid back on the bottle, Gabe was eager to continue his tale. "Before Matt's father stormed off, he hissed—and I really mean it, reminded me of my old Tom cat at home. Anyway, it boiled down to a threat. Gino would live to regret it if he double-crossed him."

"Hm. Do you know what Teo, I mean Matt's dad, was referring to?"

"Not back then." Gabe made it sound like ages had passed, thought Agnes. Then again, three or four days felt like eons around here.

"Okay, go on then," she said.

"On Christmas Eve, Gino had a spat with a guest who'd just arrived. You've seen him. The gentleman who was at my boss's place in the afternoon. Doesn't dress like the ski crowd around here. He rents a suite in the main building."

Ah, Cheryl's dad. Was bound to come into the picture again, she thought.

"How come you know about him and Gino?" she asked.

Her informant turned even redder and shifted his gaze to the water bottle he kept between his large hands. His shoulder shrugged forward like he was giving himself a shove. "In for a penny, I guess," he said, his mouth twitching. "A friend of mine told me. She's a chambermaid and brought fresh towels the guest had ordered. The standard ones didn't suffice. Really finicky, she said. Anyway, when she left the bathroom, this gent entered the suite with Gino. They were arguing and didn't even notice her. She only heard a few words, like the man saying Gino had misled him and Gino claiming he had everything under control and the deal was in his pocket."

Gabe broke off, but Agnes sensed he was holding back yet more. So far, it all sounded grist for the business mill. Nothing unusual other than maybe some rotten wheeling and dealing. She said as much and added, "No need to infer something sinister."

"True," Gabe admitted, yet didn't look convinced.

"Is there more? If it's serious, it'll be safer to share it." Hearing her own words, Agnes felt ridiculously dramatic. Maybe she was just stalling because she dreaded Jac's call. Still no clue how much to tell Jac, she thought.

By some wild association, it made her ask, "How come your friend recognized Gino? From your cabin story, I gathered you didn't know who he was when you found his body."

"He was face-down buried in the snow. I only knew who he was when they turned him over."

"But your friend knew him, didn't she?"

Again, Gabe glanced over his shoulder into the garage. "A few of us saw him with Phil. They hung out at the bar and went around the resort together. We all knew he worked in real estate and asked a lot of nosy questions. The boss didn't like him at all."

"Oh?"

"Well, how could he if Gino stuck his nose into the business, chumming up with Phil and the head bartender? Monsieur Xavier is passionate about his place. I told you. He doesn't want to sell."

"Patrons chatting up the bartender is nothing out of the ordinary, is it?"

"No, but our bartender wears several hats. He's the general manager and maître 'd. Plus, talking about sales figures and revenue in the back storeroom is suspicious, don't you think? The bar staff heard them. Our bartender also works with the boss on planning and everything in the office. He knows the business inside out. Probably way better than Phil."

"Yikes, not ethical to pass it on to a property scout," Agnes said, thrilled the proof fell into her lap without investigating. The unctuous manager was the leak Robert worried about. For once, her instincts were right in disliking a man on sight.

"I agree. The boss hit his stack when Gino told him he'd better sell before the competition would swallow him up. Told Gino to get out before he broke his neck." Gabe paused dramatically.

Clearly, the fiction writer in him got the upper hand. When Agnes cocked an eyebrow, his features split into a self-mocking grimace. "Sorry, got carried away. But it's true. Or, at least, according to hearsay."

"Let me guess. Another staff member overheard them." Jeez, you could say nothing in this place without some ear plastered to the wall.

"You can't blame them if people shout for anyone to hear. Hey, I don't gossip," Gabe said like a man accused. "I'm a writer. I only observe.

Generally speaking," he added with a self-conscious smile. "Talking to you now is different."

"It sure is," she said without conviction. "Well, I guess it'll turn out to be a mare's nest." Where had she heard that before? No matter.

She checked her mobile. "I'd better let you get on with your work." Her knee joints creaked as she got to her feet. Amazingly, her muscles didn't scream after yesterday's exertion. "Thanks, Gabe, for trusting me. I truly appreciate it."

When the tall guy got up and they stood facing each other, the tiny space shrunk and felt absolutely stifling. She sidled to the wide-open area of the garage. Its coolness felt wonderful.

"You took a load off my mind, Agnes. Thanks a lot for letting me ramble on. You're right. When it's all out in the open, it no longer looks so sinister like during the night." His features really seemed far less strained, Agnes thought. "Too bad about my true crime story," he added.

"Ah, I'm sure, with a little research, you'll dig up countless crimes to write about." She flinched at her unintended pun.

He shrugged. "Not the same as a firsthand account of finding the body."

CHAPTER 29

Meanwhile on the Afternoon of December 27

POLLY

The aluminum frame of the snowshoes clanged metallically when Polly banged them together to dislodge the packed snow. She stood them upright against the log wall by the entrance door, hoping no thieves were about to abscond them while she had a quick peek at Maria.

Not a soul in their common space. Polly kicked off the UGGS and padded across to Maria's apartment, tucking her gloves under one armpit *en route*. A soft tattoo on the door received an answer before she could even remove her elfin hat.

The blonde who sidled out in one elegant motion, an inquiring look on her face, seemed rather tall and overwhelming so close. Made no move to invite Polly in but pulled the door almost shut behind her. She peered down, saying, "Oh, it's you," like she'd hoped for a much more interesting visitor.

"Er, yeah, afraid's only me. Thought I'd pop by and see how it's going."

The Cheryl person favored her with a brilliant smile. Polly expected a pat on the head but got a verbal one. "So sweet of you to ask. We're doing well, thank you."

Is this the royal 'we'? Polly wondered. Anxious to get a foot in before this formidable lady shut her out, she stepped forward a fraction as the woman made to withdraw. "Is Maria awake? Can I say hi?" Appalled at her own pleading tone, she cleared her throat.

But blondie beat her to it. "Not now. She's resting after her lunch, er... I don't recall your name."

Obviously had no interest in finding out, Polly thought, and answered anyway. "I'm Polly. Glad to hear Maria ate something." But the woman slid inside, offering her derriere for view instead. "I'll be by again later and take my turn with the patient," Polly said lightly.

Cheryl spun around, the disconcerting green eyes assessing Polly from above. "Please, don't inconvenience yourself. Among us, we are managing very well, thank you."

"Nah, there's so little to do here right now. It's my pleasure to help out," said Polly.

"I think you'll find Maria prefers the company of her own friends and people she knows well. In times of grief," Cheryl said, lids blinking earnestly, "the presence of outsiders is...shall we say, strenuous?" She smiled politely.

Labeled a stranger, Polly felt crushed. She peered up at the imposing figure in slim black pants with a mannequin waist topped by a fluffy white sweater. Golden curls cascaded over the wide shoulders, toned by hours in the gym and pool, no doubt.

Conscious of her own messed up hair, probably sticking out in spikes whichever way, Polly's fingers plucked at her lips. Properly reduced to insignificance, she thought. All she wanted now was to get away with a last vestige of dignity.

"No offense," said Cheryl. "We are so grateful to you and your friends for taking an interest. I'm sure I can speak for Maria and thank you kindly."

This totally hurt. "Yeah, well, ta," Polly mumbled. "See ya around." She pivoted on her socks and almost ran to the door. Tears blinded her as she scrambled into her boots. Not bothering to put on her hat or gloves, she stumbled outside and grabbed the snowshoes.

She's right, her mind taunted. Maria doesn't need the likes of you. No one needs you. Remember, you don't do relationships, anyway.

Why did the pain of it hurt so badly?

CHAPTER 30

Late Afternoon of December 27

AGNES

With a parting wave at Gabe, Agnes let herself out by the garage's side door. A pale sun shone between pewter clouds. More snow in the offing. She sighed, expelling the noxious gasoline fumes in the same breath.

What weighed heavier on her mind than another blizzard was the prospect of Jac's imminent call. She'd got barely a couple of hours to figure out how much to share without throwing her distant friend into a panic. Omitting the truth was becoming a habit. Philosophically, an open question if omissions count as lying. Agnes doubted Phil and Robert kept Jac informed. Otherwise, Jac already would've texted frantically.

Aware she still stood rooted by the door, thus increasing the chance of awkward questions from Gabe's employer, she gazed down the path in both directions to figure out which way their log house lay.

"Oh, shoot. Think of the devil," she muttered. A tall guy in *Va au Diable* gear, an untied aviator hat flapping around his ears, bore down on her.

The twitch of his cheek when he greeted her showed Phil wasn't enthused, either. "Hey, Agnes. What brings you to the bowels of the operation?" he said, pointedly glancing at a bi-lingual sign behind her. 'Authorized Personnel Only. Do Not Enter.'

"Err, hi, Phil. Nice to see you. What an interesting place. Just chatted with my former student, Gabe, on his lunch break and walked him back here." A semi-truth, she thought. If Phil confronted Gabe, the young man would gab, she thought wryly. He'd assume his philosophy teacher admitted to the truth already.

Better distract Phil altogether. "Did you hear from Jac? We've been out of touch over the hols," she said, indirectly letting him know she'd no chance of passing on any unpleasant news.

"Same here," Phil said with emphasis. He wiped his sleeve across his mouth and regarded her steadily. "I would appreciate, and so would my father, if you left us to relate anything about the unfortunate accident."

"Jeez, Phil. Kind of awkward, isn't it?" Sarcasm sneaked in against her better judgment. "Jac's my best friend. If she asks me how things are going here, and I don't mention a little fatality, Jac will be furious when she finds out a guest died on Christmas."

While she spoke, Phil scowled at her. "Then just don't contact her for another day or two." Upon Agnes's headshaking, he amended, "Or yak about being stuck with the bridge down and nothing to do, for all I care. You women always find something to keep you...chatting," he ended.

Sure a less innocuous word choice had been on his lips, she thought, wow, you pompous ass.

Admittedly, launching into an account of the bridge collapsing and no way out would distract Jac. The juicy tidbit of the manager leaking confidential info would grab her interest. Jeez, Jac would explode once she discovered they'd kept her in the dark about what happened besides road closures. No matter how Gino died, the fallout would hurt Robert's business and distress his daughter on her dad's behalf.

Curbing her mental rapid fire, Agnes said, "The last thing I want is to alarm Jac. Sure, you as family should be the ones telling her. Do it sooner rather than later, is all I say. She won't appreciate you holding back on her."

"Thanks, Agnes. I knew you'd see it our way. Jacqueline thinks the world of you," the brother said. Whether the tight smile extended to the eyes remained a mystery behind the mirrored aviator glasses. She wouldn't bet on it.

"Let's hope Jac's opinion won't undergo a sudden change," she said, thinking it might be on the cards. "Got to get back now. My mom and Polly will wonder where I am."

On second thought, now that he owed her, might as well leverage the advantage. "By the way, Phil, has anyone notified Gino's and Maria's families? You were a friend of his. I figured you'd be in contact with them."

He shrugged. "What makes you think we were friends? The police take care of notifying next of kin. We wouldn't know how."

She felt tempted to point out he'd spent a lot of time with the property scout but realized she'd be risking Gabe's job. Phil was smart enough to guess at her informant. Could mention Cheryl being friends with Maria to distract him from the scent.

Before she could get another question in, he dismissed her with a cursory apology. "Sorry, but there's a lot of work waiting. Dad expects me to pull my weight around here. No holiday for me." His hollow laugh sounded unamused.

A mumbled, 'Excuse me,' and he brushed past her to the side door.

Yikes, hope he won't bawl out Gabe, she thought and rushed along the path of hard-packed snow.

It took her out of the sheltering trees right onto the wide throughway of the resort. The wind caught at her clothes. Cold seeped into her bones. Not such a bright idea to stand yakking at the door after sweating in the stifling indoor heat. She sped up to get her blood flowing. Huge piles of snow lining any free space off to the sides spoke of the staff's unrelenting labor. Floods the place in the spring thaw, she thought, imagining mountains of slush turning the road into a river. For now, all was Christmassy and bright in the errant sunrays. Despite the tragic death on the premises.

If only the Xaviers had nothing to do with it. The upcoming overseas call daunted her more than before the brother's request to stay mum. What could she say? Had a pleasant chat with your dad—yeah, right. Jac knew her so well she'd smell a rat. Again, the vision of Robert standing guard in his doorway arose. That bear of a man wouldn't harm the scout just because he was a nuisance. All roar and no punch.

Robert refused to listen to Jeong, though, as Gabe also noticed. Had Jac's dad influenced the cop, urged him to remove the body with little ado? Understandable. Who'd want a corpse and a full-blown investigation on their premises and during the festive season? Nothing sinister in keeping it quiet.

Agnes's steps slowed. Her gaze lost its focus as she pondered this. A sudden gust of wind made her glance up. She'd almost missed the path to their accommodation and the elegant figure in calf-length furry boots and fitted fur-rimmed jacket who approached from the house.

"Glad to see you, Agnes," said Bella and reached out for the obligatory cheek-to-cheek.

"Oh, hi, Bella. You're leaving? I thought Cheryl and you had switched shifts. Is Polly back with Maria?" Or maybe Sera returned from her sketching session and took over. Then Agnes noticed the serious expression on her new friend's face. "Is something wrong?"

"I'm not sure what to make of it, Agnes, but no one answers at Maria's apartment."

"What? How can that be?" Unease gripped Agnes. Had Bella intended to simply leave?

On the same wavelength, Bella said, "I knocked several times and waited for quite a while."

"Did you check with Cheryl upstairs? And with my mom?"

"Yes, I tried but received no answer anywhere. Your entire place is empty. I can just assume Maria asked to be left alone and is deeply asleep, or—"

"You must have Cheryl's number," Agnes cut in, now seriously worried. "Didn't you try to reach her to find out why she left Maria?"

"Agnes." Bella's tone grew severe like a teacher's reprimanding a pupil speaking out of turn. "Of course, I tried to contact her and my son and left voice and text messages. Nor could I reach my nephews. I assume they went skiing. The connectivity is rather spotty once you're out in the forest."

They'd experienced it already on their Boxing Day outing. Once you left the vicinity of the buildings and entered the woods, you'd be lucky to get even one bar. How frustrating.

"Maybe you're right, and Maria is fast asleep," she told Bella. "It's worrying. I'll try again. But if I don't get an answer within the next little while, it'll be best to get someone from staff to check on her."

"Exactly what I thought. Once the executive meeting is finished, I'm going to talk to Rosa and Pierre. Maybe they know more." Bella checked her mobile and shook her head. "Nothing yet."

Agnes grew impatient to see for herself what might be done. "Okay, let me know once you hear more." Surely, this was important enough to interrupt the Company's talks. Maybe not, given the bullying CEO, Agnes thought.

"The skiers should be back soon. It's getting dark so early." Bella's gloved hand quickly stroked Agnes's arm. "Not to worry. We'll find all is well, Agnes." Yet, her face remained somber.

O nce inside the log house, Agnes hastened to knock on Maria's door, to no avail. In the vain hope someone might have returned while she and Bella spoke outside, she tried upstairs with equal lack of success. She shot off a text to Polly, let herself into her own apartment, and discarded her outerwear. Swaddled in a thick fleece from her bedroom closet, she brewed a hot chocolate in their galley kitchen. For a fleeting moment, she considered a hot bath, or at least a shower, but felt too uneasy, worried she'd miss the return of the other inhabitants. No answer from Polly, either.

Armed with her mug and nibbling a protein bar, she returned to the great room, determined to wait no more than fifteen minutes before taking some sort of action. Unable to settle on the sofa in front of the cold grate, she paced to and fro, taking an occasional sip.

She almost spilled the hot brew over her hand when the outer door opened behind her. It was Sera who entered, a sketch pad tucked under her arm.

"Oh, Mom. I'm so glad you're back." Agnes placed her mug on the window ledge and rushed forward.

"My, what an enthusiastic greeting." Her mother's face crinkled into a smile, only to grow apprehensive when Agnes came close. "What's wrong, dear? You look upset."

"I just don't know, Mom. We can't get an answer from Maria, and no one else is around. Bella couldn't get in." Agnes felt her voice rising the more she said and broke off.

"Let's slow down, Agnes. Who was supposed to stay with Maria now, and why aren't they there?"

"Bella came to take over from Cheryl. I met her outside ten minutes ago, and she said no one answered when she knocked. She thinks they are out skiing, and Maria is asleep. Polly's out of reach, too."

"Hm, I see. Did you only knock, Agnes?"

"What do you mean? What else could we do? I was going to get staff in another few minutes to go in."

"I wondered if you or Bella tried the door," her mom said.

Agnes's mouth shot open, but no sound formed.

"Well, in that case, why don't we give it a try?" While speaking, Sera kicked off her boots and strode across the great room.

After several perfunctory raps, Sera gave Agnes a nod and turned the doorknob. Nothing prevented their entry.

A groan escaped Agnes. She silently cursed her Canadian politeness interfering at the worst possible times. Even now, the flutter in her stomach wasn't due to apprehension but to their uninvited intrusion. Ridiculous, she thought. They'd been in and out of this apartment uninvited since yesterday.

The living room lay in semi-darkness. Drawn curtains left a hand-width chink for pale daylight to seep in, enough to reveal the clutter. Dishes littered the coffee table. Cushions and blankets piled on the sofa and spilled onto the rug. The liquor smell was unmistakable.

Sera's look spoke the unstated question. Was this how you left it? Agnes mutely shook her head. They picked their way to the bedroom.

"Let me go in first, Mom."

"Don't be silly, Agnes. It is what it is," Sera whispered back and pushed the door wider.

The bed was empty. So was the room. Agnes slipped into the ensuite. Though messy, no one was there either.

For a moment, they stood contemplating the open closet door, clothes pulled off hangers, some discarded on the floor together with a few undies and shoes.

"One thing's for sure, Maria didn't pack up and leave," said Agnes. "Nor could she with the bridge down."

"Are you sure it's not yet repaired?" Sera asked.

"The news would travel like wildfire. I spoke to Gabe and Phil half an hour ago, and they said nothing of the kind." As soon as it was out, Agnes realized the implication. "Oh, my God! She must be out in the woods again."

"Not necessarily, Agnes. Maria might have gone for a bite to eat if she felt better. Or Jeong might have come back and insisted on moving her to a room there." Calm as ever in the eye of a storm, her mother sounded perfectly reasonable.

"Okay, you call Jeong, and I'll head over to the restaurant and bistro. Let's be fast. If she's run off into the forest again, we've little time to find her before dark."

For once, her mom went along, no questions asked.

CHAPTER 31

Also Late Afternoon of December 27

POLLY

As she emerged from the shadow of the spruce trees, Polly saw the light. It wasn't dark yet, but you could see the oil lamp blinking through the cabin's front window. Plus, the door stood open.

Hampered by the darn snowshoes, Polly hopped back into the cover of a tree. Hidden by the branches, she peeked furtively, not sure what to make of this. Did new tenants rent the dismal shack? Bloody unlikely.

Hard to credit, but if Aggie and the doc were right and someone brained Maria's hubby... What if the killer came back? Murderers often revisited the crime scene. Or so the books claimed.

Nah, no killer would be so daft to announce his presence with lights. Well, not exactly glaring, were they? Or her presence—if the girlfriend offed him.

At least, it couldn't be the widow. Polly heaved a sigh of relief. Sweet Maria's safe and sound in her bed having a nice nap, the formidable Cheryl had said.

Just then, someone appeared in the doorway with a large black garbage bag and tossed it around the side of the cabin. Two things were immediately obvious. The carrier was a girl, judging by the long braid swinging from under her hat as she turned. Plus, the bag throwing drew Polly's attention to a hanger contraption hitched to a half-glimpsed snow-mobile parked in the cabin's shadow.

The girl retreated without shutting the door.

Room service, Polly deduced and emerged from her cover. She hobbled across the clearing. Someone wants this shack readied. Or were they in a hurry to remove traces of occupancy? Her more suspicious mind wondered.

When she reached the entrance, Polly hollered a hello and unbuckled the aluminum Yeti gear, glad to feel the comfy soles of her UGGs again. Two pairs of eyes awaited her as she stood in the door frame. The male by the woodstove was still in the resort's staff outdoor garb, the inevitable devil dancing on his chest and on the rim of his beanie.

Maybe hardier than him, the girl wore a thick sweater and leggings. The only token to the indoor chill was the official hat. Unless she intended it to keep her hair free from the ashes the guy must have stirred up. A small cloud settled, and gray flakes floated from the fireplace sweeper dangling in the guy's hand.

Polly decided to do her airhead act. "Hi, guys. Saw the light and figured I'd pop by." Take me for a ghoul if you like, she added silently and treated them to an inane grin. "What a day for a cleaning job out in the woods."

They didn't respond. Chucks, perhaps francophones up here don't all speak English, she thought.

"*Bonjour,*" the guy said. "Can we help you find your way back?"

Oh, no, you won't get rid of me that fast. "Thanks, I'm okay. Just out for a wee track on the old snowshoes."

The girl paid her no heed and grabbed another bin bag, sweeping the last detritus from the table into it. The bed, Polly noticed, was stripped to the bare mattress. No sight of any bedding left.

Curious, thought Polly. A quick gander confirmed the poker still dangled innocently from the tool rack. Might as well get a bit more direct to see what they say. Pretend to be cozy with the management.

"Guess Phil wants the place spick-and-span again. Such a drag for you guys to come all the way out. What with the resort so busy as Robert was saying."

The guy visibly perked up at the casual mentioning of their boss. His partner grabbed a broom and started sweeping.

"We don't mind." Must be the official mouthpiece, Polly assumed, since the girl ignored them. "Phil treats us well. He doesn't like this place messy. The mice get in if food is left out."

Poor creatures stood a better chance of getting sloshed in this place with all the booze spills. But, hey, sounds reasonable, Polly reckoned. Probably Phil pays them extra for their trouble. Dad mightn't be in the loop. Or is he glad all traces of the so-called accident disappear and pronto? Another causal look-see, and she said, "Glad to hear it. Carry on then," like she were the queen bee. Made her crack a smile.

"It gets dark early. Don't head out too far, miss. People lose their way," the dude warned her.

"Not to worry. Got my scouting badge," she said and waved a cheery goodbye.

Back on her trusty snowshoes, she discovered a little path opposite from where she'd entered the clearing. If her sense of direction didn't desert her, she might run a neat circle and loop back to their cottage by sundown.

Good thing bigfooters could go just anywhere. This pseudo-trail went straight into the forest. Snow-covered branches hung low and dropped their load when she brushed by. Real snowshoe territory. Without the contraptions underfoot, she'd have sunk in up to her thighs. Okay, short legs, but still.

After a strenuous 500 yards or so, she hit a T-junction with a wider trail. Unsure where it might take her, she considered both directions. Safety lay in retracing her steps. Too boring. Plus, this trail had been groomed before today's snowfall. To the west, sunrays broke through tall trees, luring her like the end of a rainbow. Against the light, she saw a skier's silhouette a few hundred yards away, easy enough to recognize by the swinging poles and glide. Couldn't mistake them for a bear, for sure. Too cold for the furry monsters, anyway. They'd be snuggling in their dens, smart creatures.

Polly waited a minute to make sure. No, the skier moved away from her and into the opposite direction from where she assumed the resort. Not a tall person like Greg. Couldn't be Josh either. The guys mentioned skate skiing rather than classic cross-country as this person was doing. Not a fast skier either.

On impulse, Polly followed, keeping off to the side of the ski tracks and sheltered from sight by overhanging boughs. She wanted to be darn sure who it was before hailing them. Her hand tugged off the elfin hat and stuffed it into her pocket. No need for a jingle bell-like tune to announce her.

So stupid, her mind rambled. Should have gone and rented skis early this morning instead of snoozing the day away. Friggin' snowshoes trip you. Damnit. Polly swore as she stumbled over her own feet. Earlier, when she started out, she'd seen some novice skiers stumbling like that on the track around the pond. One pair sat on a bench, skis stuck upright in a pile of snow. What a waste of rental skis, she'd muttered. Should have traded with one of them for the snowshoes. If the shoe would fit, she grinned now.

Oh, well, doomed to play bunny and hop along. No matter. A snail skier like this one shouldn't be out alone so close to sundown.

CHAPTER 32

Before Sundown on December 27

AGNES

Wrapped in her winter gear yet again, Agnes rushed out into the cold. This time, she'd donned the warmer ski pants, too chilled still from the earlier outing. She'd texted Gabe to say she needed to see him. Alone.

A few minutes later, she sneaked in by the side door. The garage's overhead fluorescents were on. Gabe wiped his hands on a stained rag and came to meet her, a wary expression marking his features. Above his right eyebrow, she noticed a dark streak. Oil, she suspected.

"What's up?" he asked.

"Sorry, Gabe, to bother you with this, but I need your help. Gino's wife is not in her apartment. We're kind of worried but don't want to make a fuss." Yet—she added to herself.

Her words seemed to relax him. "She's probably with friends then," he said.

"We've checked the other apartments, and no one's in. I just want to make sure she's okay." His commonsense reaction made Agnes feel foolish.

"How long has she been gone?"

"I don't know. My mom and I found her apartment empty and can't reach Matt's wife, Cheryl, who was supposed to stay with Maria. The guys

186

are all out skiing and no connectivity in the woods, Matt's mom says." Aware she was rambling, Agnes stopped.

The wary expression returned to Gabe's face. "Okay, but what do you want me to do about it?" He glanced around helplessly. "My shift goes until eight tonight, and I'm supposed—"

Maybe he was right, and she was overreacting. "Could you just ask the staff if anyone has seen Maria? I'll check the public places in the lodge, and my mom is calling Jeong. We just want to make sure she's alright and hasn't gone into the woods again."

While she spoke, his mouth opened slightly in exasperation, which changed to a frowning worry. "Phil's going to get me fired if I—"

"Hang on," Agnes interrupted as her phone vibrated in her pocket. Her thumb unlocked the screen while she dug it out. A text from Sera. Not good.

"My mother says Jeong heard nothing after his earlier visit but is very concerned because Maria ought not to be out or alone." She glanced up at her former student. "Jeong said yesterday he's worried about Maria's mental health."

A doctor's concern clearly trumped a professor's, and rightly so, thought Agnes, watching Gabe reach for his work coat draped over one of the lawn tractors. "Okay, I'll text the others," he said, thumbing his mobile. "We can stop at reception, and I'll check places you can't go."

At the main lodge, they were out of luck. In minutes, Agnes was sure Maria was in none of the public areas. The restaurant wasn't open yet for dinner, anyway. Gabe's inquiries weren't more successful, but he did the rounds to make sure. Since Maria's description had circulated the day before, anyone on staff might notice her.

With every second passing, Agnes's anxiety rose. Polly still did not respond. A couple of messages told her Bella had reached no one, but she'd told Pierre and Rosa. The last bit made Agnes wonder if Bella trusted the lawyer more than her spouse. Or did she assume Pierre's rapport with the younger generation would prove helpful? It seemed the cousins were excluded from this executive meeting. And so, apparently, was Cheryl.

When Gabe returned from the bowels of the main lodge, Agnes pocketed her phone. His headshake as he crossed the foyer relayed negative results. He scratched with two fingers under the beanie, his forehead creased into a frown. "No luck."

Determined for action, Agnes zipped up her jacket and pulled on her mittens. "Will you help me search? Please? It'll be dark soon."

"Agnes, it's a huge area. I've got to tell the boss. If I don't, someone else will."

Of course they would, her mind agreed. Was she really worried Robert might have a hand in Maria's disappearance? If disappear, she did. Another idea struck her. She nodded at Gabe, saying, "Before you do, could you check with reception if Cheryl's dad, Vincent, is in, and if anyone is with him in his suite?"

Wordlessly, Gabe strode to the front desk. She waited at the outer glass door.

"They called his room," he said a few moments later. "No answer. Must be out."

"Thanks. Well, if you're sure about helping me search, let's go," Agnes said. "Don't worry, if not, I'll—"

Whatever bravado her mind might have conjured remained nebulous. For, Gabe raised his left hand while his right thumb texted furiously. He stuffed the phone into his jacket and donned his gloves, saying, "Ready?"

In mute agreement, they went back to the garage. As he readied a snowmobile, he told her, "A few of the guys are combing the resort and spiral out." His head came up with a deep intake of breath. "You realize it'll cost me my job."

Agnes groaned. How she hated to involve him. But whom could she trust? "Gabe, with or without you, I must go. If you and Jeong are right, and I believe you are, someone killed Maria's husband. She might be next." Unless she's the killer and on the run, Agnes's mind interjected.

Gabe's eyes widened as she spoke. "Pick a helmet from the shelf there." His voice now firm and determined. "Make sure it fits well enough. Cheap Canadian Tire stuff but should fit without wobbling."

While trying out a couple of helmets, a thought hit her. She pulled out her phone and texted Jac.

AGNES

Hi Jac — mind if we talk tomorrow? Am out skidooing.

Nothing but the truth, if not the whole truth. She rolled her eyes.

The answer popped in just when Gabe pushed a button, and the large garage door rattled up on its metal tracks.

JAC

No worries. Have fun:)

"That's one way of putting it," muttered Agnes.

The hellish roar of the snowmobile engine drowned out her words.

CHAPTER 33

Almost Sundown on December 27

POLLY

T he skier ahead still seemed oblivious to Polly's pursuit. Another
100 yards separated them. In the distance, trees blocked the
straightness of the path. Trail curves, Polly thought. Better speed
up or lose sight of the quarry at the bend. You never know what lies ahead.

A sudden movement off to the right, roughly halfway between her
and the skier, caught Polly's attention. Some instinct caused her to leap for
the shelter of a giant hemlock tree.

A much taller skier emerged cautiously from among the trees. The
stealthy way the dude melted out of the shadows raised her suspicions.
Nah, just your imagination, she scoffed at herself. Some side trail, most
likely.

Against the low sun, she could make out an aviator hat, flaps, and
visor down. Man, those silly hats are popular around here. Not your best
choice for skiing, she reckoned. Must sweat like hell in them, never mind
the bulky parka. Bleeding amateurs! Hog the rentals and no idea what
they're doing.

Or where they're going. No wonder they're stumped at crossroads,
Polly thought. Yet she stuck close to the trees, traipsing forward in their
shelter at the risk of tripping over a root with the alu frames.

The tall skier's head swiveled sideways. Sunrays bounced off mirrored
shades. Below them, all but a nose tip disappeared into a neck gaiter or a

scarf. Man, you must be boiling hot. Or a cold-blooder who never warms up.

Should she shout to wait up? Might be one of the guys. They all favored those silly hats. Or, at least, Phil did when he picked them up for coffee with his dad and later when he crashed Nonno's party. The height would fit. Pierre had one too. Ah, and Matt. Slid right down to his nose when the guys brought him home drunk like a skunk. Wore a parka. So did the others. The regulation black garb of the resort staff looked no different.

Not a novice skier, Polly realized now as the dude sped along the trail in hot pursuit of the slowpoke skier. Polly lumbered after them, her curiosity taking charge. Didn't hurt to stick to the side where the trailing branches hid her from observation, and a quick lunge would provide solid evergreen cover.

Always out for drama, aren't you, Poll? her mind mocked.

Didn't take long for the fast skier to catch the other. A muffled hailing or something carried back to Polly. Now, almost side by side, the difference in the skiers' stature jumped out. The slow one was a wee person like herself, Polly realized.

There was something familiar about the posture. No way. Couldn't be Maria. We're not the only little ones. Jeong's wife is short too. Hope it's not a kid lost in the woods. The thought had Polly scramble closer.

Oblivious of her, the two ahead confronted each other, skis still parallel three feet apart. Their upper bodies twisted sideways. The big dude lambasted the wee one.

"Holy cow," muttered Polly when the little person didn't yell back but brandished a pole and stabbed it right into the dude's midriff. The yeller grappled for control of the pushing pole, but hampered by his own sticks, overbalanced, and keeled sideways. Right into deep snow, skis flaying skyward, he lay spreadeagled.

The pole-wielding skier pushed off wildly and, with much increased tempo, sped away.

Polly hesitated, eyes trained on the downed figure who rolled over onto his back like a giant bug. He uncrossed his legs, the long skis whirling for a second like copter blades. Pretty agile for a big guy, Polly thought, as his lower body flipped to one side, landing the skier in a crouch.

With the one pole still strapped to his wrist, he now stabbed the snow in search of his other pole. Found it in seconds. Against what she'd have wagered, he chose not to renew pursuit but scampered through the deep snow and disappeared into the woods that rose to a hilly crest.

Show's over. Polly felt the tension recede with a long, penned-up breath. Pole-pushing arguments in the dead of the forest at sundown were not to her liking. Neither yeller nor pusher made ideal trail guides. Hedging her bets, she sprinted after the pint-size skier, who faded out of sight around the bend.

When she reached the spot where the dude had tumbled, a gap among the trees revealed an overgrown path, the fresh tracks partially covered by snow dislodged from the branches by his passage.

A creepy sensation stole over Polly as if a watcher lurked among the evergreens. No longer bothering to remain hidden, she hastened on after her lead on the wider trail. She could have sworn evil eyes bored into the back of her skull.

Yet when in reflex, she glanced back over her shoulder, the path behind her stretched into the distance with nothing but scuffed-up ski tracks in sight.

Pooh-poohing her ridiculous fancy, Polly broke into a lumbering jog.

CHAPTER 34

Sundown on December 27

I t took them a few minutes to reach Phil's cabin, but Agnes already experienced a tingling sensation from the snowmobile's vibrations and engine thrumming.

They'd agreed on this first port of call as a likely spot for Maria to go. If she knew Gino was dead. And died here.

When Gabe cut the motor, the silence of the woods became palpable. Something about the cabin appeared different. Agnes unbuckled the strap of her helmet and lifted its visor. The skidoo's headlight bounced off the cabin's window. Someone had drawn dark curtains since her last visit.

"Want to check inside?" Gabe asked and switched off the light.

"Yes, please. If we can get in," Agnes said.

He strode to the door, lifted the roof of a wooden box shaped and painted like a miniature house, and fished inside. Ah, the key in the cute but obsolete mailbox Jeong had mentioned.

Gabe's knuckle-rapping remained unanswered. He unlocked the door and stuck his head inside before motioning for her to follow. Despite the gloom, Agnes immediately saw the place had been cleaned up since their midday visit. Though unsure why the caution, she followed suit when Gabe used the flash of his mobile rather than drawing the limp curtains that effectively blacked out the remaining daylight. The inner liner's dirty gray matched the weathered walls.

Far from sparkling clean, the room appeared stripped bare. An unpleasant air freshener scent masked the earlier stench.

No sign of Maria. While Gabe pushed open the louvered door to the bathroom, Agnes focused on the area around the stove. The poker still hung innocently with an ash shovel and broom from the tool rack. The hearth appeared swept, though a gray, age-old residue remained.

Time to push on. Agnes led the way out and glanced around.

"Someone's been here on snowshoes," said Gabe behind her.

"Might've been Polly if they didn't have rental skis left." Why the imp should return here beat her. Curiosity, Agnes supposed. If Polly was out on the trails, she probably never got the SMS about Maria missing. If back at the apartment, she'd have texted post haste.

Gabe pointed to the clearing's tree-lined perimeter about 50 feet from the cabin. "Whoever it is went farther out into the woods."

"Can we go after them?"

"Not wide enough to drive through. You need skis or snowshoes. But we can drive to the other end. The footpath meets the main trail half a kilometer out," Gabe explained as they trudged through the deep snow to the skidoo.

Off they went again in the late afternoon chill. Huddled behind her driver's broad back, Agnes craned her neck from side to side for a glimpse of the fugitive. They chucked along slowly, scanning the margins of the monotonous forest along the twisting trail. Soon, Agnes lost any sense of direction. Alone, she'd never find her way back to the resort. The only means of orientation to her mind was the lowering sun in the west. Useless information with no idea of the lay of the land.

Her eyes stung from the cold and from staring into the tangled undergrowth. How could Maria cope, weakened as she was? Would Polly find her way around? Maybe the rental staff handed out trail maps. Agnes had seen none among the brochures of local attractions at the log house. Google maps wouldn't show trails. Or connect out here. On their outing the day before, they'd been in a digital black hole.

The skidoo slowed to a crawl and stopped. Her driver's head swung around. Their helmets almost colliding. He pushed back his visor. Over the noise of the idling engine, he said, "See the path over there?"

When she shook her head, Gabe told her to hang tight. He eased the head of the machine to where he'd pointed. A slim opening emerged in the shadowy conifer wall, highlighted by the headlight's beam.

"We've been following ski tracks for a while," he said. "Hard to tell how fresh they are, but for sure from this afternoon after it stopped snowing. One or two skiers turned off here. See? The others kept to the main trail."

Agnes nodded along, though her trekking skills were nil. "We must stay on the wide trail, then?"

"Yep. Up ahead is a trail crossing. A side trail there meets this little path, which also connects with the one from the cabin. Or we might go full circle on the main trail and loop back later."

"Gabe, you've lost me," said Agnes, incapable of picturing the layout. "Let's go whichever way you think best. It's getting late. All I want is to find Maria. And Polly."

Not even a minute later, they ground to another halt. The motor noise ceased abruptly. Agnes bent sideways to peer around Gabe's back. Caught in the headlight were two figures advancing at a clipping pace. Skate skiers, Agnes deduced from the wide kick of their feet.

A moment later, they were abreast. When Agnes raised her visor and cried, "Josh. Greg. I'm so glad it's you," they grinned from ear to ear.

"Hiya, Agnes. Gee, a man loves a hearty welcome," said Greg.

She jumped off and said, "Did you see Maria? Or Polly?"

"No—o." Greg hesitated. "Should we? Why? I thought Maria was ill."

"Hey, what's up?" Josh slid forward to peer into her face. "You look frazzled."

Gabe dismounted but remained silent.

"Maria's not in her apartment. She must've left after Cheryl took over from your mom at lunchtime," Agnes said.

"And you think she's out here? Again?" Josh sounded more exasperated than concerned. "Seriously?"

Already, the day before, she'd sensed he didn't like Gino's wife. Widowhood apparently made no difference.

"You say Polly's with her? I'm sure they'll be alright then," said Greg.

"Sorry, no. I didn't mean they left together. Let me explain." She gave them a quick run-down of the few facts at her disposal, avoiding any assumptions she'd made.

"Man, not good at all," Greg commented. "Sure, we'll help."

Josh nodded and said, "Wouldn't want Polly lose her way when it gets dark."

Gabe cleared his throat. "Can I make a suggestion? If you take the footpath over there," he pointed back, "we'll ride the *Diable* loop and trace back to where the path meets the blue side trail."

The guys seemed to catch on right away. "Got you. See you in a bit," said Greg.

"Wait! Did you meet anyone else while out here?" Agnes asked.

"You mean of our people?" Josh said.

"I mean, anyone."

"Geez, we've been out for hours," said Greg. "Earlier, we saw a bunch of beginners around the pond loop. Oh, yeah, Matt's skiing too. He does classic and went on his own. Too slow for us skaters. Claims we trip him."

"Okay, let's get cracking," Josh urged. "Sun's gonna be down in minutes."

Back on the skidoo, Agnes figured she'd still hear its droning in her sleep. If sleep they'd get eventually. Bone tired, the engine's throbbing muffled by the helmet, coherent thought evaded her. The shadows deepened, the sun too low to penetrate the treescape.

Would they even see anyone who stayed off the open trail? Or tried to hide, alerted by their motor? The logging left plenty of cover along the margins of the trail. Fat tree trunks stacked for removal alternated with piles of peeled skinny ones, good enough for fence posts once cut to size.

What chance did they have to discover Maria in this vast area? Yesterday, the missing woman had returned of her own accord. More or less. Maybe she and Polly were already back at the lodge by now. Blast these cellular deserts.

Agnes's wandering mind snapped back to attention when light penetrated the gloom of the dense forest. A gap among the tall trees on their right suddenly gave way to open space. Slanted rays of the sinking sun in vivid orange hues illuminated the vista. Storm clouds gathered in the mountainous distance. They must be high on a cliff over a vale.

Still distracted by the glimpse of the incredible panorama, Agnes didn't brace herself fast enough when the trail followed a curve, and Gabe slammed on the brakes. The momentum threw her against his back, the crown of her helmet connecting with his in a hollow thud. Her yelp reverberated against the thick plastic visor.

Disoriented by the jolt, Agnes peered ahead to see what spooked Gabe. But the setting sun's brilliance, hitting them now straight-on, blinded rather than illuminated a cause for their sudden halt.

From the shelter of Gabe's back, Agnes saw that the terrain on their right sloped upward at the bent. Its rugged incline appeared rocky to judge by the white shapes and precariously clinging trees, petrified by ice and snow. Some yards below the top, an outcrop seemed suspended over the valley.

The moment Agnes's eyes lit on it, her mouth gaped in a horrified gasp.

On the verge of the narrow ledge, thrown in relief by the brewing clouds, was a vividly green-haired figure.

Polly! Agnes's mind shouted, trying to make sense of what she saw. For, back turned dangerously to void, the imp was clutching the end of a thick branch or skimpy dead tree slanted down from the steep boulders above this tiny plateau that seemed suspended over the valley. Bent over, she clutched it to her midriff as if hanging on for dear life.

The sight had Agnes clamber off the skidoo and scramble up the steep embankment through knee-deep snow. Did Polly slip and hang on to whatever she could grab to prevent plunging backward into the void? With all her might, Agnes suppressed a shout that might startle Polly into letting go.

A scream nearly escaped her when she drew level with the outcrop's plateau. Crouched in front of Polly was another figure who'd been invisible from below. Both its arms slung around the imp's knees, it readied to pull the legs from under her and pitch her over the edge.

Sure now of witnessing an attack on Polly's life, Agnes hurled herself the last yards toward the two, intending to grab hold of Polly and fight the killer tooth and nail.

Polly's "No!" froze her.

To Agnes's amazement, whatever the imp was clutching moved backward by inches, straining Polly's grasp. Confused, Agnes followed Polly's stare upward along what she recognized now as a skinny tree trunk like the ones she'd seen piled up by the trail.

At its upper end, raised above them on a gigantic boulder half-hidden by stunted trees, stood a tall figure in a bulky coat and flapping hat. Backlit by the glow of the sun, both hands clutched the pole-like trunk wedged under the right arm.

In a split second, Agnes understood. The trunk moved back a few inches in readiness of ramming Polly over the edge.

"Duck, Polly! Let go," hissed Agnes and threw her full weight against the deadly pole just as it wielded a mighty thrust.

With a cry, "Maria!" Polly dove away from the brink, her body protecting the little figure at her feet.

The momentum of her lunge brought Agnes down face-first. Icy snow penetrated her mouth and nose. Gasping for breath, she scrambled back on her knees.

Next to her, in a jumbled heap of legs and arms, lay Polly and Maria.

In fear of another attack, Agnes swiveled. One fist shading her eyes against the radiant orange sun, she now saw two figures grappling up above.

The helmeted Gabe struggled to pin their attacker's arms from behind. Whoever it was fought back. Vicious heel kicks pummeled Gabe's shins. When the head came up, it set the earflaps of the hat swinging. A face gaiter and mirrored sunglasses defied recognition. Phil wore a hat like that, Agnes's mind registered.

Gabe appeared to lose his footing. The other raised one knee and kicked back so violently Gabe staggered backward. His arms lost their grip and flayed about, knocking the aviator hat askew. As their attacker tore away, the hat tumbled to the ground.

In the rays of the sinking sun, a golden halo of hair burst forth and cascaded over the fleeing attacker's bulky shoulders.

CHAPTER 35

Sunset on December 27

POLLY

"Bloody hell!" Polly gasped. Couldn't believe her eyes when the hat came off. Not a friggin' guy.

"Polly? Are you alright?" As she felt Aggie's brief hug, tears prickled behind Polly's lids.

"The f— She tried to kill us." Polly squeezed her eyes shut, then murmured, "I'm okay."

"You don't sound it yet," said Agnes and turned to comfort Maria. "It's alright. You're safe now," Polly heard her whisper close to Maria's ear.

Snowshoes still strapped to her boots, legs tingling and cramped, Polly eased from a crouch.

Agnes's hand gently freed her from Maria's embrace, saying, "You're shaking with cold. What possessed you to go skiing at all? Polly, why didn't you call to say you were going with Maria?"

The mildly scolding tone, Polly thought, covered up the seriousness of Aggie's true concern about Maria, whose pitiful whimpers wrenched Polly's heart.

"Nah, I followed when I saw Maria arguing with this guy on the trail." Polly tried to keep her voice level like nothing spectacular had happened just now. "Of course, it wasn't a guy at all, was it? I caught up with Maria on the lookout here."

"Did Cheryl take you skiing?" Agnes asked Maria.

The whimpering ceased abruptly, ending in a loud snort. "I hate her!" Then the words came in a sniffling stutter. "She—took Gino. He wouldn't—Gino loved—"

Into the renewed sobbing, Agnes said, "It's okay. We'll talk later. First, we've got to get you back." Her voice dropped to a whisper as she said for Polly's ears only, "What were you doing up here?"

Too complicated to explain how she'd followed Maria and saw her teetering on the brink. For all they knew, the killer woman was still lurking. "Long story. Let's get out of here, Aggie."

"Tell me when we're alone."

They slip-slided down to the trail, Maria between them, swaying and limp. On snowshoes, Polly could brace them when Aggie slipped.

A snowmobile blocked the path.

"Watch out!" Agnes's shout startled Polly.

Two people barreled toward them from among the trees on the hillock. Blond mane bouncing as she ran, the Cheryl person was in the lead. A few yards behind her, the guy in the helmet.

By instinct, Polly dragged Maria away from the machine. Aggie stood rooted, ready to ward off the enemy.

"Please—no!" Maria cried.

Couldn't do a thing when the blond jumped onto the seat and fumbled for the starter.

"No, Gabe!" Agnes cried as the guy stepped in front of the snowmobile.

Cool as a traffic warden, he raised his arm and dangled something before the swearing dame's face.

"He's got the key, Aggie," Polly said and felt a grin mount despite it all.

The roar of a motor suddenly drowned the flood of cursing. In the twilight, a single light approached, gained speed, and another snow machine stopped a moment later. Two riders dismounted, pushing up their visors like space cadets.

All hell broke loose. Everyone shouting, the killer woman screeching.

Polly wouldn't have thought he had it in him, but, man, could Pierre ever roar. Drowned out the clamor.

SNOWBOUND

"Enough! Chill. Phil, Cheryl, shut up." Smart guy positioned himself to have all in view. "Now, one at a time. What's going on here?"

The Cheryl person had the advantage of a cut-glass voice. She hopped off Gabe's motor and confronted Phil, totally ignoring the lawyer. "Take me back. Now!" she ordered.

Hadn't reckoned with Aggie. A prof's bellow worked just as well. "She tried to kill Polly. Don't let her escape."

Pierre stood no chance. Cheryl spun around. Her arm shot out, gloved finger pointing at Gabe. "That man attacked me. And they," arm sweeping, "just watched. None of them helped me." She spat the words with such convincing disgust it might fool anyone.

"He did not!" The fury in Agnes's shout was awesome. So was her dramatic gesture. "If Gabe hadn't grabbed this woman, Polly would lie smashed at the bottom of the cliff." No way Aggie could have seen the sheer drop.

Into the momentary silence broke Maria's loud sob. Pierre strode over to their side.

"Look what you've done," said Agnes more quietly and hugged Maria closer to her side. "Gabe, you've got to get her back to the lodge. She's in shock. Polly too. Bring them to my mom. She'll call Jeong."

Phil blocked Gabe's way, and Polly heard him say, "Take care of the women. We'll have a word later." It sounded like a threat.

Polly turned when Pierre nudged her. "Here, take my helmet. Too big, but better than none."

Behind them, a motor screeched into life and revved far beyond the proper limit.

"Hey," cried Agnes. "They're taking off!"

"Let them," said Pierre, unflapped. "We'll sort it later. First, everyone back to the lodge."

"But," Agnes sputtered.

Pointless. The machine prescribed a circle and raced away, the blonde hair fluttering like a flag.

They'd just moved over to Gabe's machine, and Aggie was tightening the strap of her helmet for Maria when a voice hailed them.

"Jeepers. There you are. We looked for you all over the place." Greg unmistakably.

The guys skated close and kicked off their skis.

"Oh, you've found her," said Josh as Agnes stepped back from buckling the helmet.

Maria's little face looked heartbreakingly fragile, framed by the large shell, Polly thought.

"Call off the hounds. All is well that ends well," said Greg. He looked from one to the other. "Why the glum faces, then?"

CHAPTER 36

Twilight on December 27

AGNES

As twilight descended, Agnes's heart sank at the prospect of trudging through the snow. She hadn't bargained ever to snow-shoe again. Yet, Polly's contraption was better than sinking in with every step. At least Polly and Maria would be safely back in Sera's and Jeong's care, and Gabe was to come back for her. Too cold to stand here waiting.

Still, seeing them take off on the skidoo, huddled behind Gabe's back, Agnes felt uneasy. Why had they been on the ledge? Though sure Cheryl attempted to ram Polly over the edge, the image of Maria clinging to Polly's knees persisted. Surely Gino's widow tried to hold on to Polly rather than help Cheryl throw her down the cliff?

Nonsense, Agnes chided herself. Maria said she hated Cheryl. They were enemies.

What she needed most right now was to talk to Pierre.

"You guys might as well go ahead," Agnes said to the skiers. "No point us slowing you down." They wore such skimpy athlete gear a slow pace would chill them.

Greg, who'd been stabbing at the ground with his pole while gazing after the skidoo that melted into the distant gloom, shifted his glance to her.

"Much safer to stay together." He nodded at the impenetrable forest and pushed off at a snail's pace, Josh beside him.

Distracted, Agnes eyed the undergrowth. "You mean there are wild animals like bears and wolves out here?" Was he joking? "They hibernate, right?"

"Don't spook Agnes with dire hints, Greg," Pierre said, walking next to her. "Sure, they've got wolves in Quebec. But you know what? Statistically, you'd stand a slim chance of ever getting attacked." His conversational tone aimed to soothe her.

"From what I've read," he continued, "in Canada, only five fatal incidents are on record. Ever. Most weren't predatory but provoked."

"Nice to know," said Agnes. "I'll mention it to the first wolf crossing my path."

"Anyway, young ones," Pierre said. "You're welcome to take advantage of our protection. Agnes and I will defend you with all our might. Won't we?"

No choice but assent. If the guys preferred to stick around, she'd have to speak quietly to avoid being overheard.

For a couple of minutes, she lumbered along next to Pierre until Greg and Josh had gained some lead. They could hardly avoid speeding up while skating.

Hardly above a whisper, she said, "You won't let Cheryl get away with murder, will you? We'll call the police once we're at the lodge."

"Murder? Whose murder?" He sounded incredulous. "You don't seriously suggest Cheryl murdered Gino?"

Interesting he should jump to the inference about Gino, thought Agnes.

As if sensing her sideways gaze, Pierre's hand reached for his hood. His profile disappeared from view. Or maybe he was freezing cold without his helmet.

"I saw her make an attempt on Polly's life," she insisted.

"Be realistic, Agnes." The melodious voice sounded as calm as ever. "There's no proof of Cheryl killing anyone."

"I trust my own eyes. The woman tried to ram Polly over the ledge," she hissed.

"What exactly did you see, Agnes? Think carefully. A report to the police requires precision."

His calm tone infuriated her. Yet, a vision danced behind Agnes's inner eye. The bulky dark figure's face hidden behind sunglasses and what she later recognized as a gaiter. Unrecognizable against the glowing sun. If anything, she'd assumed it was Phil, not a woman.

Deflated yet defiant, she admitted, "Yeah, it's murky. It happened so fast. When the hat came off, the aviator type you guys favor, the blonde hair told all."

"The hats are Matova promo gifts. We all have them. No court would rule hair color as proof of identity. Does your friend Polly intend to accuse Cheryl of attempting to kill her?"

"How do I know until I speak to her and Maria? If someone rams a tree pole into you, I'd say they mean you harm. When you're standing right on the edge, they know—" Agnes broke off, realizing she merely assumed a deadly drop where Polly had stood. The association stemmed from the vista far over the valley, glimpsed when she and Gabe approached on the skidoo.

"This is real life, Agnes," said Pierre. "Police, never mind judges, want solid evidence. Hard facts. Vincent's lawyers will make mincemeat of any unsubstantiated claim. You've heard Cheryl. The minute Vincent gets her version, he'll be on the phone to his lawyers, planning a counteraccusation of Gabe attacking his daughter."

"That's vile! We all saw he only restrained her. She kicked him while he pinned her arms to make her drop the pole. Gabe saved Polly."

"Believe me, Agnes. Any lawyer can turn tables on such a scenario."

Agnes felt like railing against the utter unfairness of reality. And he made it sound like it was the most reasonable thing in the world. She gritted her teeth and did not mask the sarcasm when she said, "Well, yeah, you are her lawyer."

At this, he stood still. His eyes blazed when he faced her. "Hold on a minute. I am not, I repeat, I am not Cheryl Vincenti's lawyer. My client is Matova INC. A corporate body. I would not defend Vincent's daughter if she were the last client left on the planet."

He laughed without mirth. "Woman, see what you make me do? The pathos. Too much, even for a courtroom."

She glared at him, unblinking.

"Right. The situation is beyond jesting," he said. "Here's what I predict. Don't hate me for it. By now, Vincent is on the phone to his lawyers and online, booking flights back home. Before this day is out, nah, say within an hour or two at most, they've got their strategy down pat. Cheryl's the injured party in their play. Do I like the drama they'll enact? No."

Pierre's speech floored Agnes.

"Hey, guys, aren't you coming?" Greg's hollering ripped her out of her stupor.

She stared ahead at the unevenly matched couple, Josh at least a head shorter than his spouse. Visions of the guys bringing home a drunk Matt in a bulky parka and aviator hat meshed with the figure on up above, clasping the deadly tree battering ram. The poker hanging innocently by the woodstove. Gino's skinny figure hastening after the guys into the bar, leaving his wife shamed, escaping from the bistro in tears.

She hadn't seen Gino's body. But Agnes's imagination readily supplied what lay in the snowbank.

With a start, Agnes shook herself. Pierre's face turned toward her. The fading light hid his expression.

What had alerted her was the now familiar engine sound. A light approached at a much greater speed than before. A second headlight weaved behind it.

"We'll talk more tomorrow, Agnes," said Pierre, his voice soft, almost coaxing.

"I don't see what's there to say. You've made the position crystal clear." Glad her tone was as icy as she felt inside out, Agnes didn't wait for a reply but bent to remove the snowshoes.

Dangling them from her hand by the straps as a sign of indifference, she strode ahead to the waiting skidoo. Gabe handed her the helmet and strapped the snowshoes to the back rack.

"Let's go," Agnes said. She didn't waste a single glance at Phil, who'd pulled up right beside them.

The noise of the engines would drown any words anyone might care to utter.

✳

T he return trip took only minutes at a clipping pace. They'd lost sight of the others seconds after their start when Phil shot past them at breakneck speed.

Gabe slowed down as they reached the first buildings. The cottages and chalets twinkled merrily as ever, festooned in their Christmas finery. Once he pulled up by their log house, Agnes got off, her fingers already unbuckling the helmet. Perhaps trained not to disturb the resort guests, he killed the engine.

"Would you like me to return the snowshoes?" he asked.

"Jeez, you know, I forgot all about Maria's skis back there." A faint droning still reverberated in her eardrums. The exposure to the motor's throbbing must cause the aural illusion, she thought.

"No worries, I'll look for them first thing tomorrow," said Gabe, sounding subdued.

"I'm terribly sorry, Gabe, for involving you in this mess." Her heart hurt thinking of what might lie ahead for Gabe if Pierre's predictions proved correct. "We should talk in the morning," she added. One thing was for sure. She'd fight tooth and nail for her former student if the Vincentis were out to harm him.

"Not to worry, Agnes. If anything, I dragged you in. Besides, this job is just for the hols. Never liked working at the pub and want to quit, anyway."

"Do nothing rash, Gabe. Perhaps—"

The distracting droning increased and vibrated in the still evening air. No illusion. Helmet tilted backward, Gabe's eyes searched the sky.

Open-mouthed, Agnes watched the helicopter approach. Like a giant dragonfly, it hovered over the frozen pond, descended in slow-motion, and touched down on its skis.

Neither she nor Gabe uttered a word. A minute passed. An off-road jeep barreled down from the main lodge and screeched to a halt right at the edge of the pond. The driver jumped out to open the rear door.

Easy enough to guess who'll emerge from the back seat, Agnes thought. The urban coat and Karakul hat were a dead giveaway. So was the long hair gleaming in the car's headlights when the woman in a figure-hugging jacket, leggings, and knee-high boots hurried to the waiting chopper.

"I don't believe this," muttered Agnes. The escape came as no surprise. Its speediness did.

The jeep's tailgate lifted. The driver grabbed luggage from the cargo space, hastened after his passengers, and handed the bags to the crew.

A couple of minutes later, the spectacle was over. The copter rose and swayed away.

"How the heck did they manage it so fast?" Agnes said, more to herself than to Gabe.

"Easy. Helis are on call for emergencies. It takes minutes to get here from their Tremblant base. Money talks."

"I guess so," said Agnes. Vincent would offer them extra for prompt service. No use railing against reality. "Well, then. I can't thank you enough for standing by me, Gabe. You've risked so much to save Polly and Maria."

"It was you who saved your friend, Agnes. There's 100-foot drop below the ledge. I don't want to give you nightmares, but it's all rock. The snow cover wouldn't have made a hell of a difference. Polly owes you."

Agnes felt the blood drain from her face as he spoke. One thing to think there's a cliff. Quite another to hear it put this way.

What drove Maria—and Polly—to seek the edge?

CHAPTER 37

Evening of December 27

POLLY

Polly hunched on the sofa, knees pulled up to her chin. Arms tightly coiled around her ankles, her fingers held on to her satiny duvet cocoon. Still, she shivered. Ripples of the shakes made her teeth chatter.

Faint sounds came from the closed bathroom door. Maria wanted Sera to stay with her. The state she was in would be too risky anyway, Maria taking a hot bath unattended. Broke your heart to see the plucky snowboard pal reduced to this. No will of her own anymore.

Went along like a lamb when Polly suggested staying with them. Agnes's orders. Just in case. Safer to have Maria where they could keep an eye on things. Sera took care of the rest. Tea at the ready. Jeong on call to come by soon after the bath. Polly sent to change into warm clothes, then swaddled tightly in a duvet. All in a day's work for Aggie's mom. No questions asked.

At the click of the entrance door, Polly's head shot up from its cushiony knee rest. The sight of Aggie's face shook her fully out of a semi-daze.

"You're back." Not a brilliant line to welcome your lifesaver, her mind commented.

"Stay put. Where's Maria?" Agnes said.

Grateful, Polly clutched the slippery duvet tighter. "In the tub. Your

209

mom's with her. Didn't get her stuff. She'll be okay with my fleecy PJs tonight. We'll sort things tomorrow. Sorry, I'm babbling." The last bit wasn't too clear, what with her teeth chattering like hamsters.

Agnes shed her jacket. "Be right back." She headed for the kitchenette.

Has her priorities straight, thought Polly. The microwave binged twice. Armed with two mugs, Agnes returned.

"Here, hot cacao to warm you up." Aggie placed the steaming drink on the coffee table within easy reach and plunked some chocolate bars next to it. With a yawning sigh, she sank into the nearest easy chair.

Polly inched over. Wedged against the sofa's armrest, she gazed into Agnes's tired face. Crimson patches from the frigid temperature and the ride or from stress marred her cheeks.

"She's gone." Agnes's voice matched the exhausted features. "Did you hear the heli? Her dad must've called them the minute she got back."

"Figures," said Polly. No need to ask who the 'she' was. "Money talks."

"Pierre thinks we can't prove a thing against her. Not that he'd want to, anyway."

At the flat tone, Polly reached out but then let her hand drop and watched Agnes bite off a huge chunk of chocolate. Maybe it provided solace.

Still regarding Agnes, Polly leaned forward and took a sip from the mug. Her head close to Aggie's, she whispered, though no one was there to listen in. "What I don't get, why would she brain him? And if she didn't, why attack me?"

"Oh, I think I can tell you—"

The sound of the bathroom door opening caused their heads to swivel around. Agnes mouthed "later" and got up.

"Ah, there you are, dear." Sera sounded like her daughter had returned from a pleasant little outing.

"Cold and famished," Agnes said, just as nonchalantly. "We're eating in, aren't we?" And to Maria, "Are you nice and warm again?"

A shy nod, and Maria stood like she'd no idea what to do next. The tiny body in sky-blue fleece PJs, covered with fluffy white clouds, looked childlike and terribly fragile.

"Here, take the sofa. It's comfy. I'll get you a blanket." Polly couldn't prevent her happy babble. Oh, man, was it good to be alive.

"Let's not fuss," said Sera. "I've ordered plenty of soup and sandwiches for eight o'clock. Maria, would you like to lie down? Jeong will drop by within the hour."

Amused at Sera's own fussing, Polly watched Maria wriggle her toes in the thick red wool socks she'd provided with the sleepwear.

Hard to fathom the girl was already a widow. The thought sobered Polly anew.

The small voice, saying, "You're all so kind to me," didn't match the image of a grown-up. Flushed from the bath, the skiing, and whatnot, the porcelain face tilted to gaze at Sera's. "Can I stay up? I've slept so much."

Aggie's mom broke into the tinkling laugh Polly adored. "Of course, dear. Do anything you like. You are your own woman."

The message seemed to hit home. Steps still a wee bit hesitant, Maria came to sit beside Polly, who resisted the urge to jump up for the blanket at the sofa's opposite end. Her pal could reach it.

"Though we're all tea-ed out, I'll brew another pot," said Sera.

"Okay," Agnes said, who'd returned from a trip to the loo, "I'll tackle the white elephant in the room. Maria, do you want to talk about it, or should we chat about the weather? I'm serious. You're safe with us. We won't make you feel uncomfortable."

Maria's glance strayed to the apartment door. Polly could guess at the other's fears. Quietly, she said, "Agnes saw her take off in a chopper half an hour ago. The woman won't be back." Strange how they avoided calling their foe by name, Polly thought. Maybe a first name was too chummy for comfort.

Either way, Maria's sigh told her she'd said the right thing. The scent of heated cookies wafting in eased the atmosphere even more. Sera offered a plate loaded with cookies oozing melted chocolate chips.

Sweet tooth Agnes nibbled away. In between bites, she asked, "How come you went skiing, Maria?" Casually, like the outing had been an everyday event.

Maria shook her head at the treat Sera proffered and took a dainty sip from the tea mug. Still bent forward, she spoke so quietly Polly strained to hear. "I didn't mean to. Like, it wasn't for the skiing. I just needed to be at the lookout again."

Polly saw her own incomprehension mirrored on the other faces. Did the Cheryl person arrange meeting Maria there? Made no sense because they were already together in Maria's apartment. Or were they?

Aggie simply asked, "Why was that?"

The answer came in a tearful whisper. "We were so happy there."

Made you want to wrap protective arms around her, Polly felt. Instead, she reached for the tissue box on the table and pushed it close. Sera suggested waiting until Maria was calmer, but the little widow shook her head and blew her nose. Quite noisily for a wee person, thought Polly.

"No, please. I want to tell you. It hurts so holding it all in."

"If you're sure, dear," said Sera and looked far from reassured.

"You'd been there before with Gino," Agnes said ever so softly. "I can see why you needed to revisit the spot."

"Yes," Maria said. "It was her. She drove me to it."

Aggie nodded. "What did she tell you?"

Across from Polly, Sera shifted forward in her seat, a puzzled frown creasing her brow. Has no idea yet who this is all about, Polly realized and mouthed, 'Cheryl.' To forestall questions, she raised one finger to her lips.

"It was horrid." Maria twisted tissues into a ball. Her voice grew agitated, like she was reliving things. "I kind of woke. Like you need the bathroom and are still half asleep. When I came out, I heard someone in the other room. I thought it was Gino."

The tear rolling down the widow's white cheek almost undid Polly.

"I hate her!" Maria cried, her face a sudden mask of despair.

Before Polly could act, Agnes was already at Maria's other side, holding her with one arm around the poor girl's shoulder, making soft pss —pss sounds.

Sera, half out of her seat, sank back to its edge, clearly not happy to let things go on. "Agnes, I think we'd better wait for Jeong," she said.

No way to stop Maria now. A flood of words broke forth. "I saw her. She stole my husband! When Gino didn't come back, I went looking for him. Phil has this old cabin in the woods. He showed us when we first came."

The little hand pointed as if it lay just beyond their door. "Gino loved the rickety thing. Said it was a perfect lover's nest. The guys laughed like it was some joke. I just knew it's where he'd go. And then I saw her come out. I hid in the trees."

It all made sense, Polly thought, busily stringing together bits and pieces while Maria was talking. Even now, Maria didn't spell out the stark facts. The one stealing her hubby was Cheryl. Or, more precisely, Cheryl was Gino's lover and had left the cabin presumably before dawn on Christmas. When Polly saw Maria return all distressed, Cheryl probably was already upstairs in her own bed.

"Did Cheryl see you?" Aggie's soft voice cut into Polly's cogitations. Spoken so casually, the mistress's name didn't drop like a conversational sack of coal. Only Sera's glance betrayed a sudden illumination.

"Not then," said Maria, quietly now. "I could see it was a woman, and she looked familiar when she passed by me. It was dark and snowing. When she'd gone, I went to have it out with Gino. But the cabin was empty. He'd left before her. I could tell they'd been drinking and...stuff." Maria swiped at her lids with the crumbling tissue.

"So, you came back here," Agnes said.

When Maria nodded, Polly put in, "Yeah, was out before dawn on Christmas. Saw Maria coming back. Man, I wish I'd known what upset you so." Wouldn't have made a hell of a difference. No way Maria had noticed what the snowbank harbored. She'd react differently now. Cheryl buried him before Maria ever showed up. Covered her tracks well, the damn killer woman.

Beside her, Maria's small fingers reached for hers. "You were so kind, Polly."

Made one go all rubbery. "Nah, not worth mentioning." Came out a wee bit gruffly. "Everyone pitched in." Some with malicious intent, her mind added.

Aggie seemed to think the same. "I'm so sorry we didn't prevent Cheryl from being alone with you. Was she the one who told you?"

With a jolt, Polly realized they couldn't be sure Maria knew Gino was dead. At a brief nod from Sera, who must've been watching closely, Polly relaxed her tightening jaw muscles.

It seemed Maria hadn't taken in Agnes's question. The vacant gaze showed she still followed the replay of this afternoon's events. "She was right there. I yelled at her to get out. She shushed me. Told me that's no way for a widow to act and poured a drink to 'settle my nerves.'"

Polly could hear the scare quotes and could picture the woman curled up in her designer wear. Had seen the outfit, hadn't she? If only she'd insisted on seeing Maria before hitting the trails.

"I was so confused," Maria said. "Why was that woman in my apartment? I wanted to scratch her eyes out. I think I screamed, where is my husband? You see, I didn't get what she told me before. Then she said, 'Your precious husband is dead. Gone forever.'"

Maria slumped forward. Aggie rubbed her shuddering back.

Sera rose, saying, "I really think this is too much for you, Maria." Polly silently agreed. It was heart-wrenching to see Maria in a state like this.

"Come," Agnes said, "you can tell us the rest another time. My mom's right. I shouldn't have encouraged you."

But Maria grabbed Agnes's hand. "No, please let me tell you. It won't stop in my head. I feel so alone."

Polly saw the questioning glance Agnes shot at Sera, who clasped her own hands tightly in front of her chest. But when she spoke, Sera was calm. "We have a few minutes until Jeong will be here."

Agnes shrugged. She patted Maria's arm, saying, "You're very brave, you know. Is that when you ran off?"

"I think I fainted or something. She was leaning over me. Her eyes frightened me, so close were they. The brandy she gave me made me cough. I told her I knew. I saw her at the cabin."

Polly inadvertently held her breath, frightened for Maria even though she was sitting right there. Safe. No longer able to stand the tension, Polly said, "What did she do?"

Maria turned, her expression deeply puzzled. "She laughed. And said terrible things." In a whisper, "Horrible lies. Gino would never do that. He loved me."

Perhaps to distract Maria, Agnes said, "Did Cheryl leave then?"

Maria nodded and told them all she wanted was to go where she'd been so happy with him. They'd stood gazing over the valley, and he'd said soon he could afford his own chalet out there.

How could a wife be so blind? Polly thought. The signs must've been there all along. But why would Cheryl want to get rid of Gino? Was the woman innocent, after all? Why then attack Polly? Did Gino end the love affair that night, and Cheryl bashed his head in?

"When I locked myself in the bedroom, she called to me she'd be leaving and not to do anything stupid. We're in the same boat, she said, and no man was worth it. Then she slammed the door, and I searched for my ski stuff. No one was about—"

A rap on the door interrupted.

CHAPTER 38

Still Evening of December 27

POLLY

"Perfect timing," Polly said to lighten the strain she felt. "Must be the doc."

Sera seemed to feel similar relief to judge by the sound of her voice as she greeted the medico at the door.

While they waited for Jeong to take off his outerwear, Polly untangled herself from the duvet still slung over her legs and leaned in to collect various snack debris. "I'll tidy up a little, shall I?" She deposited the stuff on the kitchen counter and made for the loo. Way too much tea and cacao.

When she came out a few minutes later, only Agnes remained, eyes closed, stretched out on the sofa.

Polly went close to whisper, "Where's everyone?"

"In my room. Maria wanted my mom with her, and Jeong preferred it too."

"Hey, don't get up on my account," Polly said.

But Agnes merely swung her legs onto the coffee table and patted the vacated sofa side. "Come and talk." Geez, like they hadn't done enough of that. Well, Maria had.

"What did you make of it?" Agnes asked in a half-whisper.

Was she fishing for compliments, Polly wondered. If so, she deserved the kudos. "Yeah, you sure were right. The mistress killed him."

"Not his mistress," Aggie corrected her like a schoolmarm.

"Fine, call her his lover. Same difference. Either way, Maria caught the killer almost red-handed," Polly said.

"Granted, but Cheryl wasn't his lover."

"Are you playing word games, Aggie? I thought you believe Cheryl brained him. Of course, they were lovers. Maria didn't spell it out, but it's what made her almost kill herself."

At the last bit, Aggie's eyes shot up. "Let's sort this. You're getting things mixed up, Polly. Yes, I'm convinced Cheryl killed him with the poker we found. It's the mistress bit you've got wrong."

Though she wanted to stay calm, Polly's fingers went up to dig at her scalp. Then the fuse lit. "Oh, you mean she killed him because of the real estate issue? Yep, makes more sense. Was wondering why she'd kill her lover." She frowned at her own words. If Gino worked for Cheryl's dad, it wouldn't be smart to off the dude who brought in the business. Unless... "Are you thinking Gino double-crossed Vincenti, and Cheryl got mad? Pretty weak motive, isn't it?"

Agnes straightened up and leaned close, saying, "Sorry, Poll, you've got it all wrong. Gino's lover was not a woman."

Polly almost shouted in surprise. "What?" Cranking the volume down a few notches, she said, "You're saying he was bi? How do you figure that? Man, I didn't see it."

Agnes nodded. "Well, we never really met the guy. I'd wondered for a while. Then, when I came back with Pierre and watched Josh and Greg together, I felt certain. Matt was Gino's lover. You heard what Cheryl said to Maria about being in the same boat. They are both betrayed spouses. Cheryl killed Gino. Out of jealousy or hurt pride? Homophobia? We saw her reaction to Josh. She's got quite a temper."

"Holy mackerel. Should have put two and two together." Polly shook her head in disbelief. Too distracted by the lovely Maria.

"I assume Cheryl did the same as Maria," Agnes explained. "Went out to look for Matt and found Gino. Drunk and naked. Perhaps asleep. Took the poker to him and dragged him out on the quilt to bury him in his cold grave. What with the blizzard-type conditions, all traces would disappear under a blanket of snow. Something like that."

"Or he ran outside when she came after him with a deadly weapon," Polly said.

"No. I don't think that fits."

"What do you mean, Aggie?"

"Remember Jeong told us they found Gino with his head facing the cabin? If she'd clobbered him from behind while he staggered out, he'd have fallen forward. No point in her rotating his body before burying him."

"Smart thinking. My Watson has morphed into a Holmes," Polly said, pleased to see Agnes's quick grin.

The "Yeah, right" sounded diffident as ever. Agnes looped her hair behind her ears. Then her eyes lit up. "It's another point against the accident theory, though. If he passed out while stumbling outside, he'd have faced away from the door, not towards it. And if he hit the back of his head, either going out or coming back to the cabin, he wouldn't have been face down. Never mind the unlikelihood of being clad only in briefs."

The reasoning impressed Polly. Other items fell into place.

"Makes total sense," she said. "I've got to tell you. Yesterday afternoon, Matt was freaking. I heard him argue with Phil. Now, I get his, 'What if she finds out?' He meant Cheryl discovering his affair, I bet. When Gino's body was found, he drank himself into a stupor. Remember how he looked when the guys brought him home? It all fits."

"Exactly. Mind you, it's mere surmise. No way to prove. Pierre drove that point home," Agnes said. Polly felt her searching glance. "Do you intend to call the cops about the attack on you? If so, I'll back you up all the way. Pierre be damned."

"Nah," said Polly. Though Aggie's fierce willingness to come to her aid was lovely, it wouldn't do. "We'd need more evidence to bring it home to her. You and I know Cheryl would have maneuvered Maria over the brink if she'd succeeded with me. Her lawyers would tear us to shreds."

"Polly, did you witness her attack on Maria?"

"Nah, it was different." For a moment, Polly considered Agnes's tired expression. "Here's what happened. I'd been following Maria from afar without recognizing her. Then, this other skier came out of nowhere. Not dressed for the part. I saw them arguing. Maria floored him with her ski pole and took off." Polly grinned at the memory.

Soberly, she went on, "Only, it wasn't a guy at all, was it? I caught up with Maria at the lookout. She didn't even notice me. Stared at the void in a trance. It hit me. She was seconds from taking the plunge."

Agnes's gasp interrupted. Hadn't she seen it coming, Polly wondered. Aloud, she said, "Yeah, well, couldn't let her do it, could I? So, I snuck in between her and the rim. I whispered something, but it shattered her. Broke down at my feet. Literally. Next thing, I felt this huge branch poking my tummy. First, I thought I'd missed seeing it. Couldn't be because it nudged me."

In her mind's eye, she could see it all again. "Sun was in my eyes. But there's this tall dude, as I thought then, at the other end of the friggin' pole. Suddenly, an engine roars. Was you on the skidoo, of course. Anyway, the guy's head turned, and sunlight hit the mirrored shades. Couldn't see the face. But hat flaps reminded me of Phil."

"I know. Phil came to my mind, too," Agnes said. "I'm surprised she didn't give you the push right away. One good shove..."

"Gee, thanks, pal."

"Hey, I didn't mean it like that."

"Just kidding, Aggie. A mighty shove with a tree pole would leave tale-telling marks, wouldn't it? Too risky."

"You're right. Forensics would wonder at an obvious, roundish imprint on a corpse's midriff not matching injuries caused by a fall."

"Aggie, it's my tummy we're talking about." Polly felt kind of queasy.

"Aw, I'm sorry, Polly." Aggie's arm reached to give Polly's shoulder a little squeeze. "I'm so glad the woman didn't succeed. You're not half bad, you know."

Then Agnes's face grew somber. Polly felt the eyes regarding her with serious concern. "If anything happened to you, Polly, we wouldn't even know whom to contact. We know nothing, not even where to—"

"Send my ashes, you mean," Polly finished the sentence, only half joking.

"I did not." Aggie got all flustered now. "It's just that—"

"Okay, I get it." Polly reached out impulsively to grab Agnes's hand. "I owe you my life. If I'd trust anyone, it's Sera and you. Never like sharing about myself. Guess I'm a kind of private person." Why would that make Aggie's face twitch?

"Hey, don't look hurt, Polly. I'm not laughing at you. But you've got to admit, for someone who deep-dives into other people's affairs, it's funny to say you value your privacy."

For a moment, Polly felt on the verge of taking offense. Then, a giggle bubbled up. All the pent-up emotions of the last days threatened to erupt. Of their own accord, her lips spread into a wide grin.

Only Aggie's "Psst, they'll hear us" made her suppress laughter gurgling in her throat.

"Darn, Holmes. You're right again. I'm a wee bit weird that way, aren't I? Call it an occupational hazard. My journalist training fuels my curiosity but also has me leery of disclosure. Plus, life experience taught me caution."

"No worries, Polly. I think I like you as you are. No need to disclose anything if you don't feel comfortable with it."

"One day, I will. I promise, Aggie. Right now, I wish we could figure out a way to bring this killer woman to justice."

'Twas Three Days After Christmas...

CHAPTER 39

Morning of December 28

AGNES

"Yay! The bridge is open!" Agnes hit the table with her palm and made the cereal bowl bounce.

"My goodness, dear. You startled me," said Sera. "That is good news, though. Maria and Polly might grab a flight to Toronto tonight. And we'll get a couple of days skiing." The mischievous smile told Agnes her mom was more than aware of her delight at the last bit.

She swallowed a mildly sarcastic rejoinder. After all, cooped up at the resort for days, her mother hadn't had a fun holiday. "Okay, Mom. You're on." Her eyes returned to the SMS. "Gabe says it's a temporary repair until they replace the bridge in spring. I hope it holds," she said, remembering her premonition when they'd crossed the raging river the first night.

"Remind Gabe to contact me," Sera said. "I'm sure Gwen can assist him in finding a part-time job with the university."

"He's staying on 'til New Year's. Doesn't want to leave Robert in the lurch, he says. I feel so bad about having dragged Gabe into this mess."

"Don't you think the young man is mature enough to make his own decisions, Agnes? From what you told me last night, he was aware of risking his job and preferred quitting." Sera leaned over and patted Agnes's hand. "I completely sympathize. We feel responsible no matter what reason tells us."

"Right you are, Mom." Her tentative smile disappeared when she saw the next message pop up. Bella. Her feelings about the entire Matova clan were more than ambivalent now. The easy bonding during the lovely afternoon ski and chat with Bella was overshadowed by what had happened since.

Agnes sighed. "Bella asked me to come over. Nonno wants to speak to me. No idea why." She looked at Sera. "They're leaving at noon. I guess I'd better go."

Her mom's searching glance divined her feelings. "It's not their fault, dear. Don't be hard on them."

Well, she and Polly hadn't told Sera any of what they'd surmised, Agnes thought. Only the bare facts. A smart woman, her mom would piece together what she'd heard from Jeong and Maria and draw her own conclusions. "Will you tell Polly and Maria about the bridge when they've finished packing Maria's stuff? I better go over to Matova's place now."

Bella opened the door before Agnes had time to knock. Elegant as ever, a satiny sheen reflecting from the black hair, she wore dark wool pants and a matching top. Yet, the features no longer appeared serene. They mirrored Agnes's own diffidence about the visit.

No air-kissing greeting either. As Agnes removed her boots, she noticed the stillness of the great room devoid of other occupants. Even the tall Christmas tree stood lackluster as though conscious of its imminent fate in a shredder or on a bonfire.

"My father-in-law is in the den," Bella said and led the way to a door facing the back.

When Agnes entered the small room, furnished with a table for six heaped with files, her eyes at once lit on Pierre's profile. He stood at the window, backlit by the morning sun.

"Ah, Agnes, come in, come in." Half-hidden by the open door, the head of the Matova clan now waved with the thermos pot in his hand. "Can I offer you coffee? It's Italian but quite good."

They exchanged greetings and inevitably commented on the bridge opening and the perfect weather for traveling. Yet, Agnes sensed Pierre across from her was as ill at ease as she and Bella. Only Matteo, established at the head of the table, was his courteous self. Bella withdrew her chair to the window, ostensibly to catch the sunrays while sipping mocha.

When he finally opened procedures, as it seemed to Agnes, the head of the clan, regarded her with kindly eyes. "I know you must be wondering why I wished to see you without your dear mother. I won't keep you guessing. Pierre and Bella told me all they know. And perhaps a little more than the facts."

Agnes glanced at Pierre, shocked he'd betrayed her confidence. Did he pass on what she'd told him? He didn't evade her accusing stare. Merely gave a tiny shrug.

"Now, don't be mad at Pierre, Agnes. He's our lawyer. He trusts me. It would be very wrong to hide things from me."

Would lose him his job or client if found out, Agnes thought cynically. Matova's president didn't build the business by getting hoodwinked.

He regarded her like he tuned into her mental comments. The half-smile vanished when he continued, "My grandson informed us last night that he and his wife are seeking a divorce. His nonna is not happy —Catholics believe in marriage until death do us part. I say there are exceptions. And my wife understands." He paused and lifted his cup. Over its rim, he looked straight at her when he said before drinking, "My grand-daughter-in-law has left us."

Seemingly, the coffee was of more importance. His lids closed as he drank with apparent relish. Confused, Agnes watched him closely. Was this all he'd say on the matter of Cheryl's deadly exploits? Treat them as a little domestic upheaval?

Again, she caught Pierre's shrug.

At the window, Bella rose and stood, arms hugged around her body as if chilled despite the warmth of the room. Their eyes met. Bella's gaze did not waver when she spoke. "My son also told us he is gay. Much harm would have been prevented if he'd been open about it to himself and others long ago. He could count on our support."

Agnes nodded. Greg evidently felt comfortable in his family relations, and Josh clearly was a favorite with Nonna. Yet Pierre's eyebrows twitched, ostensibly unconvinced.

"Annabella, you are a good woman and mother," said Matteo. "My son thinks differently about these matters. Matt, I fear, is not very strong."

Of course, thought Agnes. Teo was the type to bully his son into submission. One glance at Bella's pained expression told her enough. Not a topic to discuss before outsiders, Agnes figured. "Well," she said. "Thanks for sharing. I appreciate you confiding in me." Her moral sense felt outraged at the thought of the killer getting away with it. How Matova would sever the business connection, now that Cheryl no longer belonged to the clan, was another, presumably financial, matter.

The latter thought triggered an association. Might as well get clarity before the Matovas took off. "If you don't mind me asking, Matteo, will your company still attempt to buy Robert's, I mean, the Xavier's resort? To be frank, I'm told Robert does not wish to sell. Gino apparently tried to pressure him."

"I see," said Matteo. "Perhaps it's time for me to have a little talk with my old friend Robert. His son and my son gave me the impression the old fox tried to string Teo and Vincent along to drive up the price."

"Are you saying you and Robert never talked about this?" This sounded too incredible for her to believe.

"Roberto and I go back a long time, Agnes. From when we both were wild young bucks, I've come here every winter and other times of the year. Back then, he had an ancient log house with two cabins and lots of land for hunting." His eyes softened like they perceived a happy past. He sighed, and they sharpened again. "When my son proposed to make Robert an offer, I saw no reason to oppose. But I chose not to be involved."

"You see," said Pierre. "Matteo does not believe in mixing business and friendship. His involvement, he thinks, might unduly influence Robert to accept a lesser offer for friendship's sake."

Bella's nods reassured Agnes more than the lawyer's words.

"I know for a fact that Robert wants no deal of any kind," Agnes asserted. "He loves this place. His own daughter, I mean my friend Jac, told me so. And so did Robert himself."

"In that case, Matova INC will make no offer," said its president.

"Agnes." Pierre's intense gaze made her shift in her seat. "Things might not be so simple. Philippe gave us the impression the Xaviers need the money. These days, running a place like this on a shoestring is asking for trouble. Matova's offer would be very fair. When push comes to shove, Matteo here would insist on that. The vultures might not if the Xaviers are forced to sell. Vincenti, one assumes, will no longer have any interest in acquiring this object for their portfolio."

As Pierre heaped on point after point, Agnes felt overwhelmed with the responsibility she'd inadvertently undertaken without a clue as to the Xavier's financial circumstances. What if Robert faced bankruptcy and just refused to acknowledge it? If he went bust, it might be her fault for having interfered.

In her anxiety, she blurted out, "Nonno, couldn't you just help Robert with an investment? Don't they sell timeshares and things? I don't know how investments like that work, but you must truly love this place if you always come back."

His chuckle made the blood rush to her cheeks. How naïve and silly she must seem to him. She bit her lip in chagrin.

"You call me Nonno, just like my grandsons. I like it." His face creased into countless wrinkles. "And I like your courage, signorina. You take after your mother. She skis like the devil." His arm mimicked swift slalom turns as he laughed. Irrelevantly, Agnes noticed how his Italianism returned only when he spoke of casual things. Just like he felt more at home.

She noticed Pierre watching her, visibly amused. Deflated, she said, "I'm sorry. I realize it was a silly idea. You wouldn't invest money if Robert's business is not doing well."

"Matova is no longer interested in buying." An authoritative voice came from behind her. Bella, who'd been gazing at the sunshine, swung around at its sound.

It was no surprise to find Teo standing in the doorway as Agnes turned in her seat. The man's expression appeared thunderous. Matteo addressed him in staccato Italian, which elicited an equally forceful reply, the tone aggressive.

Pierre just rolled his eyes at Agnes as if to say, what else is new?

With an exasperated headshake, Bella rushed over, linked her arm with Teo's unwilling one, and shushing propelled him out of the room. She returned a moment later, alone.

"I'm sorry," said Agnes, unsure why she couldn't shake the habit of apologizing for other people's social gaffes. "I better get back. My friend Polly has offered to escort Maria back to Toronto. They're leaving tonight if they can get a flight."

As they accompanied her into the Matova's great room, Bella said, "I realize you might rather forget us after all this. But if you ever feel like getting together in Toronto, you have my number."

Matteo gallantly held out her jacket for her to slip in. "You are a smart *filosofa*, Agnes. My friend Robert and I will put our heads together. Not the company, but Matteo will see things come right."

When she thanked him warmly, he chuckled. "No, no. I like it quiet and a little old-fashioned. Like Nonno. No young yahoos partying all night."

Before she could stop herself, Agnes hugged the elderly gent.

He grinned, saying, "We shall meet again."

Over Matteo's shoulder, she caught Pierre winking at her.

CHAPTER 40

Adieu December 28

AGNES

O nce safely outside the Matova place, Agnes's breath escaped with a hiss.

The cheek of winking at her after his betrayal! She swore to herself never to trust another guy with any of her thoughts.

Heat rose to her face, not merely from the bright midday sun. Agnes stopped where the walkway from the chalet, lined by snowbanks on both sides, met the lane winding through the resort.

As her hands unzipped the top of her jacket, her mind raced ahead to her next meeting. She'd asked Gabe for five minutes of his time but needed to calm down before speaking to him.

Her eyes strayed to the cloudless sky. In the distance arose the wooded mountain range. A twinge of regret surprised her. On a day like this, skiing didn't sound all that bad. She could imagine enjoying herself on the slopes. Like the afternoon with Bella. Well, tomorrow she could enjoy a ski day with Sera, couldn't she?

The self-mocking grimace froze when a voice hailed her from behind.

"Wait up, Agnes."

A scowl in place, she turned to face Pierre, who came rushing along the path, hatless, parka undone.

When he reached her, his remark, "We forgot something," forestalled any comment.

"What?" she said and frowned.

"Turn on the airdrop on your phone. You want the photos I took at Phil's cabin, don't you?"

He must think the pics useless, or he wouldn't share them, she figured as she readied her mobile.

"My lawyer's mind tells me there's insufficient evidence for further investigation," he said, his eyes on his phone. "However, if you can convince the authorities to explore, you can pass on my contact." He handed her a card. "Who knows what they might find?"

"Yeah, right." Agnes didn't bother to suppress her feelings. "After you've spread the word, someone has sent a clean-up crew who conveniently removed all traces, I'm sure."

Pierre's head jerked up. The glare struck her as haughty when he said, "I did not tell anyone. Nor did I show these photos to anyone but you."

"Not my impression of what Nonno said," she retorted. How stupid did the guy think her to lie so blatantly?

"For the record, Agnes." His voice grew cold and impersonal. "What I shared with Matteo were my firsthand observations of the events at the lookout last night. I mentioned Cheryl came under suspicion of having attacked your friend Polly. I related no confidential conversations."

When she gazed at him, unsure whether to believe his word, he continued, "Rosa and Bella told Matteo about Cheryl abandoning her post, notifying no one, thus enabling their nursing charge to wander off. We had no word from Cheryl. Apparently, she spoke briefly to Matt about separation and divorce, citing Matt's coming out as the reason. I'm not breaking a confidence in telling you."

"Well," said Agnes, still feeling sarcastic, "thanks a lot for sharing."

He regarded her, unsmiling. "Bella thought you should know. I agreed to pass on this piece of the puzzle, as you might think of it."

A fleeting smile tugged at the corner of his mouth and eyes. It was gone so fast it might have been a trick of the sunlight.

"Thanks, Pierre." Did she misjudge him? Was the betrayal a figment of her imagination? Before she could decide, he made to go back inside.

With a last earnest glance at her face, he said, "Goodbye, Agnes. I wish you well."

Not waiting for a response, he walked out of her life.

Her eyes lingered on the snow-crested trees and ornamental split-rail fences dotted along both sides of the lane toward the main lodge. What a shame if the Xaviers were to lose it all. Some developer might transform the unique, organically grown place into a cookie-cutter, money-spinning resort.

Agnes sighed. Maybe Nonno and Robert would find a workable solution to save the old-fashioned family operation. Unlikely to please Phil. But so be it. Right now, she must focus on another errand.

Agnes veered off onto a narrow path leading to the utility garage. The resort felt deserted. Most guests must have departed after the bridge opened or gone skiing at Mont Tremblant.

She found Gabe on his haunches outside the garage, readying a snow-blower for another day's work. Hard to imagine operating the type of machinery causing him to make the gruesome discovery only two days ago. He'll remember it for the rest of his life, she felt sure.

At least he'd leave this job at the end of the week. When they texted, he'd assured her he'd contact Gwen as Sera had suggested. With luck, Gabe might land part-time employment to cover his expenses for the duration of his graduate studies.

When the sun cast Agnes's shadow over him, Gabe's head swiveled sideways. He slid the yellow ear protectors down to the nape of his neck and rose to greet her. "I won't keep you more than a few minutes," Agnes said, glancing around for somewhere more private to talk.

"There's a picknick table out back," Gabe said, interpreting her glance.

Based in sunshine and sheltered from the mild breeze, the back of the building proved balmy. Their backs against the windowless wall, they sat companionably on top of the table, resting their boots on its bench. No one could overhear them from within the garage, Agnes noted with satisfaction.

Conscious of the young guy's need to get on with his work, she jumped right in. "Gabe, I don't want to worry you needlessly, but I think we should consider what might happen. I assume Cheryl Vincenti will have twisted the facts. It's hard to guess what she told her father and if he knows or surmises her real actions."

"If he doesn't know, why would they have taken off in a hurry last night?"

"True," Agnes said. "If Cheryl told him she'd been attacked, as she claimed last night, her dad would have raised hell rather than scampering. Still, we must prepare for their lawyers to launch a preemptive strike."

Agnes glanced sideways at Gabe, whose jaw muscles clenched. "Mind you," she added, "I don't think they'd rush into a counterattack needlessly."

Slowly, Gabe's upper body turned. Their eyes met.

"Let her get away with it?" Gabe voiced the shared thought. "A killer on the loose?"

"I don't see how we can prove anything against her. On the danger of sounding defeatist, I doubt we can convince the local police to investigate if their officer filed an accidental death report."

"Won't your friend Polly report the woman for attempting to kill her and Maria?"

"Unlikely. Unless we can prove Cheryl killed Gino, any attempt to silence Maria or attack Polly would appear random. In fact, Cheryl's plan was devilish. Apparently, she prodded Maria to take her own life. Polly got in the way. Literally. Collateral damage if Cheryl had succeeded."

"So, without forensic evidence proving the Vincenti woman killed Gino, she gets away with murder." Gabe looked as disgusted as Agnes felt.

"And if no one looks for such evidence, there's no chance of finding it," Agnes said, her voice as dispirited as his.

Unless her former student's mind made the leap without her prompting, she would not suggest what had occurred to her during a restless night.

They stared ahead at the snow-covered trees sparkling in the sunlight. The noon stillness might have relaxed her if it weren't for the dark thoughts of violent death going unpunished.

Next to her, she saw Gabe's fists clench in his lap. He'd taken off the work gloves while they spoke. The skin on the back of his hands appeared chafed and red.

"Okay. I'll do it," he muttered.

"What?" she said softly.

"Sorry, just talking to myself," he said. "My mom's a cop. She's mad at me for moving back to Montreal. Can't blame her. Like I told you, she transferred to Ontario just to be closer when I studied at U of T."

"I remember you mentioning it."

He cast her a quick look. "So, you wondered about it already."

She gave a little shrug. "Couldn't help it."

He grinned. "Elementary logic." Then, grimaced. "Yikes. I hate to run to my mom for help. She still has close friends at the Sûreté in Montreal. If she'd tip off headquarters, they'd take her seriously. But I'd need you to convince her, Agnes." He looked at her pleadingly. "If I tell my mom on my own, she'll say I'd let my creative mind run riot. Mom calls my interest in fictionalized crime ghoulish."

"I'll do whatever it takes, Gabe. Plus, Dr. Jeong will support us. He gave permission and would be glad to share his findings. We recorded him for this purpose. Forensics will verify his findings. Heck, they might do so anyway. I'm sure they're thorough." Still, she couldn't suppress a sigh. "The bigger problem is to tie any findings to Cheryl as the perpetrator. The clean-up of the cabin will have wiped out all traces."

"If she killed Gino inside the cabin and dragged him out, traces of her DNA might have transferred to his body," Gabe said.

"Not if she wore gloves. On a freezing cold night in blizzard conditions, she'd bundle up to her eyeballs." Aware of discouraging Gabe, Agnes hastened on. "No matter. We've got to try, or we'll never forgive ourselves. Put me in touch with your mom. If she prefers, give her my number, and she can connect me with her colleagues in Montreal. I'll do my best to convince them."

"Okay. I will." Gabe slid to the edge of the table and jumped to his feet. "Sorry, gotta get back to work."

"Speaking of which. Don't forget to contact my mom's friend, Gwen. Hey, maybe the university has an opening for outdoor staff since that's your preference."

A smile transformed the young man's face. "Thanks, Agnes. I'd love that." A worried frown creased his forehead as he said, "When I've talked to my mom tonight, I'll text you."

Mother-son relations weren't too good, Agnes assumed. She aimed for a positive tone. "You're doing the right thing, Gabe. The rest is up to the police."

If the police succeeded and Cheryl's lawyers turned tables, Gabe might live to regret his decision. At least he had one arm of the law on his side, Agnes thought. And she herself would stand by him no matter what.

On the path to the main lodge, Agnes shot off a text to Polly.

AGNES

Meet me in 5.

She'd arranged earlier to pick up lunch for everyone at the bistro and asked Polly's help to carry it back. Easily explained as a desire to save the staff another delivery. What she really wanted was a quiet chat with Polly.

When Agnes reached the wider lane traversing the resort, the imp came jogging toward her, the tip of the elfin hat bobbing and bell jingling. A thick red fleece sweater over black leggings gave the tiny figure some bulk.

"Wow, that was fast," Agnes greeted her.

The imp grinned up at her. "Nah, I was already outside. Wanted to give Maria some space to chat with her great auntie. She'll stay with the old lady until she gets things sorted. Says she's got no one else now that Gino's gone."

"I'm glad she won't be alone," Agnes said, feeling relieved of one concern. "What's the plan, then, once you get to Toronto? The flights are confirmed for tonight, aren't they?"

"Yep, all clear. Maria's asked me to stay at her place in Toronto for a couple of days. It freaks her being alone there while packing. Then, I'll help her move to the auntie's place and be off to BC. Got to cover some environmental stuff and see some folks."

Such unusual frankness, by impish standards, made Agnes's eyebrows shoot up, which elicited a deep chuckle from Polly.

"Hey, I'm practicing. Promised to be upfront with you, didn't I?"

They'd started walking, but Agnes slowed her step. Too much to say for the short distance. Inside the building, they'd be overheard.

"I appreciate it," she said. "Goes both ways. I've got to fill you in on my morning. Let's stroll around the pond or pick a sunny spot."

It took only fifty yards for Agnes to realize the snow was far too deep for comfortable walking. They cleared a bench in a sunny, sheltered nook

233

among the trees. Agnes passed her mittens to sit on, though Polly insisted the fleece leggings were warm enough to keep her bum from freezing.

"So, what's up, Aggie?" Polly's eyes sparkled with curiosity. Yet Agnes detected a hint of apprehension lurking beneath.

When she related what Nonno, Bella, and Pierre had said and what she and Gabe had discussed, Polly listened silently. A few times, the fingers in thin woolen gloves reached up, scratching pensively under the elfin hat, making the wispy hair stick out.

At the end of Agnes's recital, Polly said, "Bloody hell. Guess we're in for it."

"I'm so sorry, Polly. Not fair to you deciding to involve Gabe's mother without telling you first." While speaking with Gabe, her conscience had pricked her not only on his but also on Polly's account.

"Nah, you've got every right to do what you think best, Aggie. It's been bugging me like hell to think that woman will get away with it."

The words eased the load of guilt a little. But other worries crowded in.

Perceptively, Polly said, "The old catch twenty-two, isn't it? Screwed if you do and screwed if you don't. You'll never forgive yourself if you let the killer escape. Going after her, we'll all get dragged in, and Maria will take the brunt of it once it hits the news and stuff. Plus, the killer woman will accuse Gabe of attacking her instead of her attacking me. Argh, what a mess."

Agnes found her head nodding along with every word. Polly's eyes searched her face. "There's more, isn't there, Aggie?"

No point in withholding the rest, Agnes decided. "Yeah. I'm worried an investigation will harm the Xaviers. Robert will be furious. I don't care what Phil thinks," she added as if that made a difference.

"But you care about your friend Jac's reaction," Polly said, acute as ever.

Agnes felt a skinny arm thread through the crook of her elbow. A light squeeze accompanied Polly's soothing tone. "Don't fret, Aggie. Sounds like Jac is a real friend. She'll know none of this is your fault. Your friends love you for being true to yourself."

Still, the worry persisted. "Call me a wimp, but I just don't know what to tell Jac," she said.

Polly's boots swung back and forth through the snow under the bench as she darted a quick glance at Agnes. "That's an easy one. Just tell her the truth."

"Yeah, right. Nothing to it." Agnes rolled her eyes.

"C'mon, pal." Polly jumped up and stood facing her. "Let's grab lunch. I'm famished." She stretched out her hand in an offer to help Agnes to her feet. Despite the grin, Polly's voice was earnest when she said, "I'm in your corner, Aggie. No matter what's in store for us."

It was late afternoon when Agnes's phone vibrated in her pocket. After a quiet lunch and a leisurely, sunshiny walk around the pond path that staff had cleared by two o'clock, the four of them were playing Scrabble in their apartment's living room. Flights booked for the evening, Polly's bag and Maria's suitcases at the ready in Agnes's bedroom, they'd kept to everyday talk.

A couple hours earlier, Jeong and his wife Su had dropped in for a final check-up and to say goodbye before departing for Boston. He'd pronounced Maria fit enough to travel. Agnes had taken him aside and told him about looping in Gabe's mother and hopefully the Sûreté. Jeong had assured her of his full support.

From what Polly said, Greg and Josh would pop in later after the ski lifts closed. They, too, were flying home tonight.

Now, Agnes dug out her phone, saying to Sera, "It's Jac. You don't mind if I take her call in your room?" Sound didn't carry as much from the larger bedroom she'd found. "Eh, Polly? You'll play for me, won't you?"

"Sure, pal. I'll win for you. Unless Maria beats us all." Polly grinned.

A wistful smile rose to the younger woman's face. "We play a lot at the daycare when the kids have their naps."

Before closing the bedroom door, Agnes glanced at the three players. Her mother, self-sufficient as ever. Polly was much more relaxed after the ordeal than on all the days before. Even Maria's eyes had lost the dazed film they'd still shown the night before. She'll pull through, Agnes felt convinced.

No way to stall any longer. Knees pulled up, she sat against the head-board of her mother's bed and eyed her mobile as though it might explode. When her thumb moved the slider to the green zone, Jac's voice came loud and clear.

"My goodness, Agnes. You take forever to answer your phone."

"And a good day to you too, Jac," Agnes said pointedly.

"*Bonjour, mon ami.* Is that better?" Jac's cheerful laugh made Agnes smile. But then Jac went on, "Now, tell me, how was your Christmas? Did you have lots of fun?"

"Well." Agnes prevaricated. Nothing for it. Jump in at the deep end. "You won't believe this, but we've run into a little situation..."

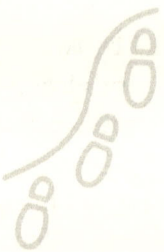

For more MYSTERIES by Eva Bernhard

Agnes Taylor Mystery Series
amazon.com/dp/B099436TY2?

Louise Penfold Mysteries
amazon.com/dp/B0FR6M4CTL?

For new release alerts follow me at
amazon.com/author/evabernhard

Don't Go Yet...

Dear Reader,

I so hope you've enjoyed *Snowbound* and felt transported to beautiful Mont Tremblant!

It's so much fun creating worlds within worlds of mystery.

Your next Agnes Taylor Mystery, **Stormy Night**, is ready for your enjoyment.

May I ask a big favor? Please tell your friends about my books and recommend them to your local library.

Would you be very sweet and post a review of my book on Amazon, please?

Thanks for your kindness!

Warm wishes,

Eva

Stay in touch and follow me on amazon.com/author/evabernhard

EB Press Release

BREAKING NEWS

LOUISE PENFOLD MYSTERIES

DEATH AT ROSEWOOD MANOR

CASCADE GAZETTE — SPECIAL REPORT

A condolence card delivered before its time has unsettled new resident Louise Penfold. Locals say the freelance editor, recently moved from the city, has uncovered troubling circumstances around the recent death of a well-known Cascade resident.

Authorities remain tight-lipped, but whispers suggest secrets at Rosewood Manor may prove darker than its fresh paint.

DEATH AT EAGLE ROOST

HURON DAILY CHRONICLE

Thanksgiving festivities at the lakeside estate Eagle Roost turned tense when visiting editor Louise Penfold and companion Nora Norton encountered a household rife with quarrels.

Sources describe strained relations among guests and hosts. Penfold, already linked to past investigations, is said to be watching closely as unease grows by the hour.

MORE INFORMATION AT AMAZON.COM/DP/B0FR9TDN2T?

Fictional press release prepared by EB Press. Events described are from the Louise Penfold Mysteries series.

The Perfect Gift...

Treat yourself and Loved Ones and tell your Friends about the
Agnes Taylor Mystery series

Standard Font and eBook Editions
amazon.com/dp/B099436TY2?
amazon.co.uk/dp/B099436TY2?
amazon.ca/dp/B099436TY2?

LARGE PRINT – AGNES TAYLOR MYSTERIES

amazon.com/dp/B0D8K71ZMM
amazon.ca/dp/B0D8K71ZMM
amazon.co.uk/dp/B0D8K71ZMM

My sincere thanks for your support!

Acknowledgments

There's never just one thing that sparks the idea for a book. But the inspiration for *Snowbound* came during a ski vacation with my son. We've been skiing together at Mont Tremblant for ages and just love it! The real Tremblant and its environs are even more beautiful than my descriptions can convey. (The locale and everything that pertains to it are used purely fictitiously.)

I dedicate this third Agnes Taylor Mystery to my son—my best friend and ski buddy—in thanks for the wonderful times we always spend together.

As with all my other books, I was most fortunate to benefit much from the feedback of my critique partners. Foremost, author Rebecca Markus, whose astute insights, suggestions, and comments keep me on track and cheer me on. Thanks a million, Rebecca!

Several others read an early version of the opening chapters and gave valuable input, notably Ione Huhtala, Mark Roman, and Ave (from Critique Circle). A beta reader, Michaela from Critique Match, gave lots of helpful feedback on a later version of the entire MS. I'm sincerely grateful to all of you.

Of course, the credit for proofreading goes to my editor, Pam Clinton. I can't thank Pam enough for always being available when I need her. Any remaining errors are mine and probably due to my stylistic idiosyncrasies.

My biggest thanks go to my readers, who make my author life a pleasure.

www.ingramcontent.com/pod-product-compliance
Lightning Source LLC
Chambersburg PA
CBHW030408020726
47493CB00003B/985